A Body of Work

A Body of Work

Colleen Anderson

BLACK SHUCK BOOKS

First published in Great Britain in 2018 by
Black Shuck Books
Kent, UK

All stories © Colleen Anderson 2018
'The Collector' first appeared in *Cemetery Dance* magazine, May 2014
'The Blade' first appeared as 'P is for Phartouche' in *Demonologia Biblica* (Western Legends Publishing, 2013)
'Shaping Destiny' first appeared in *Black Treacle #9*, June 2015
'Asylum' first appeared in *nEvermore: Tales of Mystery, Murder & the Macabre* (EDGE Publishing, 2015)
'Gingerbread People' first appeared in *Chilling Tales 2* (EDGE Publishing, 2015)
'A Book By Its Cover' first appeared in *Mirror Shards* (Bad Moon Books, 2011)
'Red is the Color of My True Love's Blood' first appeared in *Deep Cuts* (Evil Jester Press, 2013)
'Tasty Morsels' first appeared in *Polluto #8*, August 2011
'A Taste of Eden' first appeared in *Worlds of SF, F and H, Volume III* (Altair, 2018)
'Season's End' first appeared in *The Beauty of Death* (Independent Legions Publishing, 2016)
'The Brown Woman' first appeared in *Over the Brink* (Third Flatiron Publishing, 2012)
'Symbiosis' first appeared in *Shoreline of Infinity #1*, June 2015
'Exegesis of the Insecta Apocrypha' first appeared in *Horror Library Volume 4* (Cutting Block Press, 2010)
'Sins of the Father' first appeared in *OnSpec #105, Vol 28*, August 2017
'The Healer's Touch' first appeared in *The Sum of Us: Tales of the Bonded and the Bound* (Laksa Media Group, 2017)
'The Book With No End' first appeared in *Bibliotheca Fantastica* (Dagan Books, 2013)

Cover art © Jenn Brisson, 2018 – www.jennbrisson.com
Cover and interior layout © White-Space, 2018

The right of Colleen Anderson to be identified as the author of this work has been asserted by her in accordance with the Copyright, Designs & Patents Act 1988.

All rights reserved. No part of this publication may be reproduced or transmitted in any form or by any means, electronic or mechanical, including photocopy, recording, or any information storage and retrieval system, without permission in writing from the publisher.

This book is a work of fiction. Names, characters, businesses, organisations, places and events are either the product of the author's imagination or are used fictitiously. Any resemblance to actual persons, living or dead, events or locales is entirely coincidental.

www.BlackShuckBooks.co.uk

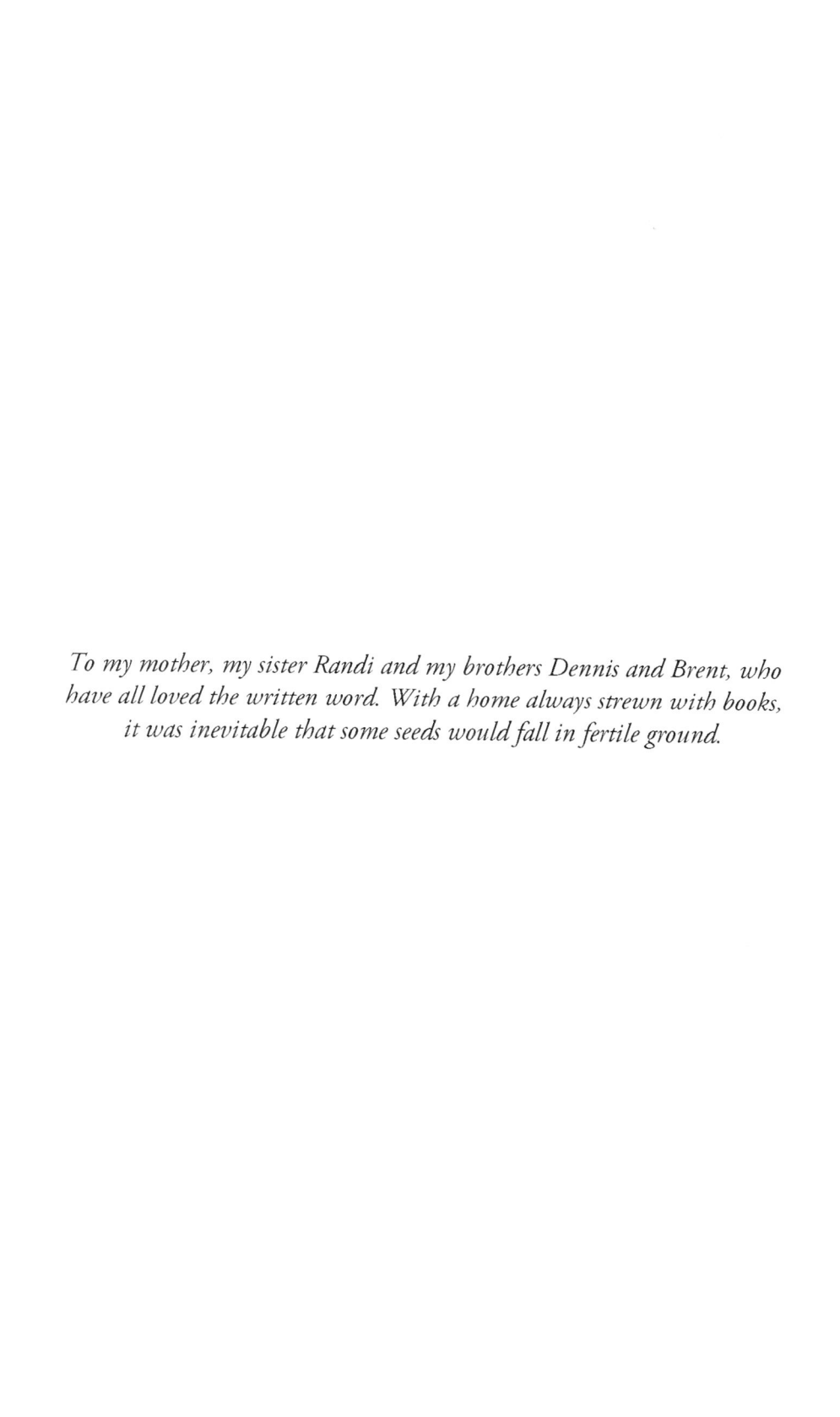

To my mother, my sister Randi and my brothers Dennis and Brent, who have all loved the written word. With a home always strewn with books, it was inevitable that some seeds would fall in fertile ground.

Acknowledgements

Writing is a solitary pursuit, but no writer works in a vacuum. Several writing groups helped lay the foundation: Clarion West for all those years ago running the tough gamut that showed me I had a long way to go, and the Center for the Study of Speculative Fiction (CSSF) in Kansas for being the genesis of some ideas. Nancy Kilpatrick and Sandra Kasturi, fellow writers with dark hearts who believed in me and have supported me in different ways, and Matt Hughes has had a hand in stirring the editing pot on some stories. British Fantasy Convention has been a stopping off point in recent years when travelling to Europe and I appreciate the warm welcome I have received from the Brits. A special thanks goes to Jenn Brisson for the awesome artwork on the cover, and Steve Shaw of Black Shuck Books who has made this venture possible. May imagination always bring new worlds to explore.

Contents

Introduction   11

Mind Over Matter

The Collector   17
The Blade   33
Shaping Destiny   45
Asylum   61
Gingerbread People   73
A Book By Its Cover   89
Red is the Color of My True Love's Blood   101
Tasty Morsels   109

Under the Skin

Taste of Eden   127
Season's End   143
The Brown Woman   157
Symbiosis   167
Exegesis of the Insecta Apocrypha   173
Sins of the Father   187
The Healer's Touch   203
The Book with No End   225

A Trick with a Pen That She's Learning to Do

What are we really trying to say when we write introductions to books, to works of fiction, or poetry, or art? What are we saying to or about the creator of said book? To you, the reader? To ourselves? Is it a monumental act of ego, as we try to editorialize or critique, try to impress with our own cleverness and understanding? But really – why write something that maybe no one but the author will read, since people notoriously skip afterwords and introductions.

Maybe it's our way of selfishly working out things about our own writing. Our relationships with other writers. Our relationship with our own unconscious. Maybe it's all a trick. Maybe it's cheap therapy. Or a letter from one author to another. A love letter, of sorts… one of praise, and maybe a little envy. Maybe it's a missive between sisters, because Colleen Anderson and I are sisters of the spirit, if not actually related by blood. But I've always thought that it's not blood that matters – it's the relationships of the heart. And mind.

I often think all fiction is a trick – a trick of the eye, a *trompe l'oeil*. Maybe a trick of the mind's eye: a *trompe l'oeil de l'esprit*, perhaps? A way to suck you in and fool you. Or better yet: fool ourselves.

And sometimes I think being a writer is akin to being a werewolf or a shapeshifter of some sort. You look normal to other people, but really, you're not. At night you become something completely other, and whatever skin you're wearing during the day as you go about your business isn't the real you, has never been the real you. And we try to hide that true self from our loved ones, and maybe share it only with other creators of weird and fantastical things. And we're faintly ashamed of what lives in our heart of hearts. We mutter about it to other writers over cocktails, like inept spies scurrying to a Casablanca that never existed. We secretly revel in all the pretense, because that's what fiction is all about: doing tricks and telling lies to other liars. Wonderful liars.

I've known Colleen Anderson a long time. I'm not sure exactly when we met, but we've travelled a couple of decades together at least, held together by that tether of kindred spirithood, despite living thousands of miles apart, convening in other cities for conventions and kvetching like there was never a pause in the conversation. I've been Colleen's editor and she's been mine. We've shared slush piles and bottles of red wine. We've moaned about our writing and our families and our exes and our currents. Cried over losses and cheered the wins. The last line of a poem she wrote called "A Strange Attraction" (both hilarious and disturbing) will always stay with me: "Repulsed, we become lovers." In a way, that line kind of evokes what this process of writing is like – a strange repulsion and attraction to the written word, to the dark side of genre fiction, to the ticking fairy tale heart of Colleen's own work.

And if her writing really is a trick, then it's a very clever one – one that seems so simple, you can miss its cleverness. You don't get bogged down with the kind of writerly nonsense you often find in genre fiction. Colleen Anderson's stories unwind neatly; you think all the threads are there for you to see – and that's exactly when she's trapped you. Because it's almost impossible not to continue to the end and see what terrible or wonderful revelation she has in store.

Whether she writes of a sentient sword or a woman telling the future through soap bubbles, a steampunk Kaiser Wilhelm, a sociopathic entomologist communing with insects, or an archaeologist seeking immortality, her stories often have a sting in the tail, but if you're a reader like me – that's often the best part. Waiting to see just how Colleen is going to *get* you when you least expect it. But it's the kindest cut. You won't even realize it's happened until it's too late.

Despite the dark themes in so much of her writing (and believe me – they're there), there's also a sneaky little thread of optimism or hope that runs through the heart of much of Colleen Anderson's work, and it's maybe why you can read her stories and not feel the kind of despair and overwrought ennui that never seems to go out of vogue these days. Instead we have a sense of wonder, and yes, a sense of darkness, and sometimes naughtiness, but more importantly – the *possibility* of things. And isn't that what we as writers want to convey – infinite possibilities and outcomes and ways of seeing things?

"What can one tell from the bones of the dead, those ivory sculptures no longer corrupted by the indulgences and errors of living? Only the greatest stories…" writes Colleen Anderson in 'The Book with No End.' And she is right. Perhaps we must divest ourselves of those indulgences and errors, our troubled pasts and worried futures, and simply create the greatest stories we can. Better to light a candle, as they say.

I do ask myself, though: as writers, *are* we lighting candles? Or just cursing the darkness? Mostly I think I'm just cursing Colleen – for her talent, her work ethic, her unbelievable tenacity, her capacity to endure slings and arrows, and just, well… her zest for life. She does all of that better than I ever could, and with less moaning. She's making a difference.

And what I guess I like most about Colleen's writing and about Colleen herself is that she's never cared if you knew she was a shapeshifter. She's never been ashamed. Her night self and her day self are pretty much the same – and she's never been apologetic about writing these strange, disturbed, weird, wonderful stories. She's embraced them – and her true self – in a way I can only envy. So, *let* her suck you in. Let the trick happen.

Colleen, Colleen! Writer, poet, editor, artist, fellow traveller in the night. *Friend.* Chica – you never ran with the wolves – you *became* one. And we, your devoted readers, can only be grateful.

Sandra Kasturi
Peterborough, Ontario
July 2018

Mind Over Matter

The Collector

This story came from an image I had of something otherworldly. From that, I needed to figure out a plot and a way for a human to be able to defeat a creature of supernatural strength and power.

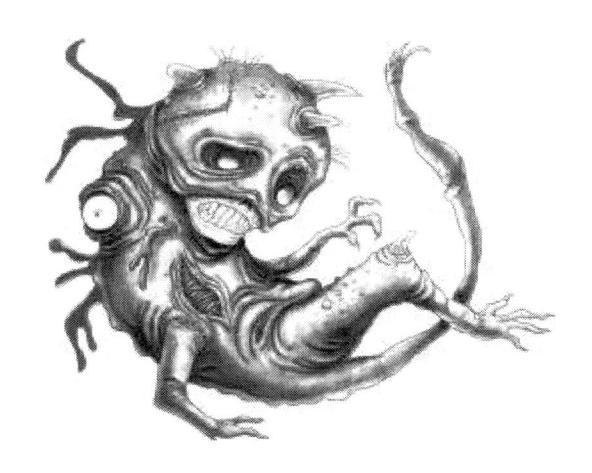

Emma knew the day was out of kilter from the start. Aldred had left without his lunch. She would have taken it later, but Agnes Cresswycke had stopped by and asked if Emma could fetch the midwife for her daughter Elaine. Some matters wouldn't wait, so Emma packed the meal, wrapped it in linen and pushed her way past the chickens and on to the midwife's. She stopped briefly to sprinkle rosemary and ground quartz on the path. Just a tiny pinch; to keep things good.

It was a hot day, one where only the crickets seemed to stir. Emma liked Falston, a place filled with many settlers such as Aldred and herself. Fresh it was, with none of the pervasive horrors they had learned to live with in their old town. They'd only been there a couple of years but Aldred had a way of getting himself known. It wasn't that he was a pushy man; he just tended to be there to help out when needed. She smiled, holding his lunch close to her chest, thinking of when she had first met him. He'd been wiry and very lean, and had a tendency to work too hard and forget to eat. Over their courtship he'd come to appreciate her cooking as well as her forthrightness, and he'd slowly put on some weight. He wasn't fat at all but now he had strong muscle, as hard as the iron he forged. Their marriage was nearly perfect.

Emma sighed and peered through the bright light, pulling her bonnet a little further forward. They'd been together five years now and had made it through snowstorms and wind to their new destination. There'd been too much to do to think much of babies. There'd been land to clear, a cabin to build and a smithy to construct. Emma had planted seeds and got the chickens settled in while Aldred had worked the forge, busy from the first day he set foot in town. They had had little time to relax, but they'd always had time to laugh.

Babies never came and Emma knew it might not happen. That would have to be. Still, it was hard to accept.

Stopping at the gate of Goodwife Margaret's, Emma called into the open doorway. "Goodwife, Agnes Cresswycke is needing your help. Elaine is contracting very regularly now and she says you should come soon."

Goodwife Margaret peered around the corner, her apple cheeks flushed in the heat. "Oh good, she's nearly on time. I'll be on my way. Thank you, Emma."

Emma nodded and walked down the road. She turned past the general store and as she neared the forge she could see Aldred bent over the anvil, hammering out a piece of metal. He stopped, hammer raised, looking like some great god, the sun shining on his golden hair. Then he fell, the hammer toppling in slow motion behind him, his knees crumpling as he folded to the earth.

Emma ran, dropping the lunch in the dusty road, her bonnet flying from her head and her skirts pulled high. "Aldred, Aldred!" She reached his side and kneeled beside him. His white face took on a bluish tinge. Pressing her ear to his chest, she heard no beat. "Don't you dare, Aldred Nelson. Don't you dare leave me."

She shook him, to no avail. "Aldred. Aldred!" Emma beat his chest, emphasizing her words. "Don't you dare. It's not your time. It's. Not. Your. Time!"

Emma refused to believe the worst. She ignored the tiny whisper that said, *Oh yes, it's his time.* Two tears fell, right on Aldred's eyes as she beat his chest in impotent fury.

His eyes flew open and he arched up, gasping for all the world as if he'd been drowning. Drowning in darkness and death.

Emma's own heart nearly stopped, so frightening was Aldred's countenance, like he'd seen what had been waiting. By that time, several people had heard her screams and come running.

Everything slowed and moved as if through syrup; no sound reached her ears. And she knew, just as she'd always known when there was a change, or shift in the world. Emma knew she had changed something. Something vital. Something that their old world had never been rid of.

Someone helped Aldred sit. Someone else gave him water and even checked her.

Aldred, pale but no longer a bluish hue, looked up at her, and in that moment sound flooded back and the world moved as normal. Emma pushed past the helping hands and kneeled beside Aldred, hugging him close. "I knew you'd be okay, I knew."

"Em, I'm okay." Aldred patted her back, but she could hear his fear.

"Why don't you let us close the forge down for today, Aldred," said Karl Veln, wiping his hands on his baker's apron. "You should go home and rest, make sure you're okay. Probably was the heat. Too hot for anything but sitting in the shade." The other folk murmured agreement.

Most of the others had never been near Aldred and Emma's old town. They didn't know what might happen now. Emma shivered. Surely that past was behind them. Surely they had moved out of range.

"C'mon." Emma helped Aldred up. He stood a little unsteadily but there were few but Emma who could have told that he was still shaky. Arlene Carmichael handed Emma the dusty lunch.

"You gonna be okay going home?"

Aldred smiled thinly. "We'll be fine. Let's go, Em. You can feed that lunch to the chickens."

It wasn't a long walk to the outskirts of Falston, no more than twenty minutes. But Emma could feel the change and the silence that cloaked the yard when they approached, and it told her that it had happened. As they pushed open the gate, they saw the first chicken. It lay on its side, and looked turned inside out; very dead, feathers gone. Around the side of the log cabin lay three other chickens, dotting the ground in red.

"Well at least I won't need to pluck them," Emma said, but her tone was anything but jovial.

"Em, I'm sorry."

She turned under Aldred's arm to face him. "Aldred, don't you ever be sorry to be alive. It's worth it. We'll deal with it. I couldn't go on without you."

His warm lips met hers and for a moment they forgot the carnage in the yard. "Emma, my love, I believe you could do anything you wanted to. Even defy death."

She turned away, not saying anything. As she grabbed a basin she glanced at Aldred. "Best go rest for a bit, love. You're safe now."

"But we'll have other worries soon enough."

Emma thought about those worries. It was not often one cheated Death, and Death wasn't the problem. It was the Collector of Souls. Those that defied their intended time often killed themselves in the end, not able to stand the constant devastation. She'd heard of one person tormented for five years. Five years of upheaval, possessions crushed and broken, of no one coming near for fear of attracting the Collector's wrath.

Emma shuddered and gathered the chicken carcasses. She gutted them inside, cutting off heads and feet and setting the rest to stew. She felt the Collector hanging near, waiting. The unseen had always had a light touch on her. And she remembered those fairy tales of people who had beat Death and the Collector to live out their years. But like all fairy tales, they were half whimsy.

Maybe, just maybe, there was some truth in those stories. If only Emma could remember any detail at all.

⁂

Next day, Emma and Aldred walked together to the forge. She carried his lunch and waterskin. He carried a pot of stew. At the forge they kissed long, until someone walking by made a good-natured comment.

Emma drew back blushing and took the stewpot. "Just you take it easy today. Drink lots of water and don't overdo it. And if you feel the least bit odd, you call someone, you hear."

Aldred laughed, a huge smile sparking fire in his amber eyes. "And here I thought we'd lost all the mother hens." He ran a finger down her cheek. "Don't worry, my love. I wish to stay alive."

As Aldred set about heating the forge, Emma ventured to the baker's door. After a bit of bartering, she traded the stew for several loaves of bread and a small sweetcake sprinkled with powdered sugar. She wrapped them in her apron and walked back to finish cleaning the yard.

Like the day before, the heat hung like a pall, and it was not yet midmorning. Birds trilled in the distance and the lazy drone of bees in the fields stroked the air with sleep. But as Emma approached the cabin she felt the twang of the air, a strum like a taut bowstring, a thrumming just under the skin. Her stomach fluttered, sending a nauseous wave up her throat. She swallowed and walked cautiously, her gaze darting left and right, the bread hugged close to her bosom. The yard looked normal. Quietly, she stepped onto the porch, and put her hand to the door. The thrumming in her veins stopped and without hesitating she thrust the door open.

Before her eyes, she watched a pot that hung in the air drop with a clatter. Then all lay still. But not calm. Every dish, glass, pot and pan had been tossed willy-nilly through the cabin. Shaking, Emma brushed broken pottery off the table and lay the bread down. She walked over to the pantry and opened the door. The food looked fine, the pot with the chicken still full. The food would be next, she knew. And more animals. An escalation.

Biting her lip, she closed the door and set about rescuing what dishes she could. She worked tirelessly, her mind turning, chewing on how to thwart the Collector. It wanted a soul of course, the one that Death had promised it. A soul in lieu, perhaps, but obviously chickens didn't count. She wasn't sure if she could make the Collector listen, if there was a way to bargain.

Before she knew it, what with straightening the cabin and the day's chores, the sun was brushing roseate fingers along the roadside. Aldred burst in through the door. "And how did my—"

Words faded from his lips. He looked around, eyes narrowing as he assessed the pile of broken dishes. Emma held up three cups, two with no handles and one with a crack from its lip. "Well, I salvaged enough for us to eat on. I wanted new dishes anyway."

In one step Aldred closed the space between them. "I'm sorry, Em." He wrapped her in his arms. "I'm sorry."

She pushed away from him, thrusting the cups into his big calloused hands. "You shush. You have nothing to be sorry about, nothing!" She picked up a cracked plate. "Do you think this matters more than the love we have? More than the depth of our lives?" She threw it at her feet, smashing it. "It matters not at all, Aldred. If we have to live in rags, under the stars, finding our food from day to day, I will not begrudge you your life. Never!"

Aldred sighed and sat. "Your love is so strong that it kept me from dying. Your strength is so much greater at times than mine. I can hew iron, I can lift trees, but you, my heart, can lift a soul." He smiled sadly. "I hope that neither of us lives to regret this."

"We won't," Emma said.

Together they cleared and set the table, putting out their supper and lighting a lantern as the day died.

"I've been thinking of those tales we grew up on." Emma waved a chicken leg as she leaned forward, nearly whispering. "They tell of folks beating Death."

Aldred frowned. "Those tales almost always talk about a sacrifice, and yet say nothing really of the Collector."

She shrugged. "Well, all creatures are bound by the elements. By the rise of sun and moon, by wind and fire, ice and rain and the very earth we stand on. I know there's something there we can use."

Aldred ran his hand through his sun-burned hair. "You understand that better than me."

They retired that night, making love like a murmuring wave, like a breeze blowing down dandelions, but both their minds drifted on more than flesh.

ᚴᛂ

Aldred left while the dew still tickled the leaves. Emma bustled about the kitchen, moving any treasures to the root cellar, but she came back quickly, feeling the twang in the air. Then she loaded another pot with stew, pocketed a knife and an apple in her apron and left. Walking brusquely, Emma made it to Agnes Cresswycke's and gave over the pot of stew.

"It'll feed Elaine and the young ones till she's back on her feet. Give you a rest too, from cooking for everyone."

"Mighty kind of you, Emma." Agnes fanned herself, then turned into the kitchen and brought over a small crockery. "Here's some jam. Did you notice how odd the air feels? Maybe a storm's coming. Thank you, again."

Emma marched back to the cottage, ignoring the hot thrum that unsettled her nerves. She set the jam pot down outside and pulled the knife from her pocket, holding it high. She pushed through the door with no thought. Only instinct moved her.

As the door slammed back on its hinges, she slashed the palm of her hand with the blade and waved it frantically about, carnelian spattering in fine drops. She yelled, "I bind you to a trial!"

As those drops fell, some hit an invisible wall, stuck and spread, to twist and shimmer until a thing never written about hovered before her. If a dried sinew, a mummified limb, could be said to live, then that was the Collector. Like old scabrous skin and burn-scarred flesh, it was of no true shape – a coagulation.

Emma gagged, pulling her apron in front of her face, backing up a step. "I—I call a trial." She tried not to vomited, swallowing reflexively.

It rasped, words like a body being dragged, no sound but in her mind. *A trial? Why should it matter?*

"You—you have rules." She clenched the apron around her bloody hand. "There are rules. Or you would take every soul."

If a scar could pause in thought, then this creature did. *Perhaps, but they are not rules of your world.*

"But they affect our world. *You* affect our world. You take what Death leaves and therefore you have rules. I call you to a trial."

What sort? it grated.

"Sort?" Her knowledge ran out.

You must know or there is no trial.

She thought furiously of trials and what she knew. "O-of air, a trial by air."

It hissed then. *And what will the trial decide?*

"If you lose, you will neither torment nor destroy anything that is ours. You will not take us. You will not transfer this to anyone else."

Through a crackling and sizzling sound—*And if you lose…*

"Then." She closed her eyes. "Then you can take my soul in return."

And the rules? You did choose.

"The rules?" She hadn't thought that far, but knew… "The trial by air; through words, questions. Whoever cannot answer, forfeits."

There is one thing…

"What?" Emma clenched her teeth. There was no stench, but it was nauseating to look at, and to feel in her mind.

It is a proper trial; however each of us can call one challenge in the element.

"Then you will not take Aldred if I fail."

⸫

Aldred and Emma arose with the first predawn cockcrow. The hush, the indrawn breath before the world wakes, felt suspended in their home. They moved quietly.

Emma hid her worry, but for all Aldred's talk of her strength she feared she had overstepped her realm of knowledge. How could she beat something as powerful as the Collector? She shook her head as she cleaned the morning dishes, glancing out to where Aldred fed the remaining chickens.

If she thought like that, she would be defeated before she started. The Collector could disappear at will, looked like nothing on this earth, but could only take the souls whose time had come. It was not all-powerful, but was bound by the elements, like all things. There had to be other limitations.

She realized she wrung her hands and stopped to undo her apron. If there was a way to stump it about its own nature… As she pulled the apron from her waist she felt the air tighten and hum about her, shimmering near the table. The Collector slowly took form.

Emma glanced outside. So it began. A wave of nausea passed through her again. Was it the Collector or the fear of what it could do? She didn't know but nothing would stop her now from trying to be free of this thing.

She sat, facing the Collector but not looking directly at its scurfy form.

It is time to begin. As you are the challenger, I start with a use of air. Then it flexed and stretched, pink-white sinew and lumpy, dried blood bolls shining.

Aldred entered and stopped, then cinched his belt tighter and quietly closed the door.

In the otherwise clear and calm day outside, a dust devil formed. They watched through the window. The dirt and wind twirled and spun faster, growing, bowing and twisting. Taller than the house, it leapt toward the stand of trees and encircled one, twenty-feet high, and snapped it at the base. The tree crashed down, limbs bouncing, and missing their home by only five feet.

Now, show me what you can do.

Emma stared. She walked toward the sitting room, thinking furiously. She couldn't fly or command the wind like the Collector. Oh! But she could command the wind. Emma started singing, not strongly at first, the fear tightening her throat, but as the song grabbed her, she soared with it. It was a song of glory and joy, of birds and spring, and the air in their small cabin grew lighter.

When she finished, she smiled and said, "This is what I can do with air that you cannot."

The Collector did not speak for a few minutes but hovered in the air, sizzling and popping. Then it contracted and said, *Now, your challenge. We do not stop until one cannot answer. Your mate cannot interfere, nor ask questions. "I don't know" is not an acceptable answer. A question asked cannot be repeated.*

"Fine." Emma breathed deeply. "Also, each must answer truthfully." She clasped her hands and stared into her lap.

She asked, "How many souls have you taken?" A simple question, but the tally may not have been kept.

Then the Collector answered with an impossibly long string of numbers. Without any preamble, it asked, *What is your purpose?*

Surprised, Emma realized that the Collector had asked a question she would have asked. She answered slowly, carefully, "My purpose. To love my husband, to work with my community, making it a better place for all, and to have a good, strong and worthwhile life." She paused, wondering if it was enough. When the Collector didn't say anything Emma knew her answer had been accepted.

They began in earnest.

Aldred hovered close until she sent him outside in exasperation. He crept back well after sunset as Emma and the Collector traded questions and answers. She slumped over the table, her hand pushed through stringy hair unwinding from its braid. She didn't know how much more she could take.

Then the Collector of Souls asked, *What would you sacrifice to have a child?*

And Emma froze. Regret and grief welled up. If she gave up Aldred, she could possibly have a child with someone else. But she loved him more than life itself. And if she gave up her life, there could be no child. She hadn't realized how much she wanted a child. And then, she *knew*—she was pregnant. Would she have to give up one? How could she decide?

"I don't know…"

It is done.

"What?" She stared, horrified. She had spoken aloud. "Wait! No—"

"Then I call a trial by earth."

Emma turned at Aldred's voice. He stood pale and immovable. "No. No, Aldred, it's too much."

"You could call a trial, Em. Then so can I." Aldred faced the thing. "Collector, I will challenge you and if I win, you take none."

I will take none of yours who walk the earth. And if you lose?

Aldred's face sank a little and he would not look at Emma as he drew a breath. "Then you will take me and only me, as intended."

"No!" Emma's fists twisted in her apron. "No! I will not let you go without me—"

That is your choice, interrupted the Collector. *But one of you will go with me when we are done.*

"It's okay, Em. We finish this one way or another."

Emma turned away, biting her knuckle to stifle a sob.

I begin. Unlike air, we will not debate words this time. The Collector moved outside.

Aldred and Emma stared at each other for several moments, then she rushed into his arms, panting, more scared than ever. "I don't know if I can live without you."

Aldred grasped her shoulders in his big hands. He held her back and looked into her eyes. "Then we'll just have to win now, won't we?" He smiled tenderly and leaned down to kiss her. "No matter what, my darling heart, I do not regret one moment I've spent on this earth."

They went outside and watched as dark gathered. The Collector shone leprous in the thin sliver of the moon's light.

The world buckled and turned inside out. Earth furrowed in great plumes, spraying dirt for hundreds of feet. Clods rained down upon them, then trees splintered, shooting sharp spears in every direction. Emma and Aldred hid within each other's arms until the death cries of trees and earth stopped. Emma stared at the devastation and knew – whatever the Collector was, it had no true feeling.

She whispered, "Aldred, it can only destroy."

Aldred stared, fists clenched at his side, lips pressed firmly together.

This is what I can do with earth.

Aldred only said, "Come." Then he stormed down the steps to the smithy. The Collector folded, twisted and popped out of sight.

Emma ran after Aldred and clutched at his shirt. "Aldred, what are you going to do? How can you possibly beat it?"

He turned so quickly that she gasped. He firmly clasped her shoulders and said, "I need your strength, Em, now, more than ever." She started to interrupt. "No, there's no time now. I just need your faith, your strength." When he reached the forge he started heating it up.

The Collector appeared, its glistening tissue stretching slowly in the forge's orange light. It hovered close without a word.

It took time to heat the forge, and when it was hot enough Aldred took a horseshoe and held it up in the tongs. "This horseshoe is worn but would still work on a horse." He shoved it into the forge's deep russet heat and left it there while he prepared the trough of water and tied on his leather apron. He grabbed his hammer and peered into the rippling heat. He gave Emma a tight smile, then sipped from his waterskin.

She glanced at the Collector. It just hovered while Aldred prepared.

Finally, Aldred was satisfied with the deep slumbering glow of the metal. Grasping long tongs in his left hand, he reached into the forge and pulled out the radiant horseshoe. Then he laid it upon the pitted anvil and swung down with the metal mallet. The predawn air shivered with the ringing as Aldred beat the metal. He hammered until there was no discernible shape and held the rectangular ingot up to the Collector.

"I have taken metal from the earth and destroyed it, but I'm not done yet." He stuck the metal back into the forge. By then the sky's cerulean glow appeared in the east. When the metal turned incandescent orange he pulled it out and hammered.

Every time Aldred hit the metal Emma's heart thudded alongside. How could they even understand anything about the Collector? She laid her hand protectively over her belly.

Several times Aldred pulled out the iron and struck it. His hair clung damply to his head, his shirt was drenched and his arms glistened with sweat. One final strike, then he plunged the metal into the trough. He held up a dagger blade to the Collector. "I have taken that of earth, which I destroyed, and I have created something new. I have made this. Can you create?"

The Collector hovered in the air, unmoving. Emma held her breath, afraid this would be the last that she saw of Aldred alive. Her throat closed, pushing the tears down. Aldred stared at the Collector, the knife held ready in his hand.

It is done. The Collector disappeared with a twist of red tissue and a snap.

Emma and Aldred stared at each other, frozen. Then she gasped and moved toward Aldred. She knew then that she never could have sacrificed the love of her life to have a child. Yet a child there would be as well. Aldred slowly lowered his hand, dropping the dagger to the ground and hugged her.

As the tension left her, the worry settled into her like a seed. Something the Collector had said during the trials. "I will take none of yours who walk the earth." She squeezed her eyes shut and prayed, but knew; their trial with the Collector was not done yet and she could never let her vigil down. Emma clutched Aldred tighter, to anchor her in the light.

The Blade

This started as a writing exercise to have a POV from an inanimate object. I loved Moorcock's Elric series and for years had several of the posters up in my place. Elric's curse was to carry a sword that controlled him more than he controlled it. It thirsted for blood and once drawn had to drink. So, how would one break such a curse if one could?

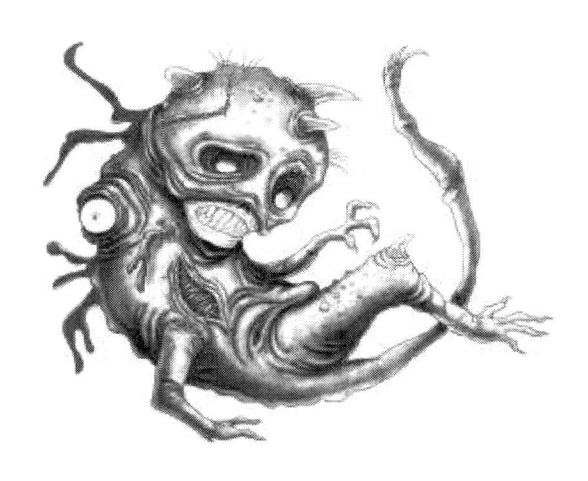

The blade's edge had been the last element in its making. Once sharper than the eye of the king's archer, it was now a pitted, scarred embarrassment of deeds. Not all of those deeds had been noble, though done by the hand of nobility. It had felt the soft parting of flesh against it many times. Flesh sweet and succulent, like the pears and peaches of the royal orchards. Flesh as scarred and worn as it now was, toughened by sun and calluses. Flesh so young and lacking the adventures of life that it had melted like butter before the blade's heat.

But a blade whether old or new does not think or really feel, unless it is imbued with a certain sentience. What is a blade to do when its awareness is awakened in the fires of its forging but never quelled with age or damage? The reason for its characteristics had been nebulous at best. Why would a sword need such awareness if it could not act independently, or could not influence others?

Its owner was dead, and the shine long gone from the blade. Of the three emeralds that had graced its hilt only one remained and it was cracked, its facets marred. The blade itself was broken at the tip, nicked from hitting and biting into armor and bone. All it tasted now was the bitter tang of rust and the dirt it lay in, next to the bones of the last that had held it.

But a blade with an intellect must think and therefore plan no matter how long it rests encrusted with grime and lichen. The first chime of sound, the laugh of young flesh vibrated the still strong metal. The tang quivered deep within the pommel and as footsteps rumbled the ground beneath the sword it mustered energy to flare brilliance through that fractured gem.

Power it still had, though much of it slumbered. The child's breath caught and as hands warmed the metal the blade vibrated keenly at the first touch of human flesh in so long. Energy fired through the minute folds of ores that had made its character. Surging molten purpose caused the sword to sing out and the child to gasp as its grip tightened around the hilt. The blade had once moved at the direction of the wielder, had supported the other's will. Now at long last it would be the shaper, and wield the mortal weapon that it now owned.

The child struggled to raise the ancient blade, grasped in both hands, nearly as tall as it was. While the forging of the flesh had just begun the sword felt the purpose as the child cried out, "I will be above all others! They will know my name everywhere!"

And thus it was done, a pact made as old as the naming of things, the will of the wielder and the will of the sword would twine and be hammered into a weapon of great potency. But even a blade whose sole purpose is to thrust, stab and cut, even one that holds the essence of power, knows that its might is only as great as the skills of its wielder. Gender mattered not to a metal of the earth. Intent was everything and this young being had a core so hot with desire that any blade could be formed anew in that furnace.

The blade had always communicated with its owner through the vibrations of air and earth. It heard, it tasted and it talked in its way with hums, trembles, shivers of energy, singing as it sliced into flesh and fulfilled its need. It could also see, of a sort, through the gems that had graced its hilt. But one fractured green jewel gave it a hazy view of the world.

At first the child lived as a wild thing, hiding in thickets and caves, filching and foraging for mushrooms, berries, a rare egg. The blade was too heavy for the child to do more than drag it behind and learn to lift it with both hands. But as the child grew and learned to hold the weapon, so it strengthened its muscles, directing its hand, vibrating wildly when the stance or hold jeopardized the strike, humming contentedly when a swing was right. Their first targets were only twigs and trees and effigies made of moss and grass. The child was diligent in practice and the first true kill was a bear that came upon them. The sword, still too heavy to wield properly, was still a weapon and the child managed to prop it up, holding steady as the bear charged and impaled itself.

The blood coursed over the blade, filling nicks and pits along the surface, causing a deep vibrational moan that brought a gasp from the child. "You are alive…"

With gentle coaxing and images sent in symbiotic resonance with the wielder, the blade aided the instruction. They skinned the coarse black fur from the beast and smoked the meat to hold them over. Spring had brought warmth and a carpet of colors so the child hid the blade and brought the fur to a local market where a furrier paid a good price. With that first coin the child bought food, a cape and a small emerald for one of the other settings on the sword's hilt.

The warrior steel hummed as the world grew a little clearer and imprinted the image of a clear crystal for the pommel in the child's mind. With such a stone it would be stronger for seeing the world about it. In the meantime they trained. A sword's life can be very long if cared for, and patience was one of its virtues, though hungers can run the length of it as well. While it longed for the din of battle and to feel its way into flesh, it bided its time in helping the child learn to wield it.

As they worked it learned the child's name was Jezaleen and it whispered its name along her flesh; Phartouche, an old tongue of long ago, the meaning obscured, though something near to *by the will, it is made*. It remembered each of its owners and the wills that had driven them. The first had been honed by power and a need to devour everything, the second by hate, and the third by valor, to save those hurt unjustly. It had not cared as long as its purpose was met.

So they spent long years of practice, Jezaleen growing tall and lean as a heron, never forgetting her promise, always asking in each town of news of raiders and armies. She would find them but she whispered to the blade that she must be able to defeat them. She was not ready yet but followed their trails of mayhem and broken bodies.

Phartouche tasted human flesh again one night when they'd been resting in the woods off a mountain trail. Jezaleen dozed before the embers of the fire, the sword across her lap. Phartouche felt the tremor of soft footsteps first and sent a shiver through the pommel that awoke Jezaleen. She stood in a crouch and pushed soil over the embers, moving silently behind a tree with the hilt held firmly in her hand.

Two figures skulked through the patchy forest light, the long points of their blades glinting. The sword felt no presence in their metal and pulled Jezaleen toward the one coming in on her left, for it sensed this was the more experienced foe. She gave no warning but spun away from the tree coming in low and slashing across the legs of the man. As he fell she swung back and ran the other man through as he turned to stab her. Phartouche moaned a warning as the first staggered to his feet and lunged at her. His blade hit her arm and she cried out, dropping the blade. Kicking dirt into the man's face, she retrieved the sword, bringing it up under the ribs of the brigand as he gasped out his last.

Phartouche sang, shivers of power, of lust – if it could be called that – shaking the blade and a bright hot heat causing the girl to cry out and drop the weapon, clutching her hand to her chest.

After, as Jezaleen patched her wound and took what she could from the bodies, she muttered on what she'd done right and wrong. The blade did not listen for once, lost in the ecstasy of the lifeforces it had drunk. It remembered those days of old, the decades that had passed with it being fed blood and power. A weapon is nothing if it does not serve its purpose. Were it to hang on a wall, be used only in ceremonies or be left to rot again in the ground, it would lose its sense of self. This would not happen again.

A blade and its wielder can live in a perfect cycle. The owner maintains the blade, the blade maintains the owner. Both can extend the life of the other. As Jezaleen gained experience she also earned coin. She took Phartouche to a weapon smith who ground off the nicks and scratches and polished away rust and pits until she could catch a glimpse of herself in its surface. Eventually, the stones were all made new, with two emeralds in the hilt and a fine clear crystal that graced the top of the pommel and became Phartouche's eye upon the world. The tip was remade so that the break was nothing but a distant memory.

Jezaleen hired out as a guard, as bounty hunter, a tracker, an assassin. Phartouche pulled her always towards the areas of violence as if the taint carried on the wind but it was a taste of metal, like calling to like, that let Phartouche direct her toward their next goal. And eventually, a decade after their meeting, Phartouche and Jezaleen exacted vengeance on raiders who had pillaged her village. Phartouche's savage bite aided her in severing their heads, six in all that she mounted on pikes and left as warnings. Gore covered her so that she and the weapon were of one crimson field, and Jezaleen laughed as Phartouche's cry chimed out across the fields.

Upon a horse, and with Phartouche strapped to her back, she moved over countryside, from village to township to castle lands, and battled all that would subjugate the farmers and the simple laborers. Wordfame spread and she became known as the battlemaiden.

Jezaleen earned a scar on her cheek, another across her hand, lessons she called them, as did Phartouche. They both healed and she always kept the blade honed and close to her hand.

A great war came to the land; a father pitted against a son, greed and fear their instigation. It split the kingdom, with neither cause being just. Jezaleen hired herself to the one with the most coin. She lead the army and fought, killing so many that even Phartouche was quiet in her hand, but never deserting her with the insight of other weapons that threatened. After weeks of fighting, famine, diseases from constant rains, lack of meals and stale water, even the stoutest heart grows weary. The war ended with nothing but grief and poverty, every family experiencing a loss and wounds in soil and souls that would take generations to mend.

Jezaleen sat atop her horse, Phartouche held across her lap as she stared dispassionately at the battlefield clotted with mud and blood and the hummocked terrain of slain bodies. She pulled out a cloth and wiped the blade clean of gore, sheathing it upon her back. "I grow ill of all this war, Phartouche. It may be time to try something new."

Glutted as it was, the blade barely heard her words over the cries and moans of the battlestricken. It could be said that the blade happily relived the brightest moments of slicing into scalp and brains or tasting the last pulses of a beating heart. Even its crystal eye saw only a red haze of the bloody arena over which the horse trotted.

When Jezaleen traveled from the contested lands, going farther south than they ever had in two decades, Phartouche only pulsated contentedly, anticipating new adventures. Most ores, most tools made of metal, do not think nor feel. Phartouche was single minded, always aiming towards its function, and over the centuries it had acquired a fearsome appetite. Too long without blood to sate the blade and Phartouche's will rose in caliber to match the mettle of its forging.

Jezaleen took a room above the only inn in a small town that prospered from being at a crossroads and the last stop before fording the mighty Zabatan River. It was a natural border between the cooler lands of the north and the humid reaches of the south.

Phartouche anticipated little more than parting flesh in battle. Jezaleen practiced against an old post, but seemed content to see what the town drew in. News came aplenty but still she remained, practicing her skills against a straw dummy. She sold the horse and rented a small open yard and began training any who would pay the coin to learn swordplay.

Eventually she moved into a small room and continued to train, but worked with the tanner down the road, learning the way of skins, how to scrape and stretch and make the hide supple or tough. One day, Jezaleen greased the scabbard well and polished Phartouche from sword tip to the crystal in its pommel. The blade hummed with purpose, knowing the time had come to once again go to battle. Jezaleen patted the blade, turning it in the golden light of late afternoon. "You've served me well, old friend. But it's time for me to hang up the weapons and take on a new trade." And hang the blade she did, on two hooks above the simple grey stone hearth.

Phartouche waited, for metal has the patience of ages, but Jezaleen touched the blade no more. In time the tanner shared her bed and they moved into a whitewashed cottage together. Phartouche came along but was shoved in a closet at the end of their bed. The soft shiver of sound that often emanated from the blade turned to the lowest of growls, but Jezaleen paid it no heed and her lover never heard it. Time passed, and who can say for how many seasons the sword was tucked in a dark alcove, no longer tasting the tang of cold or the soft caress of summer.

Shadows can sometimes give birth to shadowed things and items forgotten are not always lost. Phartouche's desire grew, and all the more so for it could feel its wielder close by. An ache ran the veins of its making. A power once bound is not severed because one wishes it. It takes special actions and so Phartouche gathered its will, the very essence of its metal, to cut, to slice, to stab. One night when even the rays of the full moon shone meager light through the laths of the closet door, Phartouche called out to Jezaleen and drew her close.

Awake or asleep she was unable to resist the pull and only came to full wakefulness as the blade plunged into her sleeping lover. Jezaleen wailed, tossing the sword with a clatter, trying to stop with her hands and the sheets the fatal black pools that welled from her lover's chest. Mad with grief, she cursed the blade then. "I will be your undoing as you have been mine."

But she grabbed the blade, her riding boots and pants, a sack and her cloak. Before dawn pushed the moon away, Jezaleen was on the road, Phartouche sheathed firmly to her back.

A year, two, five passed with Jezaleen wandering the most southernmost reaches, speaking little, taking the most distasteful of jobs. She fed Phartouche well as a guard for caravans, a scout in the mountain passes, a hunter of wild cats in the desert sands. Desolation touched Jezaleen and she spoke of the hollow wastes of her soul, but the blade cared not. As long as wielder and sword worked in concert all was well.

It was on the road that Jezaleen met another weary warrior of the bloody paths. They walked along first in cold companionship, sharing a fire and little else. Eventually the nearness of another human whose heart was scarred and world weary, one who understood the sorrows of the fighter's road, helped thaw the other's heart. A spring moved across their consciousness, drawing out hopes and dreams as if they were new shoots budding tentatively after blight. In time they shared more than words and talked of a future. He wished to use only his stave for balance, and bow for hunting game. No more wars, no more raids, no more deaths that wither a soul.

Jezaleen echoed the sentiments and though Phartouche barely cared for the meaning of words, it felt the intent. A shimmer of sound escaped when Jezaleen pulled the blade from its sheath, soft as a fire's hiss.

As they traveled through the autumn days Jezaleen and her companion stopped frequently, resting and eating windfall apples. They left behind their goods at their well concealed camp, and swam in streams and ponds. Here they forgot the horrors of war, the ways of killing, and opened themselves to the dance of loving and the healing it brought.

Frost painted a glamour of rime to the land, so that grass and gorse crunched underfoot and their breath formed fairy mists. Phartouche rang clear as a chime in such air but at this time of year all they hunted was game to feed them.

A deer trail led them to a village too far away from any beaten track to have heard news of any wars, too meager for raiders to bother with. Tucked in a vale with a small lake close by, the people herded sheep, a few cows and tended their fields. Here was where they would winter and a small cottage was easy to come by.

Jezaleen often sat in front of the fire at night, honing Phartouche's edge or polishing the pommel as she stared into the capering flames. Her partner wove sinew and made arrows and fletching. Neither of them left their weapons in a closet.

The blade felt its wielder close, the entwining of their wills and knew her heart was restless. While the chance to slake its unending thirst still remained, Phartouche was content to bide its time. After all, it had lasted centuries in the throes of power and in wars.

Spring came slowly to the veldt with drifts of crusty snow lying like slumbering dogs in the blue shadows of the lees. Animals ventured from their burrows and Jezaleen and her companion began to hunt. Yet one day she set her sword on the hearth's mantle and it tumbled off, striking the flagstones. She picked up Phartouche, examining the blade and hilt.

She said to her lover, "The crystal's chipped. I think I'll take the sword to the smithy and have the nicks polished out before summer comes."

He smiled back at her, his dark eyes pulling her in. He kissed her deep and said, "I'll try to get a pheasant for dinner. I'll see you later."

Jezaleen walked down the road to the smithy, a lightness to her step and a spark within her soul that made Phartouche thrum. It was always a sign that they would soon be on a new path. Combat and blood would warm its metal by summer's end.

At the smithy, Jezaleen placed the sword on the anvil and walked over to the smith. He was angular, leathery from the heat that had forged him as he had shaped metal throughout the years. As he walked to a barrel and pulled a ladle from which to drink, Jezaleen followed, talking. They went inside to settle the coin it would cost and Phartouche tasted the ores that lay near it, blades yet to be born. But would any of them ever be imbued with the intelligence that had kept it aware through all these years? It had never yearned for its kind for it was only one and wedded to its wielder.

The smith came out and hefted the sword, giving a few strong bursts to the bellows to burn the fire hotter. Then he pried out the crystal and the emeralds saying he would reset them, glancing to Jezaleen who stood out of the fire's heat, her arms crossed, watching.

To be immersed in the flames until its core glowed molten was like bathing Phartouche in its spirit. It hummed as the hammer struck out the nicks, it sang with ringing tones as its folds were honed and remolded. Phartouche's will never left but slowly, in the embracing heat, it changed. The lust for blood and war began to fracture, yet its purpose held. The bond of blade and wielder would outlast the fires of hell.

After a time, when the shaping and hammering had stopped, and the cooling baths hardened the metal, the smith inset the two emeralds, one in each armband. He banded the crystal and hung it from a chain. As Jezaleen took the two armbands, Phartouche chimed and subsided.

When she arrived back at the cottage, the crystal on her breast, she gave her lover one armband and she put on the other. They molded to each other's embrace, kissing fervently, fingers locked into hair before they disrobed each other in front of the fire. Armbands glinting in the light they felt Phartouche's presence. No matter where they went they would always find the other while wearing the armbands. Phartouche's purpose had changed. Where before it craved to cleave flesh, now forged anew into circles unending, it would bind flesh to flesh, bring the lovers together, forever twined with their will.

SHAPING DESTINY

I wanted to explore an unusual way of fortune telling, but in a modern world, and whether the choices we make can change a predicted future or not. To know the future, like Cassandra, can be a curse.

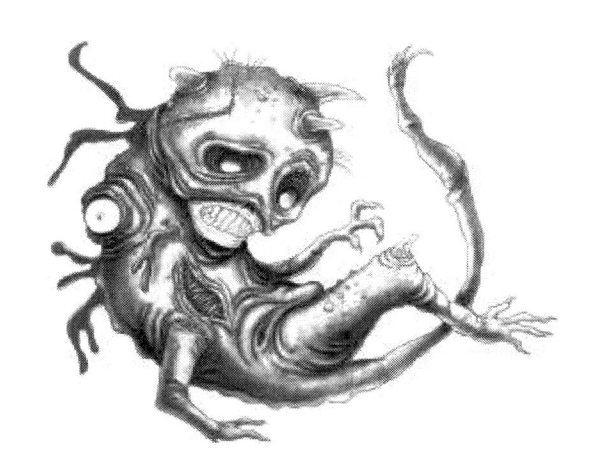

"What would you like to see?" Nerissa's gaze followed the languid path of the three bubbles as she read the iridescing futures.

The rangy man in old jeans and T-shirt sitting across from her said, "What are my options?"

"You only get one." The filmy spheres swirled and settled onto the pan of soapy water. In the first pearlescent orb he stood on the street begging for money. That could be a temporary problem or long term. She really had no way of determining length of time. In the next bubble, wearing a nice suit, hair well trimmed, he opened two briefcases filled with hundred-dollar bills. The last did not have him in it. Or rather, Nerissa saw an arm and a knife. It looked like his hands; he was grabbing a scarf, the knife stabbing forward out of the bubble's scope.

Nerissa's skin chilled and she glanced up at him. He twitched at a gold cross at his neck. With a future like that she wanted him gone. It was obvious which one to go with. She said, "You will come into a lot of money."

He clasped the cross, then released it. Rubbing his nose, he sniffed and looked at her through sunglasses. "Yeah, right."

"Seriously. More than you can imagine."

"Well." He stood, dropped a ten on the table and pointed at her in a way that unnerved her. "Let's hope you're right." He swaggered out, letting the screen door bang shut.

Ten. Maybe that's how he'd come into money, by being cheap. Nerissa sighed. It looked like she needed to put more of that Gypsy charm into reading if she wanted to make it worth her time. The allure pulled her, being able to direct a person's path subtly, and it left her feeling heady. But had she? What if she had chosen the bubble that showed him begging? Would he have come across the money anyway, or would it have evaporated, a chance gone?

A couple of weeks back Nerissa had blown bubbles for Shelagh's four-year-old. Instead of seeing just the coolly shimmering surfaces that to her had always represented something ungelled and changing, she had seen shifting, turning, twisting scenes. At first she thought them daydeams, overactive imagination, but she decided to buy her own hoop and bubble supply just to find out. From that day on she had always seen something in the bubbles.

Nerissa bit her lip. The last thing she wanted was a career in the shady art of fortune telling – she'd seen enough of that growing up. Like she needed her friends rolling their eyes and calling her Madame La Zonga or something. She had left the ridicule and suspicion behind even if her family still clutched at mystery like an heirloom. Let them have it. She wanted to fit in, not be a freak.

That first week, though, had been like changing channels on a TV, a hodgepodge of opalescent scenes until Mrs. Larkin had bustled over, talking in a tight voice. "Hello, Nerissa. I was wondering if you've seen Fraser. I can't find him anywhere."

The moment Nerissa thought of Mrs. Larkin's dog she had seen his brown fuzzy form swirl through each coalescing ball. Four bubbles drifted away on invisible strings. Fraser appeared, dead at the edge of a curb; in another a child petted him; the next showed him nosing in a garbage can, and in the fourth, Fraser was in the dog pound.

Nerissa had replied automatically, "I think I saw a child petting him a few blocks from here, towards Maple Street." The elderly, well-postured woman thanked her and strode off in search of her dog.

It had turned out as Nerissa predicted. She had danced with elation. But had she changed the future by choosing the one bubble? The vortex of playing a gimmick, fooling the *gadjo,* creating mystique, all of this waited to hungrily suck her into the old ways where nothing ever changed. Nerissa had had enough of being a Gypsy child always on the road, playing games in the cities, like trying to sneak on buses.

And somehow, people had always been able to tell that they were different, outsiders. Nerissa wasn't sure if "damn Gypsy" was a general curse for anyone misbehaving or had been thrown accurately at her people. She'd hated it, hated the family structure that still followed stilted traditions, hated the expectation that she would adhere to the same roles.

But the questions and curiosity remained and Nerissa couldn't deny the strong sense of purpose she had when she made predictions. Why now? Not mirrors, not crystal balls. Of course, she had always shied away from the mystical gobbledy gook no matter how the *compania* had badgered her. Yet the Rom ways had tracked her down in soapy spheres. Bubbles were light and airy but they weighted Nerissa with a headache.

People thought Rom lifestyles were free and easy but all Nerissa had ever felt was the oppression of succumbing to superstition, of being a cog. She'd ignored fortune telling, wasn't very good at dancing, nor interested much in playing music, and didn't want a brood of children. So she left the *compania* behind in a storm of ill will and moved to Freehaven, landscaping for the past two years. And now, now she played at the games she'd forsworn.

A rattle at the door alerted her to the next customer and she let a man in from the porch. He looked like a praying mantis, all elbows and knees, perched on the edge of a straight-backed chair. This guy twitched like he couldn't settle into his ungainly limbs.

She smiled and asked what he wanted to know.

"Oh just, um, whatever, if there uh, what the future holds."

Nerissa decided to add a few dramatic embellishments, and blew the bubbles from the thin hoop, moving her hands over them. The man's eyes didn't see the glassy bubbles as he glanced quickly at the pictures and windows draped with colorful shawls and hanging crystals that danced rainbow shards over the walls.

Her dramatic sigh caught his attention. She looked deep into his faded green eyes. "I can only tell you about your immediate future," she stage whispered.

"Yes?" His head bent forward on a scrawny neck and he pulled in his shoulders, as if to wrap his heart. "What do you see?"

The bubbles were small, almost hard to see. There were more than four, but only four scenarios showed over and over. He worked in a retail store, drove a truck, was hiking in high mountains, and was hit by a vehicle. Nerissa glanced up at him and he looked wobbly even sitting. He probably had some boring job and needed something memorable, to say his life wasn't wasted.

She threw in some Rom charm and spoke. "You will go someplace foreign." That sounded safe; besides, she hadn't seen anything tragic in that particular bubble.

"Really?" He clasped his hands sincerely and leaned farther forward, his brow wrinkling. "Where will I go? What am I going to do?"

"I'm sorry; the bubbles don't show me a lot. I could see you hiking in mountains. Maybe the Himalayas or the Alps." The breeze weaving through Nerissa's bungalow toyed with her curly locks but barely moved the man's damp looking hair.

He spoke so fast that his words ran together. "Weren't there other bubbles? What did they show?"

No one ever wanted to know that disaster and tragedy lay ahead. She chewed her lip and shook her head. The Madame La Zonga routine just wasn't her. "Fate allows you only one path. The other bubbles were much the same."

The man thanked her, left a twenty, then slipped out the door, chimes tinkling in his wake. She frowned at the soapy water. What if she chose all the destinies she saw? Would they happen whether she mentioned them or not? She tapped the pan with her fingernail. What was the point of having the ability though; to help people, to make money or was it to take control? And though she hated to admit it, there was something she really liked, maybe too much, in being able to make people's lives better.

Over the next few days, when a few friends came to visit, Nerissa had them ask simple questions about the next day or week, such as: "What will I find tomorrow?" or "Will I be meeting anyone?" Nerissa perceived small pockets of time-to-be, and what she spoke always became the truth. She could direct the future, and that left an icy sweat between her shoulder blades.

Nerissa stopped playing with prophecies for a couple of weeks. Why it bothered her was as slippery as a bubble's residue. She continued landscaping; the feeling of dirt on her hands, working in good solid earth, was tangible and real. She could see the changes she made to the land and it wasn't ephemeral like the foamy aftermath of cleaning. But... maybe she could make differences to people's lives too.

Then a postcard depicting a Himalayan mountainside arrived in the mail. She sat on her overstuffed plum couch, flipped it over and read the jerky handwriting from the scrawny man.

The first week in Nepal was amazing but then the bus I was taking was in a collision. I've had the nurses mail this from the hospital. They said I may not walk again. My adventure certainly wasn't what I was expecting.

Nerissa stared at the card, her stomach dropping like a boulder. Her palms clammy, she shivered, tossing the card to the table and watched the shadowplays the sun performed through the leaves of her potted plants. The walls almost looked alive with the passing shade. The images had been like pearls on a necklace, a string of destinies following an arcane path. Her power was to see and order them, but they were predetermined by each person's past. Should she have warned him? The sun, ignorant of the black cloud over Nerissa, was kissing the sky pink and gold when she finally pushed herself off the couch, grabbing the blue jacket draped over a curtain rod and keys from the protruding tongue of the cast-iron imp on the wall. Dusk wrapped around her like a caul. The patchy rust and yellow VW Bug in front of her home looked like a rotting lemon.

Grandma was the one who had embraced fortune telling by reading the Tarot or palms. Nerissa had always considered the mystical mumbo jumbo as nothing more than charade. Nerissa had to talk to someone and maybe Grandma knew something more.

She sat in the car gripping the steering wheel, then started to open the door again, then shut it. Turning the ignition, the Bug coughed to life, and Nerissa felt that as she sped off into the swelling night she was plunging herself into darkness.

Half an hour later she bumped along a dirt road, framed by flat farmlands and low mist rising off the ground. The Dewdney Trunk Road had always been a maze, winding through nondescript strawberry, squash and vegetable fields, with no other roads or signs. It was as if Nerissa drove back through time to a place between worlds, passing the mosaic of Cadillacs and other large outmoded vehicles. Next were a few trailers with people sitting or standing around a bonfire, faces illumined and looking wizened as the mist rose like wraiths in the fields. At the center were a few tents put together with scraps of board, metal and bright cloth. She stopped a couple of feet off a road no better than a beaten foot-track, and walked towards the fire that burned back the dark. The smoky smell brought memories of childhood and covered the fecund ripeness of cattle. No matter where the *compania* moved she could always find them through symbols marked on trees and fences.

Violin music, clapping and laughing reached Nerissa before the people materialized. Uncle Corwin, Chelsea, and Olaf sat around the fire, as well as half a dozen familiar faces.

"Eh, long time no see, little Nerissa," laughed ruddy Corwin, his crinkly silver hair catching the firelight.

She bent over to kiss his cheek. "I keep busy, Uncle, you know."

"I know. You try to forget your roots and live the *gadjo* life."

Already it began. "You forget, Corwin, I am half *gadjo*. But I'm not here for this. I need to see Tinka. It's important."

"Pfft! You need your tea leaves read, love?" Chelsea, sturdy and squat as a toadstool, asked between puffs of her cigarillo. "Having problems with one of your lovers, hmmm? You come back only when you need help, after nearly two years away?"

Nerissa's jaw bunched as the fire shadows capered over her. "I was here last year." But Chelsea had hit a nerve. She *had* only come back because she needed help.

Uncle Corwin rumbled, "A year's a long time away from family."

Chelsea sipped a beer and muttered. "We're only good enough when you want something. Just becoming another typical *gadjo*."

"Yeah," Nerissa snapped back. "And you're just typical *gypsies*." She used the *gadjo* word instead of "Rom," hoping to sting them. They were always the same, every time she returned. Like some bizarre circus, denying the world was changing around them. Always deriding her for having left the Rom way. She unclenched her fists and took a deep breath. "Look, I don't want to fight. I need to see Tinka."

The crackling fire gained volume over the silent group until Corwin nodded toward a small tent. She turned her back to the warmth and their cold stares.

Pulling back the flap, she saw Tinka sitting quietly in lantern light, a black and white ball of a kitten nestled into her arms. Swathed in a big blue sweater and the full Gypsy skirts of old, Tinka looked up from her cushions, and smiles creased her eyes.

"Ah, Nerissa. It is good to see you, child. You don't come often, but I know how it is. The tribe grows thin and the younger folk want to experience the new ways; the old ways change. Even this," she said patting the kitten. "In the old days we would never touch a cat or a dog. Taboo."

Nerissa bent to kiss Tinka's wrinkly but soft cheek, then seated herself on the worn carpets. "Tinka." She wasn't sure how to go on. "I—I've been telling fortunes… through soap bubbles. It could be… I think I might be meddling in people's lives." Nerissa cheeks grew hot and she stared down at the carpets' designs.

Tinka's eyebrows rose over her gold-brown eyes. "Oh? You never showed any power before."

"I never believed it was real."

Tinka patted her hand. "Sometimes it's all for show, but many of us have had power to see past or future, even the present in other places."

"It's more than seeing; I can direct them, choose."

Tinka grabbed her hand and turned Nerissa's palm face up. Nerissa jerked back, feeling chilled. Her scalp tightened.

"Hush," said Tinka. "It won't hurt. Palms have people's destinies etched firmly into them, though they can change too." She grunted and dropped Nerissa's palm. "Your life has a split ahead, a little unclear."

"What's that mean?"

"Depends on what you do."

She looked into her grandmother's knowing eyes. "You used to say I'd meet a handsome Rom man. Was that really what you saw?"

Tinka shrugged and rubbed under the purring kitten's chin. "Oh I saw a few things, guessed at others, wished for some. It's what we usually do."

"Do?" Nerissa frowned. "Do? Do you play people like puppets on strings?"

"Nerissa, if you've read anyone's future and you really have the gift, then you probably know they don't always want the truth. They want a dream."

"So you tell them what works for you."

"Or tell them what I think they want to hear." Tinka tapped her head. "It's what's here that makes a difference. You don't even need the power to know that."

Nerissa grew hot with anger but she didn't know if at Tinka, the Rom or herself. Wasn't that what she'd been doing? "What if they get hurt?" Nerissa stared at her hands, not feeling she could even trust her grandmother's words.

"Do you hold a gun to their heads?" Tinka pulled an olive-green blanket around her stooped shoulders. "The power of a god is no small thing, Nerissa. This gift is not that big, but to not use it would be a waste of a special talent. Not many get the choice."

Nerissa clenched her fists. "Even if it brings pain? Should I use it if it shows tragedy?"

With a sigh, Tinka said, "It's up to you to decide but life is filled with pain and joy. Let your instincts guide you. That's all you need."

She whispered, "I hated the way we were treated when I was growing up."

"Because you cared what others thought. We couldn't keep you though."

"Because I have my own path." She hugged the old woman "I better go. It's getting late."

Through the tent flap, Tinka called, "I'm always here if you want to talk. And Nerissa, you can't change the past, only the future."

Nerissa stuck her head back through the flap and forced a smile she didn't feel. "Bye, Grandma, thanks."

She heard the quiet farewell, "May *o Del* walk with you, child."

The next morning Nerissa awoke to the calling of children and dogs barking on the street. The mist in her head was soon burnt off by sunlight brushing across her room. She stretched, dressed, wrapped a green silk scarf around her neck, and went into the living room. The black pan sat with books and papers piled in it on the little wood table; the urn waited silently on the floor.

She stared at the items, then looked away. Tying her kinky hair up into a ponytail she leaned against the door frame and gazed down the street thinking time never acted the way people wished. It was as elusive as a bubble; no firm grasp. Yet she could watch time float by.

Lighting a stick of cinnamon incense, she moved into the kitchen and sat down to a piece of bread with homemade, blackcurrant jam. Resting her elbow on the table, she watched the birds in the back yard. *I need to cut the grass and do things*, she thought, then looked over at the dishes heaped in the sink. There was a lot she could do but it was soap bubbles that floated through her mind.

Brushing crumbs from her jeans, Nerissa left the small kitchen and went into the living room. She picked up the pan and the thin silver hoop beside it. She smiled at the thought of doing dishes and reading a thousand futures in the dishwater. Back in the kitchen she put everything away, then opened the back door to let a breeze through.

She could tell the future and dig up the past; find kidnapped people – or murdered children. And she could very well be alone when people realized what she did. Being an outsider for half her life had been enough. Freehaven held her new roots.

A month of normal life passed without any fortune telling but Nerissa felt guilty, wondering if she had wasted something important. And yet temptation always lay in being able to manipulate someone, to try and help them. She was still undecided about her talent and what it meant. But she feared the mire of family traditions waiting to suck her back in.

A short, sharp rap sounded on her door, making Nerissa jump. She answered, peering through the screen and felt she examined a photograph etched with time. The man behind the screen was stark – black hair, ragged pale features, black and white clothes.

"You read my fortune a couple months ago. What did you do to me?"

"Do?" She remembered his hungry look, even though he'd worn sunglasses. There had only been three bubbles. She'd picked the one she thought he'd wanted, the one with all the money. Nerissa shivered. "I didn't do anything; just said what I saw."

He glanced over his shoulder, then yanked the screen door open, snapping the clasp and blocking the entry with his body.

Nerissa jumped back, her heart thumping, but her body was confused, slow to realize the danger. "What are you doing!"

The man moved toward her, towering, his hands clenching menacingly at his sides. "Your reading... I...I got more money than I can count. But it's no good. Something went wrong. Now, I...I owe people, the wrong people who—" He stopped, his mouth moving but no words escaping. He glanced jerkily about the room, then glared at Nerissa.

Nerissa rubbed her arms, prickly with goosebumps. "I'm sorry, but I didn't know it would go wrong. I only see one image." A lie, or the truth filmed over. She backed slowly away, toward the kitchen.

He sprung like a striking snake, grabbing her about the throat. She clutched at his hands, pulling to loosen the choking hold. "It's your fault. Change it, make a new reading."

"I—I can't," she gasped. His fingers pressed into her flesh, bringing darkness to the edges of her vision. "It's your destiny. Killing me will change nothing."

His nose nearly touched hers and spit hit her face. "Read again, damn it! Read again or I'll break your neck. Tell me what's coming."

Nerissa bit her lip. She was the doomsayer, the bubble burster. She nodded and he let her go.

He let her gather the supplies from the kitchen but didn't leave her side. Nerissa sloshed water as she walked back to the living room. He pulled a switchblade from his pocket, flicked it open and sat close beside her on the couch. The blade scored her neck. "Tell me my options," he growled.

She flinched but said, "You've got to give me space, to read properly."

He moved across to a chair, the blade still in his hand. Nerissa glanced nervously at him, rubbing her neck, and uncapped the ceramic urn, pouring soapy water into the black pan. She pushed paper, books and pens aside. But before she dipped the hoop she tried to take a few deep breaths. Tinka's words came back to her. *Use what you know.*

Calm settled over Nerissa like a white blanket and she truly looked at the man – sweating, obviously terrified and he didn't think he had any choice left. He was grasping at straws. Obviously he didn't want to die but how could she direct him? She remembered the cross about his neck, and the bubble with him stabbing off screen, grabbing a scarf. A green scarf like the one she wore.

She blew through the hoop. Two oily, ponderous bubbles emerged and wobbled down into the pan. She caught the images before they shattered in a wet burst. He was stabbing forward, her green scarf in his hand; the other had him begging on the street. How could she direct this?

She swallowed past a thickness in her throat and decided to try something new. What if that was the only outcome he could see? Maybe she could appeal to his instincts and his sense of right. Nerissa dipped and blew as second time, asking as the bubbles settled, "What if you gave the money back?"

"Not possible," he snapped.

But she'd had time to see two bubbles; one revealed him dead at the feet of a man with a briefcase of money. The other showed him stabbing at her. The visions had changed but they both might still happen. "Do you still have the money?"

He nodded.

Her shaky hand pulled the hoop through the water while she visualized his choices and blew. "What if you gave it away, or to the police?" He started to answer but she shushed him.

Three soapy bubbles of varying sizes wafted into the air. The options were increasing. Nerissa's gaze greedily took in the visions. She swallowed, feeling the hard tip of the blade although it was nowhere near her.

"I...uh, you don't have great options but if, if you follow this one choice, you'll live."

"What?"

"You give the money up to the police, turn state's witness, and end up with a new identity but alive."

He stood. Nerissa refused to cower but the blade swung in his hand.

"You couldn't see all that. Lie again and you're dead. Now what do you see?"

If she had more time, she could probably manipulate the bubbles better. "Two men kick down a door, and...they shoot you. Next, you are begging on the street. And you, uh—" She stopped, the sweat soaking her shirt, giving her shivers.

"All of them." He leaned forward and grabbed her scarf, pulling it tight about her neck.

"You stab me." Her breath came out in short gasps. "You kill me." It would happen now that she'd spoken it. She closed her eyes, not wanting to see her end, imagining him begging instead.

The scarf pulled tighter and Nerissa tensed – a loud crack made her jump, and she waited to feel the pain bleed through her. The screen door banged and another loud thump came from the porch. She slowly opened her eyes, looking around. He was gone. Then she saw the knife skewering a paper to her table.

As a car screeched down the street Nerissa walked to the door and looked out. There was a black suitcase on her porch and when she looked inside she saw stacks of cash. Bringing it inside, she set it down, then wriggled the knife free from a paper. A short list of names was scratched onto it.

She touched her neck. He had stabbed as she had seen but it hadn't been her. Predictions could be subjective and only if she saw him again, which she hoped never to do, would she know if that last bubble was true. He'd made his choices, no matter how she had interpreted the bubbles. But they weren't finite. Time was a moving line and many events took place after the images she saw.

Tinka had been right. Nerissa couldn't change the past, but she could affect the future. Every choice a person made in life, whether they took someone else's advice or not, directed and shaped their destiny.

∽

She used the reward money to expand her landscaping business, and she used her fortune telling abilities, honing them to track down the gangly man in physical rehab. She offered him a job, driving a truck for her. That made another bubble in his fortune true.

Fortune telling would not rule her destiny; it was only a tool to master. The *compania* had tried to manipulate her and fill her with dire warnings of the *gadjo* because they had cared and were scared. She didn't need to ignore them, nor follow their ways. Her world involved Freehaven, and even her family. It included good and bad, the power to see the future, and the power to affect some lives, beyond just spouting visions.

Bubbles are always shifting, changing, like a person's life. Every decision directs a path in one way or another, leaving a long, well-marked trail of what has been, and an unmarked land of what will be.

Asylum

Our everyday language is peppered with idioms that we don't always realize were due to the influence of such writers as Shakespeare, Dickens and Poe. "Oh he must have a picture hanging in the closet" references Oscar Wilde's The Picture of Dorian Gray. And "The lunatics are running the asylum," comes directly from Poe's The System of Doctor Tarr and Professor Fether. That story is considered one of his comedic works and is definitely satirical. I added a darker vein.

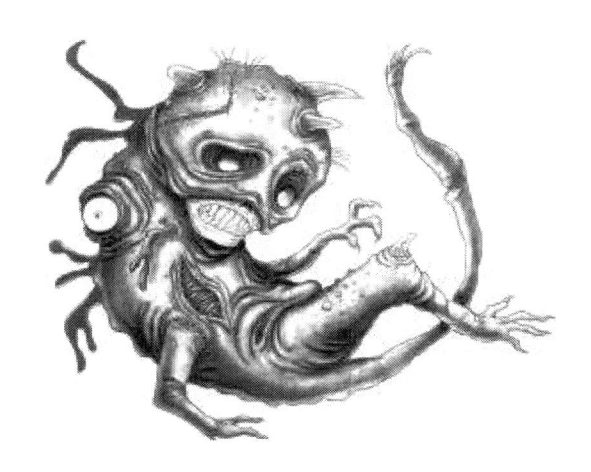

The labyrinthine country roads, land as flat as an old politician's speech, made a GPS useless near the Dewdney Trunk Road. It twines several cities, running the perimeter and weaving the farmlands together. The day-long search led me to think that Professor Fayther's directions had steered me wrong. So odd a duck was he, I had never been sure what constituted alcohol-conjured ramblings and what a small distillation of truth. Perhaps it was a wild goose chase and there was no asylum. Yes, asylum. Such a quaint word conjuring images of madmen and Gothic edifices, which was what I hungered to find. My stomach growled and I peered at the scrawled directions again. Every road looked the same, leading nowhere but to another field, or an abandoned, ramshackle house. Harvest season had ended; the sun now hunkered pallid in the leeched sky, the fields wasting to yellow.

I drove on as my need grew. Except for the tongues of pavement, I could have been transported back in time. The professor had assured me that this last relic to an archaic institution for the mentally ill still existed. Beyond the government's eye, the rich sent their embarrassments there, away from public scrutiny.

The sun was a bleary orb by the time I spied a structure in the distance. The first unusual sign in the Fraser Valley countryside was a rusted iron fence with fang-sharp spikes piercing the low lying clouds that cloaked the evening sky. Lonely birch and oak trees worked at carpeting the road with an enticement of leaves. I wanted *Gothic*, praying that the inhabitants were mad as loons and that the madhouse was decrepit, ghastly and forgotten. I was far from the nearest town.

Should I have to stay the night I would find somewhere to sleep, even if it was on an old couch.

The road curved gently, revealing the peeling facade of what once would have been a mansion, one turret and three gables visible. I parked in a yard devoid of any cars and walked up to a sturdy wooden door. My keys went into one pocket of my jacket and I patted the other, making sure all my tools were there. I could find no buzzer, not even a knocker. I looked around, noting the tarnished doorknob, the damp smell of mold that permeated the autumn air, the reluctance of the dwindling light to touch the wood. Eventually I discovered a rotting cord and, fearing it would break in my hand, pulled it. I expected a delay at best, or no answer at worst, but the door swung open immediately.

A grinning woman with frizzled blonde hair and tattoos of feathers and waves down her bare arm greeted me. "Yes, ma'am. How can I help you?"

Her retro tortoiseshell, horn rim glasses surprised me as did her nurse's scrubs, and I took a step back. "Is this the Rockyview? I'm looking for Dr. Canard."

She smiled again and beckoned me into a bright butter-yellow corridor with warm fluorescent lighting. I frowned at the boring modernity, and then watched a man approach. He was tall, bearded, with a long moustache pointed on both ends, and beautiful eyes like green glass. He looked like a hipster or someone affecting steampunk fashion, wearing a pocket watch tethered to a burgundy collared vest, a white shirt with an ascot, and slim pants. "Dr Canard," I questioned, reaching out to shake his hand.

He stepped back from my touch, opening his arms wide. "Welcome. You must be Felicia Jones, sent by Professor Fayther. You are interested in our asylum, yes?"

I licked my lips, trying to savor the atmosphere. "Yes, I'm working on my PhD in psychology, and my thesis is comparing different modes of rehabilitation used in institutions, and their effectiveness in integrating patients back into society."

In truth, I cared less about the modes and more about madness, eagerly anticipating a diet of lunatics, and their absolute lack of inhibitions regarding social conventions. What can one gain by cracking the walnut and tasting the furrows of the meat? It was into such minds that I hoped to delve, to satiate my constant hunger. I queried about a tour and meeting some of the inhabitants.

"Of course," replied Dr. Canard, "but we were about to eat. Join us – it's communal – and I can give you a tour after, yes?"

I smiled at him. "All right, I am hungry…for information as well."

The nurse grinned widely, as if I'd just accepted an invitation to a ball, and led the way, her floral tunic like a small garden. Dr. Canard brought up the rear. He chattered as we moved down the hall, his voice drifting airily behind me. "We've been trying a new way of rehabilitating our patients. We have two areas, as you will see, and they can choose in which area they spend their time. Only those with the more excitable conditions are kept confined."

We passed what could be considered a living room with a big screen TV, several computers on tables against one wall, a collection of books, and various board games. People were engaged in assorted activities and dressed in T-shirts, jeans, skirts. It completely contradicted the outer facade. I was disappointed by such ordinary attire, and I was famished. I sniffed the air, sifting the stale odors of bacon, sweat, tobacco and onions. There was the underlying tang – a frisson of copper and blood and charcoal – that told me madness lived here.

"Why does the Rockyview look so old on the outside and so very modern inside?"

There was a pause, and I looked back. Dr. Canard wore a thunderous frown, but he smiled when he noted me watching. "We use the facade to keep the curious at bay. They are less likely to…interfere."

But as we moved farther into the asylum's interior, the hallway narrowed and the color slowly changed, so that when I noted the drab institutional green and the grey and white linoleum beneath my feet I blinked, wondering if I'd only imagined the brighter corridor.

The building went deeper than I had surmised and we entered what must have been the original structure. Dr. Canard flickered into my peripheral vision and I turned. He seemed pale, as if recovering from an illness. He gestured right, toward a large room with wooden tables and simple utility chairs. "That's where our clients eat. And through here..." he now moved into the lead as the nurse who had followed us went off calling others to dinner. "...is where we eat."

The ornate room was ribbed in dark wood. Several Tiffany lamps painted rainbows on Persian carpets, and numerous candlesticks adorned a plethora of cabinets and side hutches. An oval mahogany table was the heart of the room, with seating for twenty. People entered from several doorways, some dressed in scrubs, others in street wear. As they sat, tureens and platters of food were brought in. Someone pulled a chair out for the doctor and he gingerly sat on its edge; his overly-stiff posture made it look as if he would take flight at any moment.

He smiled at me and nodded. "Go ahead, we don't stand on form here."

The food was peculiar: peaches on mashed potatoes, carrots mixed with grapes, and a whole roasted animal carcass, disturbingly the size and shape of a skinned cat, including a long tail, withered little ears, and the feline face with remnants of claws on each foot. The deep red meat was displayed on platters heaped high with a sprinkling of colored marshmallows. I scooped a bit of the tamer food onto my plate. I nibbled a carrot but tasted only copper. I tried a slice of safer looking meat, most likely ham, and tasted charcoal.

Putting my fork down, I asked, "Does your staff stay through the night?"

The doctor nodded. "They do, but not all. They have to eat after all, and someone must bring in supplies."

Several of the staff nodded. "Eat," one small woman said.

"Yes," smirked a hawk-nosed man. "Eat."

They started to laugh. "Eat. Heh heh. Oh that's good. Eat!"

The room rumbled with laughter and the nurses and aides pointed forks of food at each other and screamed "Eat!" They laughed and guffawed until they were nearly falling from their chairs, tears streaming down their cheeks, food spraying from their mouths.

"Enough!" shouted Dr. Canard, and immediately they all fell silent. The overhead lights flickered and dimmed, the glow of the candles adding to the ethereal glare.

I looked at the doctor but he glowered down the table, his food untouched.

I quivered. The energy that seemed to infect the staff ran through me as if a lightning storm were near.

"You've barely touched your food, Miss Jones."

I stared at the bizarre concoctions and watched a woman with freckles nearly the color of the carrots shovel marshmallows and meat into her mouth, barely stopping to swallow. "I'm just not that hungry."

Which was a lie. I was famished, and had been hunting a long time for just such a place as this. Out of the way, forgotten, filled with the delectable strangeness of those who untether their minds from reality's shores.

I looked up at Dr. Canard and again noticed flickering. But it wasn't the lights. I likened it more to bringing an image into focus, one that had faded over time. "You're not eating either."

His smile creased his face. "I don't often. That is, I take my meals later."

A food fight began at the other end of the table until he cleared his throat.

"Tell me," I asked, trying to ignore the strange food orgy. "What is your success rate for returning your patients to normal society?"

"Alas," he sighed. "What is normal? You see, our guests are of an unusual disposition. They will maintain to their last breath that they are fine, and refuse to see their behavioral flaws. The worst of these must be confined so that they do no damage to themselves or us."

"Indeed," called out the hawk-nosed man. "They walk like a chicken," and he jumped up and strutted around the table with his hands tucked into his armpits. "And talk like a chicken." He crowed and clucked until Canard yelled, "Silence! You give me no rest. My only boon is that you'll die or move on, and leave me in peace."

The dining room doors slammed shut. I was as much amazed by this display as I was by the doctor's outburst. In all other institutions quiet and behind-the-scenes reprimands would have happened. This was as refreshing as it was unorthodox. I couldn't help but inhale deeply, my tongue tasting the air.

A plump little woman to my right laughed. "That's nothing. Mere pranks and antics. Why, a more absurd and disturbing sort was the woman who howled and snarled and thought herself a werewolf."

I reached for a bun, thinking it the safer sort of meal from the menagerie of food, and she growled. I snatched my hand back and she lunged towards me, jaws snapping, and then leaped onto the table on all fours and howled.

I couldn't completely stifle my smile. The lunatics were running the asylum but it mattered not to me. "Dr. Canard!" I spoke loudly for the raucous staff was gaining in volume as they indulged in the one-upmanship game. "Do I take it that you have no criminally insane here?"

He steepled his fingers, glaring across them at his unruly personnel. "Oh very few, Miss Jones, very few. We have a few personalities that could be dangerous, but we take care of them."

"Might it be possible to get that tour before it gets much later? It's a long drive back from here."

I noticed he had not touched his food at all. That tang of madness was becoming thick enough that I thought I would be able to sip it straight from the air.

"All right. I think you are ready, yes?"

Just then someone shrieked and the cacophony continued. As I turned back to Dr. Canard, I blinked. Did his hand just pass through the chair?

"All right, everyone! Dinner's over. Clean up the mess, please."

As we turned away, there was little to indicate the nurses and orderlies were different from children at a birthday party.

Canard moved into the hallway and away from the brighter rooms, explaining, "These next suites, isolated from the others, offer a more sedate environment." The air felt weighted, as if it hadn't moved in years.

Canard's white shirt seemed to stand out wraithlike as the shadows absorbed the color from his clothing. He never stopped to turn on a light; in fact there seemed to be no switches, just lit sconces along the walls.

"We like to keep this institution private, with little interference from the outside world."

As he prattled on, I had to clasp my hands to keep from fidgeting, my need growing greater, almost unquenchable. "Where do you keep those with the more excitable conditions? I'd like to examine them."

Canard grew silent. I followed behind his ghostly figure that seemed to fade into the ever-darkening hallway. I had to reach out, feeling my way along the walls. A door creaked open ahead and he replied, "They're down here. You might want to grab a lantern."

"Where?" I asked, unable to locate the door he had opened. A lantern? Gone were the last vestiges of modern conveniences.

I bumped into a hall table. Barely able to see in the murky corridor, I patted along the surface until I felt the base of a small metal lamp, and next to it a box of small wooden matches. I fumbled one match out and struck it, causing shadows to caper up the wall.

I thought it unusual that he didn't help me and that no other staff were present. I turned the knob of the antique glass chimney, adjusting the flame, and it settled into an amber glow. Turning toward the door, Dr. Canard seemed to materialize in the light. "After you, Miss Jones."

A cool breeze wafted up from the dark mouth of the door's interior, causing the light to dance. With it came a complex odor.

I hesitated but moved toward the doorway, inky shadows dancing before me. The dark maw led down steep stairs to an underground chamber. The smell of rotting socks and something sharp and stinging assaulted my nose. I licked my lips and ran my tongue over my teeth.

The air was different than that above, more copper, less charcoal, as if down here madness grew in its embryonic stage. Edging down the steps, the light crawled over shapes behind rustic bars. A grubby hand reached through. "Please, help us. We don't belong here."

"Why not?" I asked, holding the lamp high, trying to get a view of the incarcerated.

"We're not mad!" A woman's voice whispered.

The basement cells were stone walls and floors, with the fourth wall nothing more than sturdy metal bars. There were four cells in all, two on each side of the wide central area, much like a prison. Each 'room' held four cots.

I set the lamp on the floor so that I could examine the lock plates set in the inch-thick bars. I ran my fingers over the metal, granular with rust. The cells must have been here a long time.

I could make out the dim shapes of three inmates, each in his or her own cell. The cloying odor of shit and sweat swirled and mixed with the copper scent.

Another, a gravelly male voice, cried out, "We were the staff here! They've imprisoned us. Please, call the police!"

It was at this that Dr. Canard spoke up. "You see, they have the worst delusions, believing they are sane."

"I see. Well, perhaps you can show me some of the others upstairs now." I turned toward Dr. Canard and he wavered into view. Of his ethereal nature, I no longer had doubt.

"I don't think so," he said. "You see, Miss Jones, you suffer the same malady, yes? This belief in being sane, of being above those you call insane and would study. It is here you'll reside for awhile until we know you are cured."

"But I'm not ill, Dr. Canard. And while you cannot leave this place there is no reason I should not."

He smiled and it was a terrible sight to see in the dim lighting. People moaned behind me. Soft weeping began. "But you shall not."

He raised his arms, pale and translucent, the weak light casting no shadow behind him. Yet for all his ephemeral nature, a ghostly wind blew dirt and debris into a dervish. My hair whipped about me and as I strove to see in the sputtering illumination I was knocked off my feet and slammed into one of the cell doors behind me.

The gate crashed open, I fell in, then the door shut, the lock snickering closed. Beyond, Canard floated in the corridor, spinning slowly as he looked at each of us.

Wiping grit from my eyes, I called out, "You can't do this! Professor Fayther will notice when I don't return. He'll alert the authorities."

Canard laughed as he drifted up the stairs, leaving the light where I had placed it on the floor. "I think not, Miss Jones. He is my jailer as I am yours. He sends me tidbits from time to time to amuse me, for my…experiments."

With that, the upper door slammed shut and I was left to view what I could of my dim surroundings. My hunger was all-consuming as I turned to survey my fellow inmates.

I had searched for years for that right blend – like sugar and spice, like sweet and savory – and it had been in madness where I found my tastes best fit. Now Canard thought he could keep me in this place that time forgot. Like him, I didn't want the authorities snooping. In the past I'd had to take pains to make my intentions circumspect, moving on from time to time. But here we would see who would be the keeper.

Two women and a man, bedraggled in rumpled and smelly clothing stared at me, their eyes deadened with hopelessness. "We were hoping you could save us," said the skinny balding man. "But you're one of us, one of us…n-now."

"Oh I won't save you," I said as I moved closer to examine him. In fact, I was exactly where I wanted to be. The feeding ground was ripe. They had stewed in madness long enough that it would add texture and sustenance for me. There was ample food in this building.

I would have to feed carefully, but one would keep me sated for a good long while. I pulled my toolkit from my dress pocket and just laid it near the lock – first, I had other needs. I reached through the bars and caressed the man's leathery cheek. "I won't save you but I can release you."

I pulled his head close to the bars and kissed him, pushing my tongue between his lips to open him up. Then I began to suck the charcoal and copper and blood that swirled in his essence. At first he was pliant, possibly surprised by my youthful exuberance and unexpected passion. But then, as I siphoned the redolent vapors and he felt his essence draining, he struggled and flapped beneath my grip like a dying fish.

It took some time to drain him. As his struggles lessened, I felt my strength growing, my skin plumping to full youthfulness. I should have gone slower but it had been so long, and I greedily sucked down his soul. As his body emptied, he grew lighter in my arms, skin shrinking, desiccating. I released him and his mummified body clattered to the stone floor. I barely heard the screams of the others as I fed on the madness.

I had sought asylum, and had found it!

Gingerbread People

In the 90s in Canada Paul Bernardo and Carla Homolka were convicted of kidnapping, torturing and killing two teenage girls. A good looking, successful couple, they didn't fit the criminal mold. Homolka received a lighter sentence because she said Bernardo coerced her to do the crimes. I've been intrigued by the sociopath mindset and chose to explore what is true evil: is it the person perpetrating the deed, or the one who makes the person do the deed?

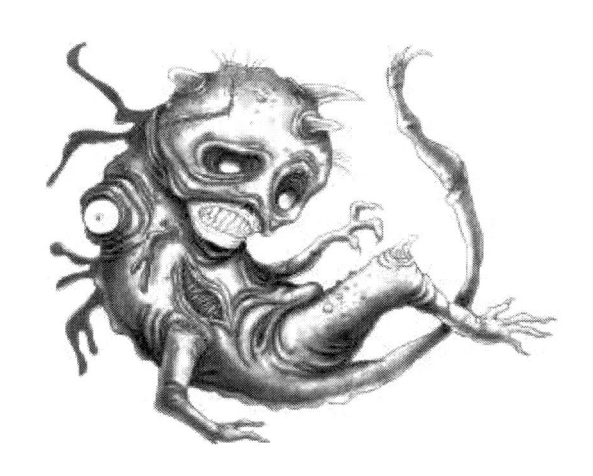

You can eat them. Go ahead. It is one way to know them.

Do you think it was like this once; lines of doughy people shivering and waiting to go to the ovens? When they came out, do you think they were toasted brown, all crisp and forever frozen...not frozen...baked in one position? Waiting for someone to taste bite into their lives, taste their stories.

I'm sorry. You don't understand. How can you?

Yes, I know why you're here and I agree to go without a fight, but I must tell you this. It's a confession, I think. They say it relieves a soul. Please...listen. I want you to know, everyone to know, so it will not happen again. That would be right, wouldn't it?

Where does it begin? With my birth, I suppose. Hans, my beautiful blonde brother, my shining star, always protected me. Mother told me he had thanked her when I was born. He did everything for me. If I fell, he held me and wiped the tears. If I was hungry, he gave me his food. He showed me things, he told me stories and he revealed the world to me.

I remember the first time Mother tried to abandon us. She and Father were still together, though they fought often. Hans and I lay in our beds, our hands clasping across the small gap as they yelled in the living room. Hans whispered, "It's okay, Gretty, I'll be here. Go to sleep and don't listen." He was the only one who ever called me Gretty.

Mother had come back from her cleaning job to find Father drunk again. "Can't you stay with Gretchen tomorrow? I have an interview for a job. And all you do is drink what you make anyway."

"No," Father mumbled. "Get a baby-sitter."

They began yelling in earnest and the door vibrated. I trembled from the reverberation of their voices. Only when Hans climbed into bed beside me, holding me and muffling the noise, did I finally fall asleep.

Next morning, scowling, Mother woke us and ordered us to dress. She gave us sandwiches and drove us to the library. "Stay here and study, Hans. Don't let Gretchen out of your sight. I'll be back at noon to pick you up."

I looked up at the great white pillars of the library and flinched. "It's okay, Gretty," Hans said and took my hand, leading me up into the forest of books. But he didn't study. He muttered and picked at the hem of his jacket. "She doesn't want us, Gretty. Neither of them do. They're always trying to get rid of us." Four years older than me and so wise. Only when I began to sniffle and shiver did he stop and give me something to eat.

Mother didn't show up at noon, nor at twelve-thirty. Hans managed to beg enough change for a bus home. When we arrived, Mother said, "Where were you? Didn't I say to wait there?"

She explained that her interview had run long, but Hans just glared at her. There were other incidents, minor really, but Hans always said she was trying to get rid of us. She and Father fought, usually about looking after me and working so hard. It was as if I caused Mother to carry the dark shadows under her eyes and rub her feet from working so much. I often curled into a chair and read a book or stared out the window; if she didn't notice me, then she would not get rid of me. I tried to be very quiet.

I was twelve when we overheard Mother talking on the phone to a friend one night. Father was long gone; no one knew where. We often came home to an empty house because Mother worked two jobs.

I had already drifted asleep when Hans's strong hand shook me. "Quiet," he whispered. "Listen."

"They're going to have to go. I have no choice, really. The doctor said I can't work two jobs and stay out of the hospital. I can't support them on one income. I'm hoping they won't have to be in a foster home for long. Maybe my sister in Churchill can take them. Their father? Forget it, he was never any help…"

※

In the morning, after Mother had left, I started to get ready for school, when Hans stopped me. "Gretty," he said while holding my hand and looking at me with his ice blue eyes, "we have to leave."

"But, where, Hans? Where will we go?" Something in my throat made it difficult to speak. Tears spilled down my cheeks.

He quickly hugged me and started pulling clothes from our drawers. He dumped my books and tossed me some skirts and blouses. "Don't worry, I'll find some place."

"But what about Mother?" I remember my heart squeezing then, but I feel nothing now.

He tossed his wavy blonde hair from his eyes and scowled.

And we were gone. A few clothes in our packs, whatever money we could find and some bread and cheese. At sixteen Hans was big. He wasn't yet six feet but you could see he'd hit it. His shoulders were broadening and he had the kind of good looks and charm that got him what he wanted. I was shorter and darker and already had a woman's body though I looked young.

The bus took us across the city, and into the next. Hans said, "We have to hide or we'll get caught and sent away forever, and they'll hurt us. This way we get to choose."

That first night I wanted to go home and take my chances with Mother. We found an old apartment building, boarded up in an area scheduled for redevelopment. Hans worked his fingers under a board and pried it off the window. After propping it back in place we walked through tin cans, newspapers and scattered bits of broken glass that glinted like eyes in the thin trickle of streetlight. It grew blacker the deeper we went and Hans held my hand to guide me. I was hungry and afraid. We stumbled over stairs and moved upward until we found a room with windows still intact and light streaming through from outside. An old mattress lay folded over in one room. We knocked drywall and rat droppings off of it, then carried it back. Hans spread newspapers upon the old brown stains and we unrolled our one sleeping bag on top.

Shadows oozed like black blood across the floor and over our feet. Chitterings and skritchings in the walls made me jump. I shrieked when a rat ran across my foot. "I want to go home," I wailed.

Hans grabbed me and pulled me to the mattress, hugging me and patting my hair. "Shh, my Gretty. Shh. It'll be all right. I'll protect you. Shh." He looked around and sighed. "This won't do. We'll survive, though." He lay me down and smiled at me, then kissed my forehead, eyelids, nose, mouth. His fingers worked at the buttons on my blouse as he talked.

I began to pull away but he held me, pinning me under his legs while he talked the whole time. "We're going to have to do some unpleasant things, Gretty, but we'll make it. I'll make it easier, I will. You'll see." He pulled my blouse off and began working on taking off my shoes and socks.

"Oh, Gretty, I love you so much," he sighed into my neck and started massaging my little breasts. His other hand pulled at my skirt. I didn't know what he was doing but I pushed at him. We had often shared the same bed when I had nightmares, but his hands moved differently. He was on top of me, pushing between my legs. I whimpered and began to cry again.

"Shh, shh, it's okay. I won't hurt you. I love you more than Mother loved us. This will only make it better." And it was done. There was no way I could resist against big strong Hans. He was my world and that did not change, though now it consumed me. It was the first time I knew he lied to me.

For a week, Hans stayed with me, only going off to find food or a warm scrap of blanket. I didn't move much and pulled back from his touch, crying and terrified. "You're a big girl and you'll be brave for me, won't you?" he would say. Each night he held me in his arms and opened me up a bit more and let the world inside.

Every day he reminded me of the bleak horror of the world, how our mother would not want us, how I could not find my way or survive. Then he showed me how to do things with my body, my mouth and my hands. He said I'd need it to help us carry on, that we were on our own, no one wanted us. I tried to do my best so that he at least wouldn't abandon me. He was all I had and I did not want to get lost in the city of shadows and hard edges.

At the end of that week he cleaned me up and dressed me, saying, "Gretty, we have to find someplace better, someplace warmer. We have to help ourselves. There are a lot of people out there, hiding in buildings and alleys waiting to prey on us. When we go out there we'll act like we own the world; they won't hurt us."

"I—I—don't understand, Hans. How do we own it?"

He applied some makeup to my eyes and lips. "Just to make you pretty, my Gretty." Then he answered, his voice quavering, a weird light shining in his eyes. "We own it by making people pay. They'll pay and pay until they know who owns them." He dabbed harder and harder at the eyeshadow until it broke apart and powdered like purple snow sparkling with dust motes in the sunlight.

Then he took me outside, winding me back and forth between tall buildings. I had only seen the outside when we arrived and I was lost in that forest of concrete and glass. Hans squeezed my shoulders and told me how much to ask for when the men came. "Remember what I taught you, Gretty, and do me proud. I won't be far. I'll protect you."

Protect me he did. My first men, though large and hairy, had been gentle. Later, there were rough beasts and several tried to hurt me but Hans always made them pay more in the end, in flesh or money.

I began to hunger. Hans had opened up a place inside me that couldn't be filled. There was never enough food and I would gnaw hungrily on a carrot or an old heel of bread.

Soon we had a little apartment with nicotine-colored walls and cracked floor tiles, a fridge that dripped and always smelled of mold and lights that flickered. But it was dry and warm and away from rats.

Eventually I learned my way around those buildings, knowing where shadows lurked and which men were too dangerous. But I had forgotten the way home.

A year or so passed. I couldn't really keep track of time when I worked days and nights, being with more men than a year has days. I started shying from Hans's hands at night, though only he spoke of love. I grew grumpier, always hungry, plumping out and pleaded to stop working. Tears trickled down my cheeks at night, like that first month when we had run away. Hans would scowl and pick at the hem of his shirt.

It was a rainy, windy day when Hans came home whistling. He was soaked through his jean jacket but ignored the puddles he made. When he saw me sitting curled up on the tattered orange couch he did a little dance, spun in a circle and spread his arms wide. "Ta da! I have a surprise for you, my little sugar plum." My mouth dropped open at his rare jollity. He smiled, his even teeth seeming to glow in the gloomy light and he kneeled beside me.

In his opened hands were five little packets, each one carefully wrapped in foil. I unwrapped one and found it in an oily rainbow of mauve, pink and green plastic wrap. I squeezed, feeling something powdery shift within.

"What is it?" I looked up at him and watched his lips quirk and tremble.

"A present for you, Gretty. It's fairy dust. It will make everything look better and brighter. It will show you a new world."

"A new world? Will it make me disappear?"

"It will make the world you see disappear. Here," he eagerly unwrapped the colored cellophane, then the plain plastic bag. Powder, as white as snow but finer, like icing sugar, glittered in his hand.

"Is it sweet?"

"In one way, yes." He laid some powder on a mirror from his pocket. "Here, try some. Just snort it like this."

I watched his eyes flutter up in his head, then bent my head over the mirror. Using his rolled dollar bill, I vacuumed up the powder. It was sharp and tingly in my nose at first but then it blossomed in my head and through my body. I let Hans take me there, half off the couch. Everything was warm, fuzzylike and at the same time so rich with bright colors and sharply defined. The dreary day disappeared.

Hans had to hide the fairy dust from me. He would coax me out onto the street and promise me some if I did well. I tried harder than ever and probably kept my first secret from him. I started charging a bit more and keeping the extra in a bank account that he didn't know about. To buy fairy dust from the king of elfland, I told myself. I was part way through fourteen and still trying to hold onto the last frail wisps of my childhood, any way I could.

I began to cook and bake. The fuzziness of the fairy dust and the warm aromas wrapped about me in the kitchen. On cookies and muffins, I slathered frothy waves of icing, thinking always of fairy dust. I baked when taking the dust but only ate when it was gone.

By fifteen I was on the street less. Instead I became Hans's delivery girl. He casually slouched into chairs, looking happy and friendly, talking about the ball game or a car; always something that the other person could relate to, something that made them feel as if Hans had always been their best buddy. People relaxed around him and he ended up making good deals. His smile, his beautiful sky blue eyes, his firm, confident handshake mesmerized people. He didn't look like a loser and they liked that and paid top dollar for the dust.

For all the men I had sold myself to, I still knew little of the world, but I knew that hidden within Hans was a fire so bright, so intense, it could wither everyone. It could rage and burn away a forest. It could blow everything out of its way. A guy tried to cheat him once and always walked with a limp after. All I did was deliver the packets and pick up money. I was Hans's girl and everyone left me alone, unless he threw a freebie into the bargain. Then I did what I had always done.

The fairy dust kept me going. But I knew that like the cookies with their icing, the fairy dust only covered up the ugly world underneath. We moved to a better apartment. Hans bought me pretty clothes and books with wonderful pictures of forests or fairy tale lands at first. Things sort of slid off me. I smiled and hummed tunes from *Beauty and the Beast* and *Little Mermaia*. The prince always reminded me of Hans.

Hans even got a real job, an assistant manager in a stereo store. For contacts, he said, though it might have had something to do with the cops hanging around for a while. Evenings we often went for walks and slipped into bars. Hans always did me up first so that no one questioned my age. Outside one bar, near the wharf, we passed a man huddled against an old packing crate. His hands shook over the little paper fire he had painstakingly built. "Any change," he rasped, but didn't look up, as if he expected nothing.

I stopped. "Hans." I tugged on his tailored shirt.

"Forget it," Hans snorted.

"But," I trotted to catch up with him as he walked quickly away, hands clenched in his pockets. "But Hans, weren't we just like him once, cold and alone?"

Hans turned so suddenly that I bumped into his chest. He grabbed my face between his fingers and squeezed, making me look up at him. Tears swam in my eyes. Hans's face seemed to waver and change and for a moment I saw a snarling beast.

"We were never like him, Gretty. He's given up hope and waits for whatever anyone will throw him." Hans wrenched my head around to look at the vagrant.

"Ow, Hans," I whimpered, "you're hurting—"

"Look at him," he growled. "Look!" Hans spun me around to face him again. The fairy dust burned away in the heat of his gaze. "Did we ever lay about whimpering and begging for forgiveness and money? No. Did we fall to pieces when Mother didn't care? NO! We went out and took what we needed. We made people pay. And they'll still pay. You know why, Gretty? Because we own the world. And we can do what we want with it."

I knew then that I could never let Hans find my secrets. That night we moved into owning the world.

Hans whispered urgently in my ear. "What do you see, Gretty?"

I walked up to that man and stared down at him. "You pitiful lump of shit. You'd be better off dead." Then I drew back my foot and kicked him in the side. He just doubled up, whimpering and didn't even try to fight back. I stomped out his pathetic fire. "You disgust me."

I turned and grabbed Hans's arm. We left, laughing. After, I was full of energy, higher than the fairy dust. I made love to Hans. And I became hungrier. There was this huge hole, like an oven in me that had to be filled or I would collapse.

We still sold drugs but Hans now moved in elite circles, dressing well, passing his precious dust to dignitaries, jaded stars and bored debutantes. I didn't go along often. They always looked at me as if they knew some dark secret that I didn't know. When we were alone, Hans and I sauntered down lonely streets and look for lonelier people. We'd visit them for a while and play with them. I would tease them, offer them a buck and then smack them, or rub burning cigarettes into their arms, or scratch bloody lines in their skins. We never killed; that would have ruined it.

Hans allowed me more fairy dust. I baked, but only cookies now, in different shapes; dogs, cats, mermaids, little men, horses, anything with crunchy little limbs that I could bite off one by one. I painstakingly decorated them, drawing out the anticipation. Then I slowly dismembered them, eating one limb at a time, chewing slowly, savoring the crumbly sweetness that trickled down my throat to fill my hunger.

Following some Neo-whatevers we ran down one of those Jews one night. And you know what, they fought even though they expected the beatings and taunting. They never gave in like that first man. More and more I began to see that even if someone didn't resist physically, there were other ways to resist. A couple of times Hans held me back, though he was the one who always thought up new ways of pain. I usually carried out the deed. "Go on, Gretty," he would say. "You get first dibs."

First dibs. As if it were a game. And yet, it was, and I had a hunger that only increased the more I kicked someone, or pushed slivers of glass into his fingers, or wrapped my hands around a throat.

It wasn't all we did, mind you. There was the everyday of washing clothes, grocery shopping, paying bills. To the outside world we were a young couple – I was maybe seventeen by then – who lived fairly well. Yeah, the world was ours but when would it all stop?

It did, you know. You don't believe me but it did. Something changed. Oh, I know it had been changing for a while. I started to get the feeling of…wrongness. Really. Still, I couldn't stop baking. I baked something every day. Always cookies with limbs. Hans would ask, "You stockpiling for a war or something?"

The freezer was full of tins designed with flowers or Santas or children on them. The cupboards were full. I never thought of giving them away. Hans took some but if I found an empty spot, I baked to fill it. I couldn't stop, unless I was eating. And yet, I found it harder and harder to eat them.

Then one night I was coming back from the store or bar – I don't really remember – and I was jumped. After they raped me they beat me senseless. What I heard first were soft clucking noises as gentle hands lifted me and brought me into a building. It was a brownstone with the thick smell of old carpet and disinfectant. That's all I knew.

I awoke hours later. A woman leaned over me; old, not ancient, with long gray hair plaited in one thick braid. A cool cloth wiped my brow. "You're safe. You were mugged, I think. We should call the police now."

I still don't understand my reaction. I grasped her hand and said, "No, no. He'll find me if you do. Don't call." Then I passed out again.

It took several days before I could walk. I looked older, more hunched than the woman, whose name was Mrs. Feldstein. She never complained, had only asked once if there was someone I should call and then didn't prod. I slept little, always expecting her to do something to me or let the muggers in. Heaviness settled over me that I didn't have the energy to lift. Someone had stopped my ownership of the world. Now, I was in the home of a caring woman. Maybe it was time to change.

I sat and stared at the window for hours. My mind was empty; no thoughts to call Hans, or to get revenge, nothing. An abyss. Then I would go into the shakes and horrible knife-twisting cramps as the fairy dust left my body. In my lucid moments I began to bake again, only gingerbread men and women. But I could not eat one. I had tried to bite off a limb but I heard tiny little cries. I had to cover my ears every time I bit one. Mrs. Feldstein ate them too, but they didn't cry out at her bites. I let her give some cookies away, hoping I wouldn't hear them. I still baked though; I couldn't stop. She didn't mind. Yet I kept waiting for her to ask for something in return.

One day she brought me a glass of watered wine after one of my lessening fits. "Here, this will ease the pain in your muscles a bit."

She sat beside me as I sipped. After a while, she said, "Gretchen, I know you've been through a lot. It's more than what happened the night that I found you. You look young, and yet you have a weariness that I haven't seen on women my age." She patted my hand, smiling sadly. "I just want you to know that you can stay as long as you want. I don't mind at all. It's nice to have some company."

I opened my mouth but only food went in; nothing came out. I knew that she, like the cookies, hid something underneath. So I sat and stared at her landscape paintings, or watched TV, or waited.

Once in a while I had this odd thought that the gingerbread people voiced the thoughts I couldn't remember having and that Mrs. Feldstein heard them. *Take me out of here,* they cried. *Save me from the hungry.* Nevertheless, I continued to bake and told Mrs. Feldstein – she said to call her Gloria – to give the cookies away, especially to needy people. It was a soothing balm.

Gloria never forced me to do anything. I had my bank account but I wouldn't go out. I gave Gloria my card and had her make withdrawals for me. I contributed to the rent; that was normal.

I think I was just beginning to forget when Hans found me. It was only a matter of time. The cookies told the tale; all those gingerbread people betrayed me, rightfully so, considering what I had done. They'd left a trail.

There was a knock at the door that afternoon. Gloria came into the kitchen and said, "Gretchen, there's a young man out there who says he's your brother."

I dropped the cookie pan and froze. "No. Don't let him in!" I grabbed Gloria's arm. She only nodded and told him through the closed door. I had to think. I had to think.

Hans banged on the door and yelled, "Open the goddamn door, you bitch! Gretty! Why won't you answer? Gretty, I thought you were dead. I love you." He broke down crying, then banged on the door until Gloria told him she'd call the cops.

Hans left but I could see him outside waiting, waiting. There was no escape. The forest surrounded me and he was king of the world. Embers that could torch a city burned in his eyes. He would always find me.

I longed for the fairy dust. Late into the evening, long after Gloria had gone to bed, I sat and rocked on the couch. She had been so good to me. What could I do? I peered through the thin curtains and saw Hans still sitting on the steps, holding his head. He could find me no matter where I hid. He had always known the trails so well.

Well past midnight I realized that if I stayed, Hans would find a way in, and if I left, he would still come back to tie up loose ends. Nothing ever stayed pure. I think I cried. I had to save Gloria from Hans's clutches. She'd given me a taste of normal and I had to thank her.

I used to enjoy hurting people but I didn't want to cause Gloria pain. I crept softly into her bedroom and looked at her sleeping peacefully. I ran my fingers along the cool brass statue of a girl picking daisies that sat on her dresser. Then I hit her over the head with it. I don't think she was dead then. I leaned close to her mouth, noticing the blood trickling down her cheek and listened for breath. I rolled her on her back and laid my ear against her breast. I was sure there was a faint beating. I was amazed at how easy it had been and I felt nothing.

A glimpse out the window showed that Hans was still there. I dragged Gloria to the kitchen and curled her in front of the stove with her head lying in the oven. I turned on the gas jets and blew out the flame.

"Thank you, Gloria." I patted and smoothed her beautiful silver braid.

Then I went to the door, opened it and quietly called Hans. He looked up, then ran up the steps and grabbed me, hugging and kissing my head. "Gretty, oh Gretty, I thought you had died." Before he could say anything else, I put my finger to his lips and pulled him inside and took him into the kitchen.

I know it wasn't right, gassing her. It should have been something more dignified.

Hans clapped his hands and giggled like a schoolboy. "Jews always end up in ovens," he laughed, holding up her head by the braid then dropping it back into the oven.

I watched Hans. I didn't know him except for the cruel glaze I saw every day. Was there something inside? I shouldn't have killed Gloria – she'd helped me when she didn't need to – but there was no other way I could repay her. In the cupboards I heard a shifting and a subtle grating noise, like limbs trying to climb their way out of tins. And voices. I heard the soft whisper of a thousand voices. *Give us our lives. Where are our limbs?*

I grabbed Hans's arm. "Listen. Did you hear that? The voices."

He cocked his head and said, "It's just the gas." The sour smell was starting to fill our noses.

Then we ran out the door and away. I looked back only once. I had left my ID behind, but then I didn't need it anymore.

After we returned to Hans's place, he didn't let me out of bed for hours. He reclaimed me and gave me fairy dust. I read the paper the next day and knew it was all a matter of time. I wondered if Gloria would have been happy with what they wrote about her. I wanted to write in and say how kind she was but I couldn't remember how to form words.

The few times that Hans dragged me out afterwards, I did my best. I think I killed, keeping them from Hans. Maybe I dreamt of the young hooker I pushed off a bridge and a drunk man, filthy and covered in sores. Hans kicked him a few times, then grinned at me. "You take over, Gretty, you have a real knack for this."

So I did as Hans wanted. I kicked the guy in the gut and balls, then bent and quickly slit his throat. It ended his suffering faster. I took to always carrying a knife with me after that.

I want it to end. There are a million gingerbread people around me and not one of them will let me taste their stories. They cry and say horrid things. Even when they aren't there I hear them; their voices even louder. Only by baking more can I quiet them for a while. I wish I could become one of them; crisp and flat and covered in glaze.

A Book by its Cover

Fashion and the quest for beauty often give unexpected results. Mickey Rourke is one example of what can go terribly wrong. The pursuit of perfection can lead to one's downfall, and seeking it obsessively can leave one blind.

Syntia is ready to become her favorite show. She even has the underwear like the Virtue Vis girls, Callista and Carlise; lacy, revealing not too much, firming and holding the breasts, making them mound up in amplitude even if she lies on her side or back. She had to try on over fifty bras to get one to fit and look the way it does in the shows. Eventually, she paid for implants, because when she lay down her breasts still sagged to the side.

She claps on the V.V. screen and sits, sipping a lychee-rice martini and eyeing her nails as the wall fills with color. *Soho Central:* who will she be tonight? Callista last week, even Bryce once; Luke has never been accessible. However, it looks like Luke will make the move on Carlise soon. Syntia grabs the programmer as the music fills the speakers and muffles her in sound.

She checks herself in the mirror that covers one wall before activating the ocular implants with three rapid blinks of her eyes. A seductive glance, she pouts, lips dusted with faint, shimmering mauve, then she slouches further into the form-fitting couch. Perfect. Not too much, not too subtle.

Her fingers tap the programming console as the images fill the dimensions around her. Now to play Carlise and get Luke where she wants him, where she wants to be.

V.V. Interactive TV. Syntia loves it. She loves being involved with the beautiful ones. They are all so glamorous and there is no reason she shouldn't have it as well. Callista and Carlise, models with smooth creamy skin, clothing that fits and moves perfectly on their sculpted bodies. Thin arms, firm thighs. Syntia has been practicing. She hungers to play these characters who entwine their lives in the fast times; the movers and shakers who built their empires on fashion and love and money. The men are gorgeous, tailored, successful, caring, with bodies the envy of any god. They *are* someone. Echoes of Syntia's mother saying, "You'll never amount to much. You don't have the drive."

Syntia wants more, always more. Soon, hopefully, the viewers will be playing Syntia on their Virtue Vis sets, programming her viewpoint into their consoles so that they will be her in *Soho Central*. She isn't sure how it works. An actor is integrated with the viewer but still acts true to the plot, which means there must be constructs, but Virtue Vis maintains that all their actors are flesh, and the viewer is just seeing what the actors see. And if they are real, then their fame can be hers. Syntia could lead a life as lovely and exhilarating as Carlise or Janeen, but for real.

Syntia sips her martini, and through the implants looks at her new surroundings. She sees Park Avenue as Carlise does while walking. Syntia has her stop and look in a few windows. The digital readout in one corner outlines the script. Viewers can direct the actors' minor actions, and view the show from a character's point of view, but the script is locked in. Carlise has a meeting with a fashion designer. No matter what one makes her do she will inevitably move toward that goal. Every once in a while Syntia tries some deviation.

Syntia-Carlise stops in an antique shop. The lean, craggy man walks over and smiles like an alligator. She smiles back and says, "I'd like to buy everything you have in the store."

The man smiles again and says, "Would you like to charge that? I can have everything sent to your place by this afternoon."

She walks out, snapping, "Never mind." The programs aren't always the most entertaining. It would have been nice to see shock or surprise on the guy's face. But still, most characters respond to her voice imprint and will follow a circuitous route. There are almost infinite numbers of minor characters for the viewer who deviates into little shops or such, but there's not much depth to them.

It had been expensive to buy the Virtue Vis entertainment system, so expensive that Syntia has foregone luxuries, such as eating. Besides, being slim helps her look like the actors, and it is well worth it. She's tried out for various shows. But that was before she started perfecting her image.

Syntia, as Carlise, bumps into Luke on the street. They share a taxi with opaquing windows. He confesses his undying love, his loyalty and search for the perfect woman. She coaxes him into parting the zip seals on her skintight pants and trailing his lips along her lean hip. It is still Carlise doing this, and no matter what Syntia sees or says, she still cannot experience the sensations. It would have taken millions for that type of set.

Luke and Carlise are still entangled when the taxi stops. Luke's business partner, who has been trying to bed him to gain investments in his new company, opens the taxi's door. Syntia as Carlise smoothes her pants, slides out of the car and smiles at the woman, then walks away. The episode ends.

Syntia sighs and deactivates the program, then checks her hair in the mirror. Still perfect, no strand out of place. She rises from the couch, one fluid movement, graceful, no jerks. As always, she is unsatisfied, hungering for the lifestyle she cannot yet afford, for being someone she cannot yet be.

Time to go out. None of her friends will go with her to The Club. Too trendy, they say. Snobs, they snort. Syntia knows better. It is just the envious sniping of those on the outside, the lesser class, jealous that they cannot attain that higher level and be integrated wholly with society's stars – those who really shape the world. She strips, then pulls on an emerald lycrex gown. It billows gracefully over one hip and cuts away to reveal her angular hipbone on the other side. It slips off the left shoulder in lightning jags and clings to her breasts like a lover. She turns before the mirror, arching her back just so. She smiles the Mona Lisa smile, the knowing smile that is just right: not too many teeth, not too goofy. Years have been spent perfecting herself and she knows others would love to see through her eyes.

She checks her makeup. Next to acting, it is what she does best. She likes to sculpt people's faces into masterpieces. Beautiful, living art from indistinguishable canvasses of flesh.

The cab is waiting when she arrives downstairs. Cars line up behind it. Syntia moves slowly, flowing, then stops to pull a smoke from her arm pouch. She bites the end, the other end flares red and she inhales before getting into the taxi. People stop to watch. She knows it, but will not look. Those who are truly the elite do not need to prove to themselves that others find them attractive. Even in the dark obscurity of the cab Syntia remains poised. One never knows where a hidden cam might be.

The Club, the in-crowd is here. Atmosphere shoulders its way through the lights and music. There's no room for the uncultured smell of sweat. Syntia glides to a table, not too close to the front, not too central. Heads turn. Here she can watch the watchers without being evident. She leans back into her seat, one manicured hand slipping into the arm pouch, deftly removing another smoke. The end flares as she bites down, and smoke drifts lazily in the nearly clear air. Syntia prefers the smoky variety. They present an air of mystery, of sultry sensuality that envelops her. The smoke curls from her mouth, as if reluctant to leave her.

Slowly, she rearranges the folds of her gown over the covered hip. Who is here? Any talent scouts? Any agents or actors? The drink arrives in tinted glass, a mystery to those who wonder what she drinks.

"Hey, Cynthia, long time. You're looking good enough to mold in holo."

Syntia glances up. "Markian, it's Syntia now. Ess Y En, no aitch." Markian is a round-faced young man, pleasing but moving nowhere fast. She wants far more.

"Whatever. You're still a deadly Syn to me." He straddles a chair. "Buy you a drink?"

She holds up her glass and smiles slowly. "I already have one. Thanks." She looks away and stares at the dance floor where those who dare to ruffle their exterior dance, avoiding a fatal fashion-marring sweat. She only dances when she can find the right spot on the floor, visible to those seated, giving a rare show, sure to look good from every side. After all, she has studied the shows to see how the stars dance, and has practiced before the mirror.

Syntia knows that image isn't everything but it serves to give you everything and get you where you want to be. And she intends to be there. Soon.

Syntia chats with Markian for a bit, remaining aloof. There could be other prospects, other possibilities to entertain. Markian moves off when Syntia declines to dance. She taps her holo-engraved nail against the glass, once, twice, but not so that she looks nervous – just bored.

It is time for a thorough look around, like Callista does in *Soho Central*. Take a sip of your drink, savor it; tilt your head to the left. Then slowly open your eyes; keep them heavy-lidded with sensuality, and roll your head until you're looking over your right shoulder. Not so much like you're inspecting the crowd as actually enjoying the visceral pleasures of the surroundings.

Visceral. Syntia could do with some heavy visceral pleasure. Her eyes catch on the man sitting to her right. He stares at her; she does not look away – doesn't show anything. She brings her drink to her mouth where her tongue laps the edge. He is stunning: chiseled chin, beautiful catlike eyes, nearly black hair in the latest style. His clothes look Armand and uncreased. The smoke from his cig forms a nimbus about his head. It is hard to tell in the flickering, swaying lights but he looks like Luke from *Soho Central*. Could it be?

Her heart knocks at her chest, reminding her of where she is. *Don't look too long,* Syntia tells herself. Not good to appear too eager. She lowers the glass, letting a half-smile touch her lips before she looks away and signals the waiter.

Syntia looks down and opens her pouch for another smoke, trying to formulate a plan to attract this particular man. He might have connections. A shadow blocks the lights reflecting off her lycrex gown. She looks up, unsurprised. It *is* Luke, and he holds a smoke out to her.

"Here, try mine." She takes it and bites the end. He doesn't ask, just sits beside her and orders a drink when the waiter brings her scotch.

"I'm Kieran King."

She clasps his hand firmly but doesn't shake it. "Yes, you play Luke on *Soho*. I'm Syntia Alleen."

They chat, warming to each other, gauging their moves. She gives him sultry stares. He gives her endearing smiles. She brushes his hand once. He leans in and lowers his voice.

"What do you do?" Kieran asks, leaning back and draining his drink.

No point in beating around the bush. None of, 'I'm sure you hear this from every woman.' Just, "I'm in cosmetics, but I want to act."

More chat, then she asks him, "How long have you been an immersive actor?"

He smiles, a secret hidden behind his lips. "I do more than act. I only do that to keep a handle on what the industry needs. I'm the designer of Virtue Vision." He hands her a card with holo image.

She reads it, trying hard not to shake with the good luck she sees before her.

Virtue Vision
KIERAN KING
President
Our reality is yours.

Luke, the character, and Kieran King, good looking, rich, who will have pull in the right places. It is all paying off. She hands back his card.

"Keep it." He stares at her and says, "You are exquisite."

"Beauty isn't everything," she begins, the obligatory protest. "I'm like a book. The cover usually tells something of what is inside, and each page that you turn reveals a bit more story." It's one of her favorite lines. It shows depth.

"I'd like to explore this book," he grins. "Look, I might be able to help you audition for a part in *Soho*. We need someone like you. Janeen might be leaving us soon."

Curious, she asks, "Just how do you get an immersive program and an actor to mesh?"

"Come." He stands. "I'll show you the equipment."

Syntia takes her time. This seems so easy, too easy… but then she has worked hard to make herself into a Virtue Vision girl. It's no more than she deserves. She finishes her drink, feeling warm from the alcohol caressing her veins, then rises in one fluid motion, and exits beside Kieran, knowing everyone is watching.

⚜

They arrive at the Virtue Vis complex. There are filming studios and offices. The office is more of a high-story castle. To her surprise, Kieran does not take Syntia to the penthouse suite. They stop in the basement first. He holds the elevator door open, as polite as his character. Luke the virtuous, the man who's made it to the top without harming others, the man who is loved by all – perfect.

He stops her in the lobby where there are plush green, form-fitting couches. He gives a short history of the operation, then puts a hand on her shoulder to guide her through another door. She turns to say something, and meets his mouth, crushing against hers; his tongue, sliding like wet velvet over her lips. His hand reaches behind her and pulls her buttocks towards him. His hips grind against hers. His mouth trails down her neck, biting softly.

Syntia gasps, giving her best performance. It is all an audition and men like to think they have the sexiest vixens in the world. But it is not all acting and fire spreads from between her legs. She touches one zip seal and releases it. He's already found the second, and her dress slithers to the floor like an abandoned skin.

Stockings and shoes are off in a minute. She's naked and releases the zip seal on his pants but he takes her before his clothes are dropped. He presses her down onto the couch, thrusting in – hot, sliding, moaning. Syntia doesn't mind the suddenness, relishes it. This is the ultimate power a woman can have over a man, to make him lose control. She arches her back, runs her nails under his shirt, moans deliciously into his ear; all he could ever hope for. Syntia is in control, loving the feeling but not giving in to it. Anything for an acting career.

But Kieran breaks through her control. He thrusts deeply and bites into her shoulder just below the neck. She yelps, thrown off balance as his teeth break flesh. Then he's pumping hard and Syntia gives herself to the moment.

A moment of rest, of acquiescence, before Kieran grunts and lifts his head. He smiles and kisses Syntia. She feels languid, limp, alcohol and sex making her like a sated cat.

"Let me show you where we make the programs," Kieran whispers into her ear. "We use a special implant." He picks her up, her weight nothing in his muscled arms. She wants to ask for her dress but feels too lazy, sleepy, and just lets him carry her. He walks past darkened doors explaining that Virtue Vis has top-of-the-line software, programs on the cutting edge. Full body integration for the viewer is just around the corner, and at an affordable cost.

She wants to look around but can't, realizing there is something off. She's never been this drunk. Syntia tries harder to lift her head, to move, to say something, but only a grunt escapes.

It is only when Kieran enters a low-lit room, one with many form-fit reclining chairs, that Syntia realizes her mistake. "We get only the best for *Soho Central*," he is saying, "and half a dozen other shows we run. Of course, virtual constructs are used in tandem with the interactive actors. The best actors are the ones that every viewer wants to be. Why are they so good as immersive actors, Syntia? Because it is their lives."

He's laid her down on one of the chairs. Out of the corner of her eye, she can see that some of the chairs are occupied. With all her concentration she manages, "K-Kieran, something wrong…can't move…numb."

He smiles an almost loving smile as he smoothes her hair from her eyes. "You don't think that was a love bite I gave you, do you?"

He takes certain small tools – wires, jacks, computer chips – from the counter in front of the chair. There are monitors lined up on them and some flicker replays of earlier Virtue Vis shows. He does something at her temple and at the base of her skull. He holds up an IV needle as if showing her a prize snake.

Her tongue is starting to work and she can turn her head but she can't lift her arm. "What…you doing?"

"You, Syntia, will be the newest actor on *Soho Central*. People will be able to access your personality and live through your eyes as you live as a projection in *Soho*. You'll meet all of them. I'm sure you'll all get along. After all, *Soho* will be your only life. You'll have some freedom to move in the scenarios but you'll never be far from me. I'm sure you'll be a great actress of the immersive world."

A pit is opening in Syntia's stomach. Panic wells blackly through her vision. "What do you mean? Why can't I move?"

"You're so perfect. It's what you wanted, isn't it? To be an actor, to live this world." He injects something into her arm and she cannot twitch so much as a muscle.

She always wanted to be an actor, live the lifestyle, but she never thought of the sacrifices. Syntia whimpers, trying to struggle, but the neuro-toxin has paralyzed her. Her mind, though, is fully active. Yes acting was her life but this isn't acting. This isn't life.

She gasps, "But you're not like this. You were so caring. Luke is so good and strong."

He stops and looks at her. "Didn't anyone tell you not to judge a book by its cover?" He flips a switch, punches some buttons. "You always have to look beneath the surface." He leans in close. "And that's where you'll be. Welcome to the stage of immersive acting."

"I don't want this. Please. Let me go."

Syntia feels her consciousness slipping into another dimension, but she struggles to hold on. "What are you going to do with me?" she whimpers. Already she can see and smell the streets of *Soho Central*.

"Oh don't worry," Kieran smiles and sits beside her on the reclining chair. He begins to undo his shirt as he strokes her breast. "I'll take good care of you."

Red is the Color of My True Love's Blood

I actually do not like many time travel/loop stories, but I have bought some when editing. There are also some Doctor. Who episodes, which are particularly fine writing, yet others that stretch beyond believability or following any thread of sanity. This story explores obsession and madness. Like Groundhog Day, we sometimes get stuck in our own worst nightmare.

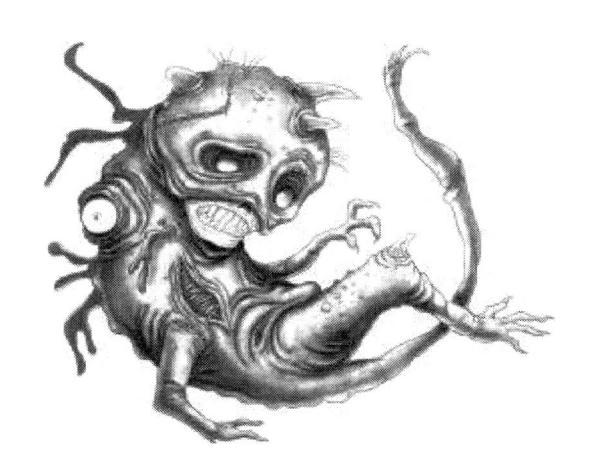

My hand touches the cool metal of the door knob. I've been humming a tune. The problem is when I do this I sometimes zone out, forget what I was doing. And I've been to Jordy's door so many times before that it's almost automatic.

But what's different today is that my flight was cancelled due to the weather and I thought I'd surprise him with dinner. I push the door open with my shoulder and carry in the bag of groceries. Music drifts like a wraith down the hall, and amber light capers over the living room walls illuminated by a fire crackling in the fireplace. The scent of sharp pine resin mixed with an odd metallic smell fills my nose.

I turn right into the open layout kitchen, maneuver the bag onto the counter, then return to the living room. I check the logs in the fireplace and warm my hands for a minute, staring into the fiery dance. The axe is lying in the middle of the floor. I take a few moments to absorb the heat, the scent and the space of Jordy's home. Soon this will be mine too. I pick up the axe and prop it against the fireplace, near a fresh pile of wood brought in to dry. There is a sticky residue on the handle. Back in the kitchen I wash my hands.

I smile; just like him to put a fire on and then forget its ambiance as he goes back to his thesis. He's so close to the end now, which will be a cause for celebration on several levels. Not only will he be done with years of school and have his PhD but I'll get to move in. We both agreed that it would be less distracting for him in these final stages if I moved in after his defense. But that's now only a month away and we've been distracted enough by each other as it is. I'd love to just crawl into his bed and wait for him there but it could be hours until he notices.

I'm still humming, unpacking the crusty baguette, the head of lettuce, the basil and crimson tomatoes for an al dente pasta sauce, and am reminded of Jordy's thesis. It's a fascinating subject, and really, how we first met. He's looking at the psychological and mythical symbolism of the color red. Every color has its significance but he's always been drawn to red. Perhaps I have too.

Maybe that's why he noticed me with my spiked, red only-a-bottle-can-give hair. That and my photo show, Nature's Rainbow, with pictures of nature that brought out each color; the wild green of trees with young leaves, the blue of a gentian against a lake reflecting the sky, the red of an apple amongst turning leaves. He had wandered in, his dark wavy hair falling over one eye, spending so long before each picture, especially the ones with red. My show had had two photos for each color, the second one showed a juxtaposition of manmade objects with nature – the blue of a car against the backdrop of sky, a red lacquered wood-handled knife spattered with blood from a slaughter – to show how humans encroach upon nature.

Jordy's thesis goes into more depth than my show, more history. He could have written a book on each color but said red was the most vibrant. It's the lifeblood, and looking around his place I see that accents of scarlet embellish each room. The rust red wall in the living, the trim on the counters is cinnabar. The carpet is beige with random speckles of dark ruby, which I've never noticed before. When something is drawn to our eyes we suddenly see it everywhere.

A thin, cherry border encircles each dinner plate, and his cutting board is red marble. I've laid out the ingredients and put the pan out but I better check to see how he's doing before I start. I should let him know I'm here.

I stop for a moment. Something seems odd, out of place. But then that would be me, my schedule disrupted. I smile. It's worth it to get to spend a few moments with Jordy. He doesn't complete me necessarily but he makes me happy, is counterpoint to my thoughts. Where I see patterns and shapes, he sees lines and symbolism. We mesh well like that. He is like a great scarlet balloon rising into a summer sky and bringing joy. His laugh always lightens me.

Jordy is one of those people who like to work with extra stimulus, the music or a radio going in the background. I like the opposite, a cone of silence in which to concentrate or sort out the natural sounds. But I guess I only believe that as more than one person has commented on my humming. It's a subconscious thing that I don't even notice most of the time.

I like the glow from the fireplace, the warmth and the softly sinuous shadows. It makes me think of centuries ago when people lived in the mysteries of color. Jordy said that Christian religion used red to represent saints, and of course blood, the active humors and the earthly connection. Even Catholic cardinals, like the bird, wear red. Brides in China, and women in India do as well. Studies show that people get fired up (fired up!) by red, but interestingly orange is used on inmates because it supposedly calms them. Or is it just that they're easier to spot if they escape? Maybe I'll do a series next on colors tied with emotions. Green is jealousy. Yellow is cowardice.

Color is so integral to many things, and the patterns and shapes of color do form my focus in photography. People or places don't matter as much as the colors they embody. Blue for calm, black for death, white for spirit. So many ideas attached to what nature provides. Blood is red. Red is anger, love, war, passion. Blood is used to curse, to heal.

Jordy said numerous cultures, such as voodoun, use blood for rituals. Some just try to predict the future, or contact a dead granny to find out where the jewels are buried. Yet other rituals call on gods and spirits for knowledge and retribution. Curses are always about getting even, a punishment to fit the crime. If justice can't be brought upon the perpetrator, then the curser can get those from the other side to mete out an eye for an eye. People make up so many things.

One night we both had too much wine, laughing about all the superstitions attached to colors. When Jordy knocked over the glass, slicing his finger on the shards, I held my hands to my face in mock horror. "Blood sacrifice," I giggled.

Instead of wiping away the blood that crawled its way from the small cut, he chased me around the living room with his finger held up like the wand of doom. "I'll teach you," he yelled, laughing. "I will curse you."

He caught me as I pretended to cringe in dread. My face clasped gently between his palms, he leaned in and kissed me, blood smearing my cheek. Into my kiss, Jordy whispered, "I'll curse you to always love me."

And I do. I love him like I've never loved anyone else, but that is only because we're compatible, understand and trust each other. I loved him from the beginning. And we both are fascinated by color. I uncork the pinot noir, pour a small amount and take a sip, toasting our lives to be. The wine needs to breathe and I set it aside to walk down the hall.

I peek into the den on the left, expecting to see Jordy chewing his knuckle as he works through his concluding chapter, but he's not there. Only the bluish glow of the monitor's screensaver shows he was in the den. The air is dead here, papery. He spends more time on his laptop than sitting at a desk.

Maybe Jordy took one of those 'cerebral naps' as he calls them, the ones he claims sort out his thoughts but which I think are just procrastination. Still, he's done some amazing work and the end is very near. I love him as much for his brain as his awesome humor and great body.

The music contours the bedroom and spills out the open door on the right. That's odd if he's sleeping, and I slow. Should I wake him?

As I reach the door I pause with my hand on the wall, not wanting to disturb him. The light is low. Why would he be burning a pillar candle beside the bed if he's napping? Then I see Jordy's tight little ass moving up and down, up and down. I am glued in place, filter slowly what I can't comprehend. He says, "You are my firebrand. God, how I burn for you," and a small feminine laugh follows.

I'm doubling over, clutching my stomach as though he punched me. A gut shot, the air is sucked from me and I back out the door. Our endearments. The words he says to me. The special phrases. My vision begins to fog with a red haze.

I'm back in the bedroom. I don't recall moving. I see only red. I smell salt and musky sex and something else, something coppery, metallic. They don't perceive me as I draw near. Humming, I raise the axe over my head as Jordy's head turns. The axe falls, of its own gravity and volition, sheering off his lower jaw, spattering scarlet everywhere. It sounds like he's gargling and I realize I've severed Jordy's lying tongue. He's a mess, no longer pretty. Still interested in red, carmine, carnelian, ruby. I can't leave him like this and the axe blade falls again, biting with lover's passion into his neck. My last kiss. He twitches and falls. Blood geysers, oozes, blends with his burgundy sheets.

A keening comes from beneath him, high pitched, like a teakettle. Humming, I let the blade shut her up too. I keep expecting to hear metal hitting wood but it is only a thunking, wet meaty sound. There is blood, so much blood, a red speckled pattern upon the carpet, and something gray. Jordy's wasted his brains. Too bad. He was brilliant.

The haze in my vision begins to recede.

What have I done? There is cloying gore everywhere. I gag and back out of the room. The punishment should fit the crime or there will be hell to pay. People say these things, the clichés, the color codes, the blood curses. I didn't mean to do this but red overcame me. I've done too much. Red is everywhere in Jordy's apartment.

I stare at the fire, let the axe thud on the carpet. Red-handed, I stumble to the kitchen, wash the sticky residue off of my hands. But everything is going black. I don't see red, just black, an end, a finale. The punishment should fit the crime. I stumble toward the door, humming.

※

My hand touches the cool metal of the door knob. I've been humming a tune. The problem is when I do this I sometimes zone out, forget what I was doing. And I've been to Jordy's door so many times before that it's almost automatic.

But what's different today is that my flight was cancelled due to the weather and I thought I'd surprise him with dinner. I push the door open with my shoulder and carry in the bag of groceries. Music drifts like a wraith down the hall, and amber light capers over the living room walls illuminated by a fire crackling in the fireplace. The scent of sharp pine resin mixed with an odd metallic smell fills my nose.

    I turn right into the open layout kitchen, maneuver the bag onto the counter, then return to the living room. I check the logs in the fireplace and warm my hands for a minute, staring into the fiery dance. The axe is lying in the middle of the floor. I take a few moments to absorb the heat, the scent and the space of Jordy's home. Soon this will be mine too. I pick up the axe and prop it against the fireplace, near a fresh pile of wood brought in to dry. There is a sticky residue on the handle.

Tasty Morsels

I'm working on several motifs here: the Errol Flynn charming rogue, who wins every battle and charms the skirts off of the gals; the wolf and Little Red Riding Hood, the age-old trope of hunter and hunted; and the ancient worship of Diana, all tossed together in a science fiction setting. Like the previous tale, overconfidence can lead to unseen outcomes.

I set spies on Red while I conducted my affairs. At first it was an idle game for spare moments but one by one my spies said she'd given them the slip; then my intrigue was piqued.

Pale as new spun silk, she often wore a nondescript gray coat and hood that blended with overcast days, if we had them, or the hue of the moon's ragged face. On Mars, the slightest pink would have tinged her. Even her hair was platinum. Only her glacial blue eyes pierced with coldness, held the color as if leached from others.

Red's name came not from her looks, nor her passion, for no one that I knew had come close enough to experience it. She was a lily white virgin ripe for the plucking, if one could get past her safeguarded nonchalance. If she was a nun, she displayed no compassion. Red could have been named for her bloody-looking nails, enhanced in some way; perhaps a nanotech hardening compound as a protective device. But really her name came from rumor, and only that. She'd never been pinned with any crime, yet. We wouldn't see her for days, and then she'd appear, sitting at some table, drinking alone or tabulating on her rasa. Someone usually said, "Ah, Red has come riding home again," a tradition of our own. Then the coms would fritz with news of a gangland killing and we would wonder where she'd been.

The same happened whether I was on the moon or slingshotting to Earth. The last time we heard of a killing, Garo had said, "Do you think we'll see Red riding in?" Before he'd finished speaking, a crimson skimmer coasted into the landing bay beside our much larger ship, and sure enough, Red exited, plucking off the protective caul of her helmet. Not so much as a cool nod acknowledged us; she walked by, oblivious.

Red wasn't known as an assassin. It was rumored (as everything was about her) that she ran weapons, wetware hacks and other contraband, but none could say exactly. She was an enigma, pallid and circumspect.

Yet she haunted the stygian levels of the dour Moonbase towers, and the crumbling forests of buildings in the wildest port cities on Earth. Even amongst the humming gray girders, the shimmering glass under false light, she glided like a bright moonbeam, or a ghost. No one frequented these places if they could be somewhere better. We conducted our business and left the moment we finished. Red was a true creature of space though, and her color reflected it.

Even before I clawed my way through the gangs and packs of petty thieves with no vision, I could choose any woman. I'm blessed with natural good looks and not many could resist me; dark eyes, head scarred in intricate whorls, earlobes distended to just above my shoulders, a dozen rings in each; tall, muscled and slim. Charisma, intelligence and fashionable clothing can forgive a host of crimes. Having been master of the largest cartel for quite a while, few have captivated me for long. It's the chase and the luring that I desire, and good sex too, of course. Liken me to a wolf, or should I say, a Hwulf among the sheep. Sheep are always meant to be taken.

This particular sheep was different from the rest and as time accumulated her absences and arrivals, her aloof ways, she became a prey most succulent. My greatest challenge with Red was her lack of involvement with those around her. She walked a narrow path but it's easy to leave enticements along the way. I am a connoisseur and to devour gluttonously demeans the morsel as well as my palate. Much better to stalk quietly, catch, then marinade in delicious anticipation before the final savoring.

I run a tight ship, or I should say ships, and my power attracts many to me, for adventure or danger or profit. I can use that, but I always watch my back, even my friends, for they are only a credit away. I chose long ago to find my own path, taking as much as I could anyway I can. I never stop, whether building, buying, drinking or seducing.

It was Garo, on one of his binges, who discovered one of Red's haunts. I found the bar, a rustic place of plain gray girders left over from the early days of colonization. The Lunar Module was too old to even be in fashion but a good place for being left alone. I made sure I was seen there several times before she appeared.

One day she showed up, a foamy green drink in front of her, her rasa glowing as numbers scrolled past. The hot and noisy bar rumbled, packed with miners, as well as other private types, in from the asteroids and years on Mars. I sat across from her, a shimmering glass of vodka in front of me. As always, she didn't look up, so I studied her. Her unzipped suit opened to just between her breasts, the white well of flesh like marble. One would have called her serene, until one had seen her eyes. Somehow her tensile strength distinguished her from a frail albino even more than her icy eyes.

Eventually she looked up and I nodded. "Hope you don't mind me sitting here. Crowded." I waved my hand at the crowd. "I'm—"

"Hwulf." She looked at me, faint curiosity the only emotion showing in her eyes.

I raised an eyebrow. It's not uncommon for those in these parts to know who I am. "And what may I call you?"

"They call me Red." Her long fingers gently clasped her glass and she tossed back the drink.

"Can I buy you another?"

She cocked her head to the side for a moment, then said, "If you wish."

The drink came and she sipped, her eyes always watchful and penetrating. When I asked what she did, she only said, "I'm an entrepreneur. And you?"

I smiled widely. If she knew who I was, she probably knew what I did. "I'm in shipping." Red remained silent, so I asked, "Which is your favorite place, Moonbase or Earth?"

She raised a pale eyebrow, leisurely sipping the emerald liquid. I was mesmerized as that alcoholic river flowed over the banks of her lips. "The Moon, though Earth does have its uses."

I laughed. "You were born here, weren't you?"

She smiled slowly, "As much as anywhere." Then she rose, shutting her rasa. "Thanks for the drink." And she glided out, between the other people, barely causing a stir.

There is a counterpoint to everything in the world: black and white, good and evil, active and passive. As much as I crave a constant stimulus I grow tired of it and need time alone, where I energize myself for the tasks ahead. There is a time when one must digest what has been tasted.

Though I watched for Red, my pursuit allowed me time to ponder. I had a sense of her trail from the docks. Each time she returned to Moonbase I was farther along her path, hidden but watching her eddies and tides, how she moved, the ripples in her wake. Besides Moonbase conveyance tubes, transportation didn't amount to more than bikes in the closed air environment. Patience and time was all I needed.

I also found a disturbing kernel within that had nothing to do with my penchant for collecting rare delicacies. Long familiar with the dark scope of my soul, it was more that I detected a searing spot of light, a longing that welled up and threatened to consume me when I had time to ponder the depth and vagaries of my life.

Tracking Red, who was as unconcerned with the world around her as I was concerned with it, I wondered; did I make more impact with riches and starships than she did gliding silently through? And more and more, was I addicted to stimulus or could I survive the realm of only myself? The jungle of other peoples' lives was a more intriguing pursuit, and that thought jarred me. Was I finding my self so hollow that I had to fill it with trinkets and conquests?

Denial and fear are strong nectars. Consume or be consumed. My thoughts spiraled into mortality, which had me experiment with stimulants, a weak salve for the yearning that opened like a wound. I hungrily watched Red as she'd walk by. She always wore the long gray coat. Her clothes, though similar, varied through a pallid range of gray, blue and glacial green.

Of course I staged a few more encounters, managing to draw close and breathe in the cool scent of her. I met her once coming back from Earth. Her skimmer and blood red nails were the brightest things about her.

"Is that how you get your name?" I asked as she checked the compartments, shut down the electronics and pulled a large gray sack from her stowage.

Over her shoulder, she smiled enigmatically and tossed my way, "Possibly, but I doubt it. Surely you've heard the rumors."

I was just on my way out to check one of my operations and as I zipped my suit, noticing that my navigator had finally made it, I smiled back. "Rumors are just that; perhaps a smidgen of truth stirred with a healthy dose of speculation." I moved closer to her, feigning inspection of her ship. "This is a nice piece. Lightweight, durable, good for covering long distances fast."

"Or short distances faster." She hefted the duffle onto her shoulder.

"What do you call her?"

Her smile hit only one side of her mouth but touched her eyes for once. "You think it's a she? Well, you're right. I call her Grandmother. She houses me from the cold of space, guides me where I'm going and doesn't tell me when to be home."

Laughing, I saluted her and boarded my ship. My trap had been sprung. I had her now.

Needless to say, the pursuit continued. I could scent the change, her interest growing like roots that seek the deep dark earth. My mystery remained, as did hers, but she had let me into her world. Intrigued by her alabaster inviolability, could I breach her statue calm, reach in and lick the embers to flames? Was she attracted to the darkness within the forest of my soul; would she penetrate it with her moonbright essence? Chaos always wins, entropy winds all things down, even resistance, and I should have remembered that.

Evening never fell on the moon's bright side; instead the dome covers flavored the towers in false shadows. In bars that tried fancy facades like a gutter rat eats caviar, I listened to a live band play air pipes, nautilus chambers, and glass chimes, lending an eerie forlornness to the frenzy of people trying to stave back the darkness within. I wanted to howl with the madness rising within me, to shout back the inky blanket that threatened. Bright lights, jewels, flavors, scents; this is what keeps me alive. I feed on life.

Then she entered, a cool ivory luminescence in all that mire. I shook my head, mesmerized. My goal had become elusive, overwritten by a different lust. A craving arose, to see Red quenched that need slightly but it wasn't enough just to look. She was dazzling; not the sun burning out one's corneas, but a light that was inescapable just the same. One rule; never trust anyone, especially those of any underworld. No matter how alluring, never care.

Red scanned the crowd with barely a tilt to her head. Before she moved on I angled across her path, picking up a glass of Shimmering Grove, which I handed to her as she turned back from glancing into one dark corner. She cocked her head to the side and smiled slightly. "Thanks."

I leaned in through the noise and stuttering red-blue lights, surreptitiously breathing in her aroma, as subtle as a mountain breeze. "What brings you to this place?"

She smiled and snorted delicately. "The same as everyone else and yet, different. Let us sit."

The place could not have held many more people, or even cockroaches. We found a booth but on one side, squeezed together. I began to absorb the vibrations, working the subtle flavors of her into my senses. Red wore no adornment except for moonpowder gray pants and hooded jacket. She stood out against the darker people around her. My thigh lay against the length of hers and I knew despite herself that she was electrified by the touch when her breathing sped up.

Leaning forward, I held up my drink of chilly, dark Lethe liquor and tapped her glass. "Here's to you, oh goddess of the wild places."

Red looked down, smiling, before she drank. That smile drew my curiosity. It was not one of shyness, nor even delight at the compliment. But more a knowing smile, which I did not understand.

Then she asked me, her arctic eyes staring into me, "Why are you here?"

"To drink."

Her eyes narrowed. "Don't be coy. You know what I'm asking."

I snorted. In business I detested subterfuge and demanded people speak plainly. And here she was reminding me of that. "You're right. You're beautiful."

She waved her hand casually at the room. "There are many beautiful people in many places."

"And you intrigue me. You are mysterious. Controlled." I kissed her cheek. "Sensual."

Her eyes closed and lips parted slightly. For all of a couple of seconds. She looked at me, "You know nothing about me."

"I'd like to find out, if you'll allow it."

"You may wish you hadn't."

I tilted my head. It was true we didn't know what she did, and the assassinations happened where she always seemed to arrive from. But how many people would meet those specifications, arriving daily from a district or a planetoid where someone had been murdered? Thousands, really. "I doubt it. All knowledge is worthwhile."

She drank, letting the river of green pour into her mouth. Licking her lips, she grinned, almost feral, unnerving me slightly. "Even if in the knowing, you condemn yourself to the path."

"It's always the way," I replied as I lightly laid my fingers on her knee.

She stiffened, then relaxed back, her shoulder touching mine. Heat fired along my fingertips, up my arm, lancing to my groin. I had her. The first barrier was down and she would be my latest treasure, perhaps the greatest. But I could not rush it now.

I leaned in and whispered, "I must go, but it has indeed been a pleasure. I hope we can meet again."

As she turned to answer I kissed her softly, her lips smooth and pliable, like living velvet. She didn't respond for a moment, her eyes widening in surprise; then she tentatively returned the kiss, a need slowly feeding on my small caress. I left her then, a look I couldn't describe in her eyes as she bit her lip and watched me go.

Anticipation can be its own narcotic. But sooner or later you want to taste more, to finally devour and glut the senses. No longer was I content to pursue at weekly intervals or longer. At some point the chase must end and the meal begin. After a few nights I stalked her to another dark little den of evening pleasures. Quieter, more refined, I slipped into the chair across from her and proceeded to order a sensorial feast, light but seductive. Laced with various wines and alcohols, for the first time it looked as if Red's edge had softened.

A touch is like a questing animal, beginning slowly, almost tentatively before braving a greater distance. So my fingers quested along her legs, across her back, defining the fine line of her chin before caressing her neck and shoulders. My breath first warmed her, thawed her glacial demeanor, an advance scout for my lips that grazed the mysterious curl of her ear, the slender neck, that same jawbone, to the lips. And once the advance forces had conquered the outer defenses I took her into a full penetrating kiss, my hands lightly tripping over her body, teasing her delectably hard nipples through her shirt.

At first her reticence formed a barrier, but even the greatest fortress can be breached. A floodtide, my whispered endearments, a kiss to her ear, a light nibble on the neck, overwhelmed her, had her gasping, blindly seeking parts of me to kiss as if I could give her sight into seduction; and in a way it was exactly what I was doing, leading her along a new trail.

Yet I left Red again, panting, wet, her face flushed with the lightest pink. This way I assured that when I did take her, she would be complicit, no longer fighting against my wild longing. Did I worry at my scruples, at the fact that I would probably toss her aside when satiated? I assumed I would immerse myself as usual in work and vice.

What I did next should have warned me I had gone too far. I've always kept my goals in focus and usually achieved them. I continued the spying, the slow encroachment into her zone. Each time I followed a bit farther until, one day, I saw her enter a building after holding her wrist to the keypad. A place of permanence then.

But I did not breach the place. Instead I let myself be seen, leaving a restaurant or pub just as she was arriving, or sometimes lingering to keep those flames burning. Once I caught her as I was leaving an establishment and before she entered, pulling her around the corner of the pub. The cool metal singed my palms as I placed them either side of her shoulders, her back braced against the wall.

"Hwulf! What?" Her blue eyes slitted to hard lights. "You're lucky I didn't gut you. Never surprise me on the street."

I leaned in, my lips centimeters away. "Now, Red, don't you like surprises?" I whispered. "The unknown, the anticipation…"

"I—" She pressed her lips to mine, her tongue snaking between, tasting my teeth and tongue. Momentarily caught off guard by the passion in her kiss, she had me hesitant for once. But only for a second before I responded. Her teeth nipped my lip, drawing warm coppery nectar. My hands pressed her to the wall so that I could look at her, into her. Had I misjudged her virgin state or had I stoked the fires well, very well indeed?

Laughing, I clasped her face and kissed her, rubbing my knee up between her legs. "You are delicious, my dear."

She moaned, undulating into my hands, which bared her breasts. My serpent tongue slithered over her flesh, circling the fleshy pebbles of her nipples. Red pressed one into my mouth, clasping my head between her long nails. I gave a final long languorous lick and pulled away, my finger touching the tip of her nose. "I have a meeting now. I'll see you later."

I left, but when next I returned to the building that cloistered her, the shadows held me like a lover. Not one person passing noticed my marriage to the darkness. I waited and watched, even though I already had obtained Red's flight schedule for the next week. It is good to know who else frequents an area and to study the lay of the land. Red exited her place, in skimmer suit, helmet in hand. I waited a good hour after to make sure she didn't return, or any other "friend" show up.

Red and I are loners in our ways. I established levels of employees and hangers-on but on my most crucial matters I conduct them alone. Red always traveled solo, a solitary white light. It surprised me therefore, when I cracked the building's defenses, to hear movement within. The door opened to a landing, embraced by horizontal bars painted green. I propped the door with my foot as I looked around. It was difficult to tell the full size of the cavernous room, as if gloom and colors pooled, waiting to be unleashed on the world, or moon. Two sets of stairs lead into the space proper, though room was a term I would use loosely.

I would have called it a forest of fabric, ceramic, plants and sparkling trinkets. A bed nestled to one side, draped in red, gold and emerald silks, an autumn of decadence. Lights like many feral eyes glinted in between the textured swathes hung from the twenty-foot ceilings. There was no other room or kitchen that I could see but all was layered like foliage, with darker shades of crimson, eggplant and ebony filling one corner. So unlike the austere, controlled and somewhat cold vision of Red was this room that I was stunned.

The rustling I had heard upon entering grew louder, a slow waking. Likewise, I came to my senses, alert to danger. A man emerged from the canopy of fabrics in one corner, a resigned slump to his shoulders until he looked up and saw me. Confusion wrinkled his brow. He was not young, nor old; thirty I would say and good looking, haughty though that seemed to have been worn down.

It would not serve my plan if Red already had a paramour. Already the complications multiplied; that she might not seem as innocent as she was, but intrigue still piqued me that she could fool me that well.

"Who are you?" the puzzled man asked.

"I might just be the path to your transformation."

I pulled out a card and quickly inscribed it with my stylus, encrypting a code and an amount. Holding the card out to him, he cautiously ascended the steps.

"If you take this and leave, never to return, you will have enough here to set you up for life. Should you accept, and then return, your life will be cut short."

He snorted, his brown eyes like pools of stagnant mud. "It already was. I'll take it and never see her nor you again." And he was gone through the open doorway, a whiff of fear trailing in his wake.

A subtle scent of pine and humus, wildflower and spring rain overtook me. My hairs rippled with possible dangers in Red's lair. I hesitated. But the snare was laid and I had to explore. My foot left the door and it gently swung closed, a metallic click sealing the artificial environment of the moon. I left the stairs, aware of the carpet's soft pile patterned subtly in overlapping leaves. I had to feel it.

As I moved into the room, passing through groves of soft and scratchy fabric, the sound of wood on nut, of seed in pod, of rustling fibers, of water on rocks came to me. Slowly it permeated, melted away the metallic clutter of Moonbase. A quietus descended that these sounds only enhanced. I wandered a forest of touch and sound, of scents and sight. Immersed, I did not realize I was snared until I looked up at some slight change in sound and realized I knelt, naked, having shed my clothes, the last vestiges of civilization and technology. I was born anew to the sensorial world. For one who had always cherished the visceral pleasures, this was a heightened state beyond the pale. It was as if I had come home.

Red's voice fell upon me as gentle as a moonbeam. "It looks like someone's entered my sanctuary." White fingers scythed apart the emerald and gold gossamer. I stood, uncaring of my nakedness.

"It is more that I have gone to ground here." I walked to her and she did not seem surprised. Desire filled me, to be bathed in the whiteness of her body, its pure light touching my flesh. I reached out, running my fingers over her cheek and chin, down her neck and over her breasts. I pulled the zipper. Her jacket slithered to the floor and joined the other clothes, becoming part of the sumptuous environment.

In moments, or was it longer, she was naked, her nearly silver body shimmering against my darker skin. Her fingers explored the whorls of my head as my lips sought clavicle and breast, elbow and shoulder, neck and ear. Down I moved, nipping at the sweet spot by the point of the hip, licking in lazy spirals around her navel and down to her pubis. My tongue parted the platinum grove, seeking the omphalos, the great center of all. Red gasped and shivered, folding over my back until long fingers walked down my spine. Her tongue flicked out, trailing dark fire along my flesh. Groaning, I clasped her buttocks and pulled her closer, inhaling her musk, which was just like a forest of pine and cypress and other earthy scents I could not discern.

As Red kneeled before me, she placed a hand on my chest and pushed me back to recline on that carpet of woven leaves, yet I heard them rustle.

I was so stiff that when Red hovered over me the lightest brush of her thighs electrified me, sending my cock jumping like a jackrabbit. Then she let her luscious lips hold the tip as she slowly, excruciatingly slowly, rocked her hips back and forth. Her eyes closed as she threw her head back, the white orbs of her breasts above me like moons.

Flashes of cognizance made me wonder, was she a virgin? Her skill was consummate. She lathered me until I could not bear it and then slid the head just past the first luscious folds. In control, she lowered herself in increments so small I was desperate, yet never wanting it to end. Then Red rode me, time meaningless, ceaseless. Shadows came and went, colors shifted about us and we were lost in the timeless realm of sensation. Red stopped for a moment, her eyes widening, and then she kissed me, her nails biting deep into my chest as she slammed herself down upon me. Moaning, I rose up to meet her as her hips sped up. Our flesh joined and parted, and I slipped deeper and deeper into liquid velvet. Moaning, gasping, Red clamped me, my balls tightening with delicious pressure, her muscles milking me into a world-bursting orgasm. She screamed her ecstasy as our juices mixed, hot and molten, welding us in one ultimate moment of perfection before she collapsed upon me.

Later, I moved her hair from her ear and whispered, "Tell me your real name."

Her lips smiled against my shoulder. "You could call me Selene or Diana."

I must have faded away for a bit for when I opened my eyes again, Red was dressed in red; a skirt, a blouse, bare feet. I was no longer on the carpet but naked upon the bed. I could not move and she grinned, all teeth. "Ah, Hwulf, you are my greatest treasure yet. I might just keep you. At least for a while, no matter what."

Confused, I asked, "Were you a virgin?"

"I am and I am not. There is a divine cycle," she replied as she walked around me.

"Who was that here before?"

She laughed, the first I'd ever heard from her. "That was my lusty woodsman, but you let him go, so now you get the role."

"Red, what have you done to me?"

Sitting beside me, she trailed her crimson nails over my chest. "Ah, that. Let's say my bark isn't as bad as my bite, or my scratch." She scratched lightly with her nails. "Just a little something to keep you calm while I change the locks."

I didn't understand then, but I believe I do now. Now that I'm the one caged. I would say that I'm a captive; that I am frantic to escape. She did change the locks, to something high enough tech that I couldn't break them, not without tools that I didn't have. But am I enslaved if I willingly have given myself over?

Time has ceased to be linear and some days I feel I am truly in a forest; the foliage…the fabric seems to change, to engender shadows and spirits. It brings memories of the wild, of a time untamed. I have found myself howling, but not in terror. I have found a peace amongst the jewel tone cloths, the acheronian shades, a place both solitary and always mobile.

When we named her Red, it had nothing to do with her color. Now I knew it was more as if the moon bled, not in sacrifice but in rampant chaos.

Under The Skin

A Taste of Eden

I wanted to try a steampunk story, but not set in Victorian England. I needed a king or queen who loved gadgets, and found that in Germany's Kaiser Wilhelm. When professional competition and jealousy mix with passion, we oft don't see the warning signs until too late.

"Wunderbar!" said Kaiser Wilhelm II. "Simply wonderful! An Eden!"

Genevieve Dupuis executed a full curtsy, head bowed and eyes downcast, though her cheeks flushed with pleasure. Months of painstaking work had now won her this moment of triumph. She straightened and lifted her eyes to see the Kaiser, in the uniform of an Uhlan regiment, though with a cape carefully draped from one shoulder to cover his withered left arm, wander into the bejeweled grove Genevieve had labored to create in the palace grounds.

Leaves of multi-colored gems gently shifted and chimed as the breeze filtered through the artificial forest she had fashioned from a range of bright metals, the trunks and branches shimmering with dappled light, while the ground was speckled with flowers of amethyst, garnet, ruby, sapphire, coral, tourmaline, and chalcedony.

"Magical," the emperor said and Genevieve took a breath. Now was the moment to ask for the next commission, to turn this singular achievement into a blossoming career. But as she opened her mouth to speak the carefully rehearsed phrases, disaster struck.

The disaster came in the form of the most stunningly beautiful woman Genevieve had ever seen: ebony hair, carmine lips, eyes of an impossible blue, and a face copied from one of Raphael's angels. She appeared from nowhere, insinuated her way through the gaggle of courtiers, and knelt before Wilhelm, offering something wrapped in silk.

"Your majesty, may I present a gift to add to your forest?"

Wilhelm had never liked the unexpected, but curiosity won out and he waved away the equerry who was rushing to his aid.

The kneeling woman flipped back the square of silk to display a little bird made of brass, with some sort of gem glinting for eyes. "A nightingale to sing within your jeweled forest." She touched its throat and the metal automaton began to sing, its beak clacking mechanically, but the voice somehow that of a real bird.

The emperor laughed, took the creation from the woman's hands, and walked into the garden, where he positioned it on the golden branch of a nutmeg tree. Liquid notes continued to pour from its brass mouth. The courtiers moved forward to coo and fawn over the Kaiser's new delight, leaving Genevieve alone on the lawn, her moment dissipated and gone.

She turned and took two steps toward the exit, to find her way blocked by the usurper.

The woman smiled a perfect smile. "I wanted a word with you."

Up close she was even more stunning, a radiant firebird compared to Genevieve, for whom "mousy" she had always thought was almost too kind a description. Genevieve frowned and crossed her arms across her flat chest, steeling herself not to soften under that warming smile.

"I wanted to congratulate you on your creation. The forest is remarkable."

"No thanks to you," Genevieve said. "The Kaiser has already forgotten it."

The woman's cool fingers grazed her arm, sending a shiver through her. "I apologize, but this was the only time I could win His Majesty's notice." She tilted her head and took Genevieve's hand in a grasp whose warmth was startling. "Let us start afresh. I'm Mita Leopoldine Freiin von Bauer and I would like to work with you. You are a genius."

Genevieve kept her lips pressed together, though she did not pull her hand away.

"Please," Mita began, "I do not wish us to be enemies. Come by my chateau this evening, where we can talk."

"I cannot." The woman's magnetism disturbed Genevieve, summoning up half-formed emotions that were new to her. She stepped around her and moved toward the exit.

"Then come by tomorrow. I will send a coach around at seven."

Genevieve threw up her hands and without turning, said, "Fine! Tomorrow!" She left before she started screaming.

※

But when the coach came she did not answer the door. She was busy making new automata for the emperor's forest. A week after the unveiling, Genevieve brought the Kaiser a rabbit sculpted from finely cut strips of silver and tin, with ears that twitched and swiveled. Once wound up, it hopped about, stopping to sniff at the artificial plants as if to eat them. When it lollopped beneath the gemstone leaves it moved with the grace of an actual animal.

Wilhelm laughed and thanked her. But then Mita von Bauer was suddenly there, presenting the Kaiser with a crude cat of copper and brass. The cartoonish face was missing whiskers and its roundish shape was barely reminiscent of a feline's graceful body. Two rough pieces of green glass passed for eyes and the limbs' motions were mere jerks. But when it meowed or growled it sounded exactly like a cat, with a full range of feline utterances. Those who attended Wilhelm in the jeweled garden watched his face carefully and when he smiled they clapped.

Genevieve was the empire's most accomplished fashioner of robots and automata, but neither she nor her competitors had ever been able to produce true voices. Now, wearing her shapeless pants and old woolen coat, she watched the flawlessly fashionable other woman bask in the emperor's regard.

Mita approached her and smiled. "You never came." Genevieve's gaze floated to her competitor's red lips and she forced herself to look into the woman's blue eyes. Then she looked away.

"I was busy." Her hand gestured toward the rabbit. It seemed silly now.

Mita did not take her eyes off Genevieve. "Please come to my château. I guarantee to make it up to you. We shouldn't be enemies."

"How do you capture the sound?" Genevieve asked.

She ran her hand over Genevieve's shoulder and down her back, raising a shiver. "Come for dinner. Let us see if we can work together."

Genevieve found it hard to speak. "Yes, all right."

※

The elegant aristocrat sat across from her as they sipped a *digestif* in the sitting room. The flavorful dinner of Cornish hens and fresh fall vegetables had been superb, though Genevieve had nervously drunk more wine than she was used to.

At dinner they had chatted about inconsequential things; the weather, the best places to travel, lightly over politics but not in any depth. Now Genevieve, emboldened by the spreading warmth of the Armagnac, said, "How did you manage to mimic the sound so closely? My best efforts produce only rough approximations."

Her host arose from the divan, picked up the cut-crystal decanter and poured more for both of them. She set the vessel back on the small table and sat beside Genevieve, leaned in close, staring into her eyes. Genevieve felt Mita's breath against her lips as she said, "We will have plenty of time to talk of work. Now is the time for adventure."

Genevieve looked into the little amber pool in her glass, hoping her flush didn't show. Then warm fingers gently tipped up her chin. The knowing smile on Mita's incarnadine lips captured Genevieve's whole attention. The woman moved in closer, lightly touching Genevieve's own breathless mouth.

Mita's lips trailed over Genevieve's neck and her eyes fluttered closed for a moment. Nothing like this had happened since her school days. She had been working so long, and always alone.

Genevieve tried to sort her thoughts as Mita pressed against her, returning to kiss her lips again. Shivers of pleasure ran through her and her hesitancy broke. Now Mita was pulling the clothes from her and Genevieve's hands were equally busy.

Mita's mouth and tongue trailed over the flat planes of Genevieve's belly and dipped in to tenderly burrow between her legs. Genevieve gasped as the warm velvet of Mita's tongue penetrated her, and she pulled forward to trail her fingers over the woman's ivory back, managing to work the rest of her petticoats down. For a moment, she thought, *Is this wise?* But then Mita's ministrations overwhelmed her.

They lay upon the carpet, clothes a chaotic mound as their bodies glowed and sweated in the amber firelight. They writhed and loved and explored until the embers had burned low in the grate.

"Let's work together," Mita murmured into the curve beneath Genevieve's ear.

She shivered, feeling a stir of arousal in the languorous aftermath. "All right," she sighed.

Then Mita sat up and smiled with such triumph that Genevieve suddenly felt the cold that was seeping into the room. She sat up, wiping hair back from her face. "I must go or I'll not be fit to accomplish much tomorrow. I have a client coming by."

Mita rolled onto her belly, chin in hands and watched Genevieve carefully. "Of course, my dear. I will have a servant bring a carriage so you arrive safely." She rang a bell, then stood naked, wantonly, and ran her fingers over Genevieve's breasts as she dressed. "We'll see each other soon."

She turned and left through a door on the far side of the room. Genevieve watched her leave, then dressed hurriedly before a servant entered.

Weeks humped up against each other like eager children waiting for a cookie, and before Genevieve knew it, fall was nearly over. She had spent a great deal of time in the lush environs of Mita's body. Together, they had received commissions from the Kaiser, or rather he commanded speaking animals from Mita, who subcontracted the building of a dog, a lamb, a wolf, to Genevieve. While Genevieve worked, Mita watched her closely, asking questions, acquiring skills and abilities that made her a better craftswoman. Yet when it came time to imbue them with sound, Mita took the automata and withdrew to her secret workroom, somewhere in the depths of the city.

"Are we not partners?" Genevieve would ask, but the answer always came from Mita's tongue and fingers working their insidious magic. Genevieve's desire ran like an opiate and she fell to the allure as surely as the last leaves dropped from the trees.

⚜

Genevieve was working on a snake, jabbing it ferociously with a screwdriver. Months had passed, during which Mita had revealed nothing beyond her luscious body. The sun cast long shadows from the autumn sky and Genevieve looked up. Tossing the screwdriver down, she took off her work apron and pulled on a thick wool coat against the chill. She hailed a hansom cab and arrived at Mita's chateau as the sun was setting.

The servant looked surprised but bowed to her as she stormed in. She found Mita in the drawing room, donning a cape, jewels sparkling in her raven-dark hair.

"Mita."

Mita turned slowly. "Ah, darling. I wasn't expecting you."

"We have to talk. I'm starting to feel like I'm just your assistant."

Mita picked up an exquisitely beaded reticule and laid a gloved hand on Genevieve's cheek. She smiled, tilting her head to one side. "We *will* talk, my dear. You know I do love *talking* to you. But right now I have a meeting." She leaned in, giving a quick kiss to Genevieve's lips. "I'll see you tomorrow."

⚜

But Mita did not come the next day or for several afterwards. A week later, Genevieve was in the emperor's forest, summoned by Wilhelm to explain why Mita's nightingale had stopped singing. She made her way among the metal trees, and heard the titters and growls and hoots from Mita's magic housed in Genevieve's exquisite casings. She saw the damned snake twining itself around a bronze tree trunk. It hissed at her.

But the nightingale was silent. Its sheen had dimmed. Voiceless, it no longer imitated life; instead it looked more like something reanimated from death, a monster from the grave making a mockery of the living. And now that she moved among the creations, Genevieve saw that Mita's other earliest automata no longer meowed nor barked.

Genevieve was deep in the grove when Mita also arrived in answer to the Kaiser's summons. She was dressed in peacock green and gold, ever the superb ornament. Genevieve moved back into the shadows as Mita approached the emperor and curtsied elegantly.

"Your Majesty, I would like to ask for an imperial commission."

Wilhelm turned and raised an eyebrow, then stared up into the tree where the nightingale sat lifeless and unmoving. "Perhaps, but look, your first creature no longer sings. Do you think you can make one that lasts longer?"

Mita tilted her head, a tiny smile playing over her lush lips. "It has to do with the life force of the creation, Your Majesty. Small creatures, small lives. Now if we go for a horse or even an elephant—"

Wilhelm waved away the notion with his good hand and wandered through the forest, squinting up at the jeweled leaves. "Too big, not right for this marvel. It should crown this, not stampede through it. Perhaps a child. Can you do that, make a child's voice? If so I will grant you a yearly allowance for five years to work on larger commissions. Perhaps create a zoo of mechanica."

The emperor's back was turned as he spoke, but Genevieve saw Mita's face light up with greed. And some other emotion that was even less pleasant to see.

After that day, Genevieve did not tell Mita that she knew of the new assignment, nor did her supposed partner mention it. But clearly Wilhelm's command to build a child had drawn a line between what had been and what was now. Mita no longer sent a carriage for her and when Genevieve made her own way to the chateau, Mita's servant would say that his mistress was not at home.

But Mita Leopoldine Freiin von Bauer was not one to blend in with the common people on the narrow streets of the old city, while Genevieve was the daughter of an engineer and had lived a simple life before her studies. It was not hard for her to observe without being observed, or to ask questions of tradespeople and cab drivers. Soon enough, she had found her lover's workroom: housed in an old stone abattoir that was filled with people carting carcasses and slabs of meat during the day, but quiet as death after dark.

She watched Mita come and go, on several occasions. On the fourth night, having established the woman's routine, Genevieve waited an hour past Mita's departure, then made her way into the building. She lit a small lantern, casting its golden eye over the large room and the chunks of red and white marbled meat hanging from the rafters. The place did not smell of rot and looked clean. The meat cutters had washed everything down at the end of their day, and water shone blackly on the floor and wooden tables where butchers cut up flesh and chopped bone. She crept between gently swaying sentinels of pork and beef, unnerved by the shadows and oily pools.

Genevieve noticed stairs to a floor above. As she moved toward them the lantern light winked over something on the floor. Bending down, she found the ring for a trapdoor. *This will be the lab,* she thought. She pulled and the wooden square eased up silently.

As she descended, the lantern's dim light showed her stacked crates and unrecognizable apparatus. A bluish glow emanated from her far left and she went toward it. She felt water dripping on her through the floor boards above as she wove between shelving and packed crates, tables littered with cogs and wheels, some with tubing, and others with brass or tin limbs. Most were either animal forms or completely unrecognizable but the refinement increased as she made her way toward the light.

She stopped to inspect some of the material on the benches and became aware of a low electrical humming. Genevieve moved toward the sound until, rounding one row of shelves, she came upon giant blue-white glass spirals of light, thrumming with contained energy. *Tesla coils.* She'd used similar devices to animate some of her automatons. But these were massive.

The Tesla coils stood like sentries over a table on which lay a human-shaped robot. Torches and tools for welding were on a nearby bench. Genevieve set the lantern down, no longer needing it in the pulsing white light, and walked between the electrical pillars. Dripping water flashed like lightning as monstrous shadows capered and danced across the lab. Cautiously, she looked for movement. Why would Mita need so much power for such poorly constructed machines?

As she edged past the coils, Genevieve felt a charge ripple through her body; her hair lifted away from her neck. The air smelled tangy, yet musty, and something else…musky, elusive, and reminiscent of her childhood.

The humanoid shape on the table was crude, blue glass eyes staring, arms stiffly at the side of the comical tubular body. *More a marionette than a person.* It was the size of a twelve-year-old child, and by far Mita's roughest work. Obviously, it was for the assignment the emperor had ordered, but why always the sloppiness in the forms?

Genevieve took up the lantern again and looked around the shadowed room. She saw cages on the floor and knelt before one. In each one lay a lifeless form: dead, dried-out husks, a nightingale and a peacock, a cat – recently dead of starvation from the looks of it – and a wolf. The latter was not yet dead, but lay on its side, its ribcage barely moving, the grey matted fur showing its emaciated form.

Why had Mita starved these creatures? Genevieve's arms prickled with cold. What kind of person would cage an animal and not even feed it? And then she thought, *Of course. Here is Mita's secret.*

She clasped her mouth. Then she rose and, splashing blindly through puddles, stumbled back to the table, seeing not the shadowy scene around her but the terrifying pictures in her mind. *A child*, she thought. *She will steal a child, and starve it to death.*

But there was no child here, caged like the animals. The automaton was built but Mita was not ready to work her foul magic. How could Genevieve stop it? She studied the child-shape, noticed wires leading from the Tesla coils to the robot, but little else. She ran her hands over the cool metal surface, finding little remarkable. A latch on its side opened to reveal rudimentary cogs for movement. Then she found a second, almost delicate knob at the automaton's hairline above the ear. A puzzle latch, but Genevieve twisted, pushed and turned it until she found the right combination to release the catch.

The curved door swung across the robot's forehead, revealing a large tinted crystal. Genevieve frowned. She had used crystals and had only approximated sound. This one was different though and it definitely glowed blue. She leaned over the machine, her hand resting on the sturdy metal chest as she reached to pull the crystal free. The moment she touched it a power slammed through her, sucking the breath from her lungs.

She tried to draw in air but felt herself suffocating as hot white light blinded her. *The circuit*, she thought. *I closed it.*

Genevieve opened her eyes and knew something was terribly wrong. She was cold, couldn't move, and her breathing seemed odd.

Mita's brilliant eyes were looking down on her. "Ah, you're awake. Good. Don't try to talk just yet. It will take a few more minutes for everything to calibrate."

She moved away. Genevieve tried to turn her head, following her voice. Her head finally twisted a fraction, giving a view of one Tesla coil, its captive energy spinning like a dervish up the column, much faster than before.

"I was always afraid it would come to this. Your curiosity is insatiable." She came into view, the Tesla light limning her black serpentine tresses in silver. Shaking her head, she sighed. "You know you brought this on yourself. But it's all for the best. You've provided me the chance to capture my first human soul. You will be the test."

She adjusted something out of Genevieve's view. Human soul? Genevieve couldn't even frown. Her thoughts were disjointed: automata, normally run by gears, common steam engines, sometimes electricity; capturing pure animal voices, so close to the original that one couldn't tell the difference; dead animals in cages; the human soul for a human voice—

Genevieve jerked, heard the creak of metal as she tried to turn her head further. Now she succeeded in looking to her right. She saw a body lying on a gurney. Her vision was fuzzy but the shape looked familiar. The clothes too, and the soft brown hair. *That's me.*

Mita eclipsed her view, her edges blurry. "My, you are determined, aren't you, *darling*?" She walked over to Genevieve's body and leaned over, smoothing hairs from her face. "I'll miss our lovemaking." Mita kissed Genevieve's lips. Genevieve felt only revulsion, willing her flesh body to strangle Mita. But it did not move, except for a shallow rising of the chest.

"W-why?" a tinny voice croaked.

Mita grinned. "Good. It's working." Her face clouded and her eyes went dark. "Why? Because I can. This is only the beginning. I will form an army that will obey none but me. I will have *power!*" Her fist snapped shut and again Genevieve saw that emotion that Mita had revealed behind the Kaiser's back. Now she knew it for what it was: the mad lust of a tyrant.

Then abruptly Mita was laughing and tucking up some strands of her hair. "It was pure luck, really, finding this location. The water was essential for the soul-capture. Still, I'm not sure how well I can keep humans, or for how long. Then there is the problem of what each of you might say – I may have to collect mutes. And then there's the… impermanence."

Mita waved a dismissive hand. "That's neither here nor there. The life force is what will fuel my indestructible army. Now I must go." She smiled sadly at Genevieve in the brass golem's body. "You were a lovely dalliance, even though you were no more exciting than a pet mouse."

Humming, Mita left in a swirl of taffeta. Genevieve could not cry, nor form a fist of wronged fury. All she could do was lie upon the table, encased in inferior metal, and *think*. The first thing she realized: Mita needed time until she could find a way to extend the captured life inside metal bodies. An army whose life force dwindled and died would be no use. But the experiments would hurt many.

Genevieve had to survive. And she had to get beyond this immobility. *Concentrate*, she told herself. *Learn to control this metal body*. She would start with raising her right arm.

Hours passed; a day? In theory this body should move on its cogs and gears, if she could just find a way to motivate it. But it was a rough prototype, the crude joints not even oiled. Again and again, she sent the message to the arm: *Move*! Again and again, nothing happened.

Until it did. With a jerk, the metal arm moved. It creaked into view, the charging cables from the Tesla coils still attached to the wrists. Genevieve wished Mita had asked her to make this robot. She would have given it intricate joints and ball bearings for smooth, fluid motions. Instead, she was like a turtle on its back, only her right arm moving back and forth, like a marching soldier. But now she managed to get the other limb in motion, and began to work on curling the fingers.

Footsteps reverberated on the floor above and the trapdoor clunked open. Genevieve stilled herself.

"Hush, hush, Come down and I'll give you a lolly," Mita's voice cajoled. Her gown swished against the wooden crates. "Now just sit here."

Genevieve creaked her head to the side as Mita sat a young boy of about six upon a chair and gave him a sweet.

As the grubby child unwrapped the parchment, Mita put a cloth soaked in ether over his face. He slumped into her arms and she carried him to an empty table, briefly glancing at metal Genevieve.

The woman positioned the unconscious child then moved to the table next to where Genevieve agonized. Another automaton lay there; Mita opened its head plate. The blue crystal glowed weakly against the pulsing light. She picked up two cables.

Genevieve croaked out, "Mi-i-ta."

Mita's back stiffened and she put down the cables, turning toward the sound. "Really, what is it now? I'm busy."

Genevieve rocked on the bed. Mita laughed and moved closer. "You're moving! What a brave little mouse! I'll keep you to entertain me."

She threw back her head and laughed. The laughter stopped when Genevieve's metal fingers seized her wrist. Genevieve could not know how tight her grasp was, so she used all her clumsy strength. Mita gasped and paled, then started pulling at the fingers.

"Mi-ta, you…must…stop."

Mita pulled back but Genevieve held on and brought her other arm up, and now she gripped both of Mita's wrists.

"Let me go!"

"No." Genevieve's voice was a metallic croak. "You… let… me… go."

Mita thrashed left and right but Genevieve did not loosen her grip. The cylindrical body rocked on the table as Mita thrust and pulled, back and forth. Now metal Genevieve slid over the edge of the table, pulling Mita down to the floor, falling on her, pinning her. The enraged woman kicked and strained against the metal grip.

Mita's flailing foot connected with the table that held the second robot – the table on which the live cables rested. The conduits slipped off, falling to the floor, arcs of light snapping between their naked ends. Then they hit the water.

A crack of light and sound, a shriek, and Mita's body arched, her arms jerking like a string-puppet's. The flash blinded Genevieve. She was in darkness, and it felt as if a cold wind rushed through her. Then she was doubled up, coughing and gagging, vomiting as her body convulsed. Shakily, she looked around. A burned metallic smell filled her senses. Her vision wavered. Her pounding heart was all the sound in the world.

The automaton lay on Mita, blackened flashmarks across metal and flesh alike. Genevieve pulled herself up, wiping her mouth on her sleeve.

※

Spring arrived heavy and leaden. Genevieve made one last round of the jeweled forest. Kaiser Wilhelm had ordered it rid of all automata, even the rabbit. Now a few real nightingales and larks flitted through the branches, and even a cat or two prowled the artificial woods while workers polished the gems and metal to maintain their splendor.

She was leaving Germany. Great steamworks were being constructed in England; she would pursue her work there. As she turned to leave the garden, a telltale glint of gold slithered by. Reaching out, she seized the snake, then smashed it against the ground. Coils and springs bounced loose, green gems scattered. Genevieve ground her heel against the metal and said goodbye to the false Eden.

Though one of its serpents had been all too real.

Season's End

Peter Pan is a (relatively) modern version of the Green Man. One of our more modern fairy tales, he is a symbol of regeneration and eternal youth, like Tammuz or Dionysus. What happens when Peter Pan, the eternal youth, is unable to return to Neverland? And if there is an eternal youth, is there an eternal mother or an eternal lover?

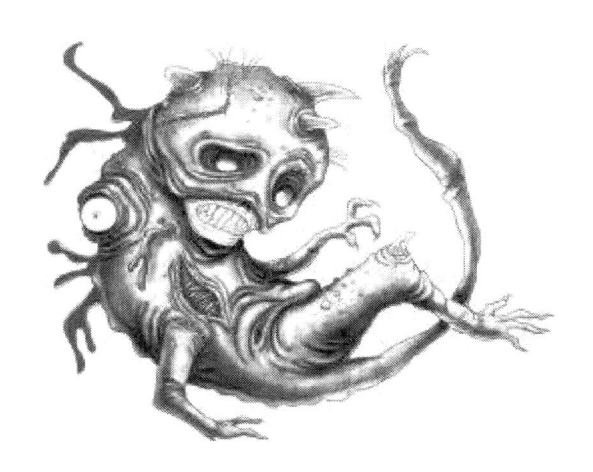

A howl threaded through the warehouses as I peeled russet and gold leaves from Jack's face and arms. A small childlike whimper bled from him. The sucking sound made me shudder.

"Shh, Jack, shhh. It will be over soon. This is the last."

Cool wind whistled through derelict buildings and silos that held some strange blood leached from the earth's veins. Water scabbed in thin layers of ice over cracked asphalt. Shallow oily pools winked when the moon hid behind scudding clouds. Only the skeletal limbs of a few trees creaked at the lot's perimeter.

Biting my lip, I pulled another crackling brown and yellowed leaf from his cheek, its veins breaking as Jack's were revealed beneath. Yellowish fluid welled. His green-gold eyes flashed, then darkened to brown with each tearing away. The pain unearthed him and his mind revolted from the present.

He moaned, "Willow," his voice merged briefly with the wind, "we're lost."

"Always, Jack, always. Now lie still so I can apply the skin." We had indeed lost our way, had to blend in until we could find a path back. How do you search when days, seasons, years repeat on an endless wheel, round and round and round? Jack had never really learned this, though there was an animal ken to him always. As the worm knows to burrow, the rabbit to shed its summer coat, the kitten to begin to walk, so Jack too had that instinctual grain. But what good is that when an animal goes to ground?

I opened the dinged plastic cooler and pulled out the bag, undoing the seal and carefully unfolding the skin. It had an unpleasant cold, rubbery feel. Still, we had been lucky enough to find a girl dead by the river. Skinning her was little different than taking game.

Another hoot echoed over the area, followed by laughter. I jumped, but carefully set the flesh across Jack's arms, trimming away the excess with my hunting knife. He hissed and went rigid but held still. This was the last of two weeks replacing his skin in patches, slowly removing the dying leaves, hiding what he was. Rooting here would be the death of him. Taking the smoothest piece from the belly and cutting a large oval, I made small openings, then laid the flesh over his face, like forming a pie crust. With the flats of my palms, I applied pressure until I felt the flesh adhere. Jack's never-ending cycle took over, beginning the healing as best it could, given the circumstances.

I saw shadows in the moonlight and whispered, "We have to go! They're coming. Can you move?"

He groaned and sat up, a frightening marionette's patchwork face staring back. Poor lost Jack. I pulled him to his feet and passed him the T-shirt. With clothing and night's camouflage, the piebald nature of the grafts wouldn't show. Gingerly, he pulled the shirt on and I motioned him away, under the shadowed awning of a squat building. I passed him his jacket as he staggered behind me.

Time slows in other dominions but it doesn't stop. We had eventually grown and all my play-acting at house and mothering finally spun too thin. I hadn't let little boys fight over me. I had fought for myself instead.

Jack hadn't liked it but memory for him is as fleeting as time. Yet here I was, mothering him again, keeping us both alive. He knew the tricks of nature; I knew how to adapt to man-made places. We had never trod the man-made world for more than an eve, but now we'd been stuck here far too long.

We ran crouched like twiggy things, our feet smacking and cracking the surfaces of hoary ice.

Voices echoed off aloof buildings, circling around to confuse us. I found an open bay door and pulled Jack in. Its cavernous interior birthed shadows, wooden crates crowding the back quarter. Jack lurched behind me, and wouldn't last much longer. I moved back through the rows of twelve-foot high sentinels, then chose one set of crates to climb upon. Jack's bare feet found purchase as easily as mine. Grabbing his arm, I heaved him over.

"Lie flat, be still," I whispered as we crouched down in the center of the pallet. He lay spread-eagled on his back, I on my stomach, knife in hand. Listening, waiting, I looked at him. His eyes were closed and the skin looked raw-edged, black in the darkness. Hair like tangled moss spread out about him. But then, it was just hair and his chest rose and fell, rose and fell, and I put my head down to wait and think.

I was the responsible one; he was the one of instincts. Flitting back and forth between the lands as if they were Sunday outings had broken the pathways; trails entwined and twisted. The realm beyond, the never lands, had faded behind the haze of corrosion belched from automobiles and smokestacks. The poison had mired Jack ever since. And I with him. He could no longer fly.

A little boy in skeleton leaves, their stark ribs showing, carefree, petulant, brave with great deeds, ruthless in his wants. We'd changed, coming of age, coming into an age. How long had he been a boy before I joined that madcap band? Those other lands had gently shifted the seasons, the leaves starting fresh upon him, dropping away with a gradual release, until Jack stitched them into clothes, the slight brown grain of his skin showing through. Sometimes he was smooth as birch, sometimes, rough as cedar.

Unending games – rolling through the landscape, like puppies chasing sticks, kittens batting their first mice. Unheeding, uncaring, artless and heartless. We had been all that, except for me playing stern mother, task mistress, bringer of order. I had grown tired of playing nurturer, of domesticity while the rest went wild. Had I caused the alteration, destroyed the natural balance?

Jack had cared more for upsetting balance than keeping it. A wild boy, a nature boy, shifting, sickening, losing his instinctual way until one day we didn't know where we were or when, the other boys disappearing one by one, like mist on a hot sunny day. I finally recognized it after so many goings to and fro – the world of man and machines, the world made ordered. Jack had grown no new leaves in all that time.

Voices called and feet left hollow sounds to spill up and tremor us. I placed a palm upon Jack's belly, kept him still and held my breath. I peered between dirty straw strands of hair.

"Hellooo," they called. "Come out, come out, wherever you are. Let's play a game."

We knew those games. The outsider singled out, the exile made scapegoat, the one left for the predators. My tears had stagnated, months, maybe years ago? Time had meant so little that we could not order it now, except to know Jack's cycle had stopped. Neither leaves nor witticisms floated from him and I felt a terrible truth shiver me. What would happen if he ended? Had he *ever* ended?

He'd been there forever, peppering children's dreams, tempting us to venturing. Now we lived a nightmare. Even before we'd left the leaves had begun to fall from him, sporting black spots and worts, a system decaying.

The voices of a half dozen sounded inside and out, going from building to building. Footsteps dopplered away and for a moment, maybe longer, Jack and I slumbered. Darkness still clasped us when I startled awake in complete silence.

"Jack." I gently shook him. "They're gone and so must we go, before the workers show."

He rolled to his knees and numbly followed, his stillness more eerie than the lack of life around us.

We scrambled down. Jack hugged himself and I hurt to see him so. Cold grew clouds from my breath but Jack's was a thin trickle, like steam. We'd wandered through a bald park of sickly grass and naked trees. The pathway didn't matter unless we found the hidden ways. We snaked through streets, still devoid of people.

"Jack, I don't know where to go."

He only grunted. Then; "Any way, any where, any when if we could. Could we, lovely Willow, Wendy mine, Margaret maiden, Kore sublime? Could we…"

"Shhh, shh. I'll find a place." This wasn't the city I had once known nor imagined. I'd been young then and memory is a painting that always changes. My stomach flopped, an unpleasant fish sensation that had taken residence of late.

We wandered down the city's grand parade, stores displaying dreams, make-believe, things to pad away the fears. These were their never lands. The naked alleys revealed only rats and escaped garbage limned in lamplight. The naked limbs of trees arched over, their branches clicking like bones. I shuddered but not from cold.

Had the affliction begun here, where forests were hard to find? The black spotting on his limbs, the strange stunting of his toes… Autumn had always grown into barren months, but he had harbored an animation, the feralness of a lean winter, hunting as the days sped by. Would he see spring? I'd learned a lot from Jack, my playmate, friend and lover. If I could find a portal, I could open it. But I couldn't find the path. Nor could he. We no longer flew but only stumbled along, searching, ever searching.

Morning crept closer. I steered us toward some modest homes. Sensing for life, I found a vacant dwelling, and using street wiles known everywhere, I coaxed the locked door to ease us in. Jack collapsed into a stupor and I joined him for a while until the floorboards bruised my hips.

Midday, I sat up and clawed through my tangle-mop of hair. Jack lay asleep, a deadwood look. I peered close; skin adhered in sections, but not as well as the previous grafts. The mottled blue with green looked like rotting food. I bit my lip. This was not the normal molt; no new buds peeked from his pores. Winter was when he had looked most like a boy, a man, when he grasped the thread of time's tapestry and rode the pattern of introspective thought.

My jeans were smeared with myriad bits of the outside world. The torn leather jacket that I had pilfered on our exile was too big, an old and beaten thing. The empty home held nothing in any cupboard or corner, devoid of all inhabitants. Not even a mouse to feed Jack. I worried about leaving him, but he was in no shape to hunt.

"Jack." I leaned close and touched his arm. "My love, I must find food. Stay here."

Not sure if he heard, I left before night descended and dark's denizens hunted again.

The sky remained as insipid as old porridge and people huddled like turtles into coats. I managed to beg a bit of money, buy some tins of fruit and filch more.

I found one teen, hair spiked like a surprised cat, his face scarred with patterns and symbols. "What month is this?"

"Good drugs?" He smirked. "It's July." He turned away, pulling a big coat tight.

I grabbed his sleeve, yanking him to a halt. "July? But…it looks like winter."

"Duh, where ya been? It's been like this for five years now."

He eyed me warily when I asked what year it was. "2024. You should lay off the blast. It's warping your mind." He shrugged me off.

I stood frozen as people jostled me. One hundred and twenty-some years. I'd suspected. But worse, where had summer gone? Something icy hollowed my gut, as if someone cored me. Had *I* broken the pattern? Had we brought the end nearer? When I was a child, the innovations of coal heating, the betterment of society, the glory days of machines had been present. The future had been a shiny penny. But had we not tempered blight with beneficence?

Walking woodenly, I returned to our hideout. I passed sallow-looking people; healthier than Jack, but it explained the ferocious gangs that had chased us, relentless, hungry, hiding from their worst fears. The world was dying. The listless eyed me, and the hunger was not far behind.

We had spent our endless, childish days moving in perpetual and meaningless conflict. I had balked at the mender in me, but I couldn't fix Jack or myself, adrift in this chill, this lackluster landscape. Jack had to get back, find us a way where time stood still and we could slide in between again, like we had in the carefree days. Carefree ways, the ways of yesterday.

I returned as dusk descended early as if it were November. July dared the dark to cough up the long days of light, and failed. Jack flipped and flopped upon the floor. I grabbed wood from out back and built a fire, then stripped off my shirt and jeans, and bathed with cold water. Next I washed out my clothes as best I could, laying them to dry. Jack stirred from dormancy. His skin looked too patchy, flesh like a Frankenstein doll, other areas showing grayed woodgrain, splinters popping out as he bent his fingers.

I cut up apples into canned pears, poured in some sunflower seeds, added yogurt. I ate a bit of the blandly sweet concoction, then knelt by Jack. "Hey. You need to eat."

He groaned and rolled like an old man. There was nothing boyish left. Eyes dull as old ash barely looked at me. "Wendy, Willow, you're so good. All that's good…" He trailed off, staring at the food.

"Here." I pressed it into his twiggy hands. "Eat."

As he listlessly scooped the food I explained the world outside. He weakly shrugged. After he rested, I fed him a second helping.

Late in the night, when the fire turned into sleepy orange eyes, I felt Jack's fingers trace my hip. I rolled over. "Can you do nothing?" I asked his dark silhouette. "It's all so…broken. So…dark."

Fingers, chilly and stiff, touched my cheek. "Nothing." He shook his head. "I remember bits, seasons, the land… I can't see the lines, the dust trails of fairies. There is no way back any more. They have captured me, after all."

I didn't know if I wanted to go back. I was stuck in this ugly, cold and gray world. He used to make it okay, an adventure into other places, ones we could always escape to or from.

His lucidity was rare and he leaned down to kiss me.

We'd been tangled in a web of confusion, pursued and searching secret exits for long enough that we hadn't stopped, breathed, touched. Now, Jack ran his hands over me, rough as a laborer's. Already in my underwear, I peeled him from his clothes. For once it was not the painful removal of leaves out of sync with their normal falling. Desperation fueled us but it was awkward, not beautiful nor poignant. Parts of his flesh were clammy, and other parts rough, slivery. I grimaced through the pain and was grateful I could not see the patchwork job we'd made of him. Instead, I imagined him supple, pinky brown flesh tinged softly with green, fronds sprouting upon his head. I remember the feeling of his leafy abundance – lime, shamrock, emerald, peridot, earthy and fresh and rustling. Even his crackling crispness, the sloughing away of fall and winter had always been exciting, redolent with the scent of pine, spruce and sage. In the end I held these images strong, and we were both soothed. As we curled into each other like drying leaves, I asked, "How do we find the ways, Jack? The world is sick too."

"I don't know," he intoned, all lightness buried deep beneath the cobbled flesh. "I can't sense…anything, as if there had never been a never land, had never been a faery. Did I imagine it?"

I chewed at my nail. I might survive, but Jack turned with the seasons, capricious, blowing this way and that, unfettered by moral codes. He had never really scared me, even at his most untamed. Nature was unheeding but never intentionally vicious. Cruel cuts had been part of our world. I drifted into exhausted sleep.

Late morning, I awoke to a creaky sound. Jack's breath sounded like wind through wood. Through the bare window, clouds still covered the sky. I studied him. Spots blistered carnelian or black, pustules on his face and arms. Rotting garbage, leaves and rinds wafted up to cloy my nose. I closed my eyes, trying to will away the evidence.

I left food, mixed in a tin, and went to find more. Should we just bend to the ways of the world, accept the inevitable? Jack had always been a fighter, a force of perpetual motion. Yet that machine had stalled and stopped. His descent went far deeper than ever before.

Mother, mender, fixer, keeper. I had denied being all those things when I had finally grown, but as I swallowed back nausea and a shakiness that had rattled me of late I wondered if it was more than being astray on a trail. I used the subtle gleanings I had absorbed from all those years in places unnamed. In some ways, Jack and I had stayed true to our natures, never taking much from the other's world. In all that time, in all those journeys, it had always been make-believe, always games. Emotions flew by like clouds on a windy day, adventures switched like hairpin curves, and we had never minded. Just as we implant memories, and events impregnate us with a certain depth, so it seems that Jack, despite the chaos, had dropped his seed in me. Something had stuck.

After all that time pretending, and *now* I didn't know if I could handle it; in this place, at this time.

Things outside our hideout hunted, hooted, screeched and searched. Eventually they came scratching at the windows, faces human and feral. I moved us twice, then went to ground. Quiet, I cautioned, would have us go unnoticed. Yet still I heard the skreeking claws, the hollow howls. Still they searched and dug and lured from the shadows. Shadows can obliterate the sun and the light within one's heart.

I stood in a monochromatic world; grey roads, pewter sky, the stark fingers of trees cracking and falling upon the ground like discarded bones. Jack withered, the world crumbled, and as the breeze slid cool fingers over me I pondered ways to persevere. Jack lingered in pain, maddened. I could only make him comfortable, avoid the predators, and hope. We were running out of time.

※

We hunkered down. I worked and stole and scavenged things, using creative whims of yesterday to fuel a desperate need. I administered poultices and salves, broths and tisanes, mixed with earthy things, but nothing worked. My belly grew rounder. Jack lay listless as decaying cedar. I searched for answers, but when doorways disappear as if they never were, as if magic didn't exist, how do you heal a being made of the world's wonders? Grief weighted me.

I couldn't assimilate this place of mild workers coexisting with roving bands of the untamed. It was as if nature brought its wildness to the core of civilization and planted it within an equal and opposing force of people. And always the sky never lifted the grey lid that put a pall on everything.

I scavenged food yet again, digging through old bins. Hunters appeared, these ones human hyenas, decked out with axes and lasers, the red light shattering fog that rolled in. I weaved my way back to our hideout. Rumbling, low and ominous, followed me and the earth jittered. I ran.

Jack should have grabbed that wild nature, absorbed it, regenerated. He could reassert order just by being himself, but it wasn't happening. Something was shifting.

The discontented rumbling grew and shook the house to shifting lintels and steps, fissures cracking the walls. I jumped up the stairs and pushed the door open. Wood snapped and groaned as glass shattered. I ducked the flying shards. Jack's ennui barely changed.

As the house shimmied and juddered, I gathered our measly supplies, shoving my hunting knife back in my pants, then hoisted Jack. His skin slid like sludge, blisters peppering his flesh, and a grey mold furred him with an unhealthy lanugo. I had seen mushrooms past their prime molder this way.

We burst from the tilting house and I followed the smell of water, Jack leaning, staggering, stumbling while I propped him up. I didn't look at what dropped off of him. The human predators shrieked at the shiftings but followed us nonetheless.

The ground vibrated as we shuffle-ran, tripping. I headed downslope over crunchy grass and dirt. We no longer held the breathlessness of flight, nor even the exhilaration of running. Tension wound me. The lonely streets and houses waited, paint faded to soft browns, pale yellows, old green. Wood and glass fell. The sky was a metal lid lowering upon us, shutting out warmth and light, and as the day grew darker, where the buildings didn't tremble, the mouse-shifting of people scurried away. The earth heaved and growled again, tracking us, and the last denizens fled.

What emerged became more sinister than the gangs that had hounded us. Packs and hunters always find the weakest, the ones to ferret out. They came, silent, deadly, determined. Oozing shadows, oily and obscuring, congealed around us. We neared the water, a small lake bound by tangled grey vines, deadened trees, browned leaves. Even here the land resembled Jack's malaise. We hit the shore in full darkness, no stars piercing through. I steered by the sound of water sucking lecherously at the bank.

Dropping to our knees, Jack rolled onto his back, his eyes reflecting the black pits of heaven's ceiling. Tick-tocking alligators and wretches with hooks would have been preferable.

He mumbled. "Wendy, Willow, Margaret, Heather… You were once my queen… Below the world, our underworld, a realm, a dream… we guided, loved, Persephone, the cycle, season me…"

Round and round, he circled me with words twisted together. The ground shivered and shimmied some more. My chest tightened as the shades approached, pooling over the ground. I held my knife, crouching over Jack's prone form. We could fight to the end, but against a shadowy foe? I stared down at Jack, unrecognizable as that capricious boy, the fey child, or even the rogue adventurer. Laughter had dried up, blithe attitudes rotted, and I knew, as if a clarion bell had rung.

I had to fight, to bring a healing. I had to play mother, mender, fixer, again. I had fought myself all along, yet had always held all facets, no matter how I disguised them. I had to end the cycle for it to begin anew.

I turned toward Jack, and knelt. "I'm sorry. I love you." Then I plunged my blade through his heartwood, severing him from the world. He gasped, his chest arching up as if to push the blade deeper, eyes opening wide and sparking one last speck of green. He exhaled and collapsed in on himself. Brackish fluid trickled from him.

I shed no tears, had no time as I pulled the knife free. A sucking reluctance held it a moment longer. Then I spun and waited for what crept through the stalagmite trees.

Just darkness, natural and uncaring. Pinpricks of light pierced the sky's canopy.

☙

I buried Jack under leaf mold and browned pine needles, with muddy clumps and small stones. He returned to what he might once have been, entombed in an underworld he had ignored. Perhaps it was only fitting; he had spent years above ground, zipping through the air in light, and then many days on the ground, in light and shadow. Now shades took him, Hades reclaimed his own. And all I did was usher Jack along.

When he was born, I named him Peter and he had that spark of green in his eyes. I found a small house by the lake and stayed near Jack's grave. The shoreline is a cornucopia of verdant life, attracting people. Even the sun cracks the sky's shell of clouds and pours its golden yolk through from time to time. This altar has a man shape, and where Jack's mouth was, ivy spews forth. Seedling trees, peridot moss, tender young daisies and crocus bud from chest and limbs. Each day it moves out farther. Each day, another plant joins this Eden.

I had relied more on his instincts than mine, but in the end, mine prevailed. I still cannot feel the never lands, the lost realms, but there is something deep that hums as if these two places have shifted and blended. I look at my lively baby, fists sporadically pumping as his chubby legs kick in joy. There is the slightest tinge to his healthy skin and small nubs are appearing. Soon he will grow his first leaves. He may one day wear the mantle of many names. He will be Peter Pan, Jack o' the Green, Hades. He will be a new green boy.

And I, I will continue to be mother, mender, fixer, fighter, and tend this garden.

The Brown Woman

We often hear of green men, but what of their female counterparts? Gaia, or any of the fecund earth goddesses from different pantheons speak to an age-old relation between the female and regeneration. As the world shifts and changes, as pollution and cities take their toll on nature, what then happens to these entities of the green? This idea came to me while travelling down a highway and wondering about those medians of green cut off from the rest of the land.

The Brown Woman's haven lay in the middle of a long strip of narrow land. On a raised mound of meadow grasses and sun-warmed boulders she often rooted her lower limbs and dug extra rootlets throughout the soil to see and feel and taste her realm. Shedding the thick brown bark she wore when she traveled her land, she became the peridot shoot and swayed supplely in the breeze to reach thin, continuous branching limbs high into the air. Rounded, pointed and jagged leaves rustled in her crown, and insects buzzed around her. She danced in the dark of night and creatures sang in chorus to her moves.

One lightless night something foreign moved through the Green. Unknown vibrations made her root, tendrils gripping the earth, and she quickly pulled leaves and loam over her. Her two limbs, now four, now eight, branched, thickened and darkened. Then something flashed through the glade, disrupting her every cell to the heartwood, deafening her senses. Moments bloomed and died.

When the Brown Woman recovered, she pulled up her secondary roots and taproot and moved to investigate. A large larva lay like old leaves on the earth. Drifting closer on vibrating roots she circled the larva. Dark browny sap puddled about it, stinging her senses, and the ground thrummed with its lingering spark.

The Brown Woman watched. A pungent scent rose from the larva, strongly enveloping her, and she stayed cloaked in early morning shadows. She did not yet move to where its juices seeped onto her land. In her way she felt a reluctance to touch it. It rumbled, and its vibrating soul touched her in odd patterns.

When she brushed the larva briefly through the end rootlets of other trees she felt a withering, a pain that filled the mossy places in her mind. The larva spasmed and shrieked! She heard a strangled animal noise.

She retreated, and twined her limbs, now more like hands, through her lank, viny hair. The slow *thump thump* of the larva's life force pushed at the invisible hedges that held her to her land. At first she could not move. No instinct guided her one way or the other. This new thing was different and required something more than she had ever given.

In her way the Brown Woman talked, to the seeds, the mosses, the lichen: she knew the patterns that rippling water made with leaves and trees. Through the wave of her limbs, unfolding leafy tips to caress bark and loam, she communicated to the scaly slitherers, the burrowers, the furred hoppers. She lived with purpose. She knew what hurt and what nourished, and she touched her world as it flourished and died.

When the Brown Woman thought, leaves unfurled. It was a slow process. She sucked minerals and saps from the earth and trees; leaves, pine needles, berries, bark, water spirits, and from the furred creatures who gave their trunks when they departed to the beyond. She could heal infested leaves and blighted trees, but she did not know what to do with the suffering larva.

༄

Once she had moved freely as the wind-born seed, but with the seasons, camouflage became her way. Even now she must be careful that no furless being saw her. There were great gray wounds that encircled her Green. The large ones – was the larva one of them? – sought to pen or destroy the Green. Many times she had discovered the flattened forms of the furred creatures that had encountered the gray wounds. Always, when she sent out a tentative tendril, it would wilt and wither and she would abandon it, feeling unwhole.

Now there was a wound in her Green and it came from the larva. It hadn't moved. The Brown Woman shakily pushed away from the warm tree bark she leaned against. She ambled closer on two barky limbs and branched her awareness to warn her if other larvae lurked nearby. Using knowledge as old as the first seedling, she pushed leaves and moss into the larva's hole and stanched the crimson sap oozing from it. Snaky white shoots slithered from the ground, wrapped and caressed the larva's limbs. It did not move, but breath still issued from it.

Then she found a sun-dappled mound to stretch out on and absorb the heat and air, and replenish herself.

In the dark she sometimes stood full beneath the bright nightbloom, branches outstretched; she breathed the calm, only slightly tainted air. It was at these times she felt the need to push forward from her haven; to move unrestrained through the other emerald and amber lands of the great orb. She felt then that the hollow within her, the missing core of her knotted trunk, would be healed.

Once her kind had been many, root systems interconnected, partners meshed to aid growth and nurture seedlings, and watch trembling rootlets. With the swarming of the furless ones across the great orb, her world shrank; she felt as the flower feels without the bee. She could keep her Green alive, but could not make new growth. Throughout her land, from the withered tree branches and flowers with dusty, dry petals, she felt the aching hollow. It mattered to feel the fecund earth pulse; to hear the whisper of plants and trees caressed by sighing air. Because it mattered, in a semi-conscious way she made her decision about the larva.

The next darktime, she returned full-leafed and succulent, a sleek wandering branch, and moved from tree to tree, watching. She sent out the slimmest white tendril into the larva's mouth to choke out its life force. *Awareness. He only knew he had not ceased to be, hoped to see the land once more. Loved the earth, the trees.*

The Brown Woman felt something different. It filled a different hole in the larva. It intrigued. Instead of ending the spark she deftly inserted a feeder root. Shivering, she cautiously layered warm moss upon its body and lightly touched it with a frond she unfurled from one of her limbs. It became part of her Green and so she tended it best she could.

The Brown Woman rooted. The larva ventured back to consciousness. It slowly opened its eyes, gritty from the mosses and dirt that covered it.

The Brown Woman watched it shakily raise its head and stare about. The whites of its eyes shone like the shining one at its fullness. It looked down at its body, inhaling quickly, then shuddered and writhed.

The larva's eyes opened wider. Working one limb free of the new shoots it raised it to its mouth and touched the feeder root disappearing into his cavern. Air rasped in and out. It gagged and yanked at the root. Through her plants, the Brown Woman reached thin fibrils into the soft tissues and stroked the sleep spot. The larva grew subdued, breathing raspy, while she floated within it.

The watchful quiet closed in, pressed damp, scented fingers over his skin. He felt as if every sprouting shoot, every grub, worm or beetle burrowed beneath his flesh. There was no pain, just a distant throb as if he was squeezed, then let go.

He heard the distant roar of cars and knew they were just a crawl away, but the earth entwined him as well as any tree's root. He could lie there for years and not be discovered. He felt blood, an uncomfortable stickiness, seep through old wrappings and water the ground beneath him.

The forest crept in on him, breathing moist decay. Dark grew at the edges of his vision. Small soft things crawled throughout his stomach. Something foreign scraped through his veins, leaving an odd burning vibration, not hurtful but unpleasant in its alienness. It would be all right to die, in the arms of the earth.

The Brown Woman withdrew her tendrils, uncomfortable with the sensations. The images she had felt were unknown, too concrete. She left the area and returned in mid darktime as the larva tried weakly to lift its free hand and found it bound. Its head moved only as far as the sturdy vines allowed; the rest of the body embraced the ground tightly, wrapped in rootlets and moss, protecting him from the chill night.

The Brown Woman detached herself; from the trees she flowed toward him like hastening shadows. She made a wind of bark and leaves and loam, forming a shaped that looked like one of the larva's kind. Leaves coalesced to form green and brown calves, thighs and arms. Warm, worm-riddled loam and gray branches entwined to create belly and buttocks. Supple branches curled with tight leaves and shoots, flowers and seeds; she made a face with verdant hair, eyes and a petite nose. The larva squeaked like a small furred burrower.

The Brown Woman reached out; a long limb snaked towards him. It squirmed, twisted from her as she touched the wounds. Sounds gurgled around the feeder root, and water frothed from its mouth. Insects and clumps of moist dirt tumbled onto his belly that quivered as slippery centipedes and moist purple worms wriggled and crawled over him.

The Brown Woman knew the limbs were mostly of bone, which she absorbed for nutrients. She reached in through pores and soft pink openings and slowly, ever so slowly, grew invisible rootlet strands. When they found the denseness of the calcium limbs they twined about and gradually rooted into the softened center of each bone. She detached herself from the rootlets and knew they fed on the core of each limb and changed it. She shivered.

She looked at the mouth and managed to duplicate the opening. With lips of beige, fungal sponginess, she bent over the twitching form and put her lips on its own. The larva jerked but the Brown Woman did not let it deter her from dropping tiny spores into the humid interior. Soon the airspaces would change and still the horrible wheezing.

The next day, the Brown Woman inserted several limbs through his red sap cavern and let the shoots rip and burrow through the organs. She almost faded away from the onslaught that hit her.

Something tore at his liver, intestines, heart; clamped down and pulled – veins and sinews flared hotly. To his core, he felt the charring. Nerves flayed from bone and skin, hurtled him into hibernation from all his senses.

At times, the Brown Woman watched as a small insect or a seed grew into the skin – flushing it pink before fading to a whitish green, then disappearing. Red sap still coursed through the hills of muscle, and through the forests of veins becoming vines. The red sap slowed and lightened in color. His moss – hair grew lush and green, more like a pelt every day. She saw the dark haze of pain wither and slough off like dried lichen from his chest wound.

She had done all she could and was not sure what would come next. The Brown Woman felt changed. Strange images formed within her crown like those she had first felt from the larva. Her own sap quickened. She was old, so old, and this new green being was so very young. The Brown Woman could only tend and see if he grew strong.

While the green being healed and changed, the Brown Woman roamed the deepest part of her verdant realm and watched the insects burrow into the earth and crawl along the trunks of trees. Made from brown earth, bark and lichen; of dead leaves and fungus, she maintained a body resembling the larva's. She felt the color of leaves change as they drank in the heat from above, and fed on the deep marrow of the great orb from below. The chirps and low grumbles of the forest denizens soothed her against the ever-present threat of the gray wounds. Here she remained safe, and content to feel the earth continue its movement around her.

Other days found her staring from the edge of the treed area to the short grasses beyond. She yearned to reach those new green mounds and grasses, and thought of testing the long dark scars; then he would call her. She felt his thoughts as he became one of her realm, one with her.

He remained bound by vines for several moonturns until his wounds healed and his original organs fell in moldering clumps for the maggots. Lush green covered his chest, and sturdy emerald stalks supported him. The Brown Woman did not hope for his gratitude; she had no concept of it. She healed as she lived and found the hollow within her not so large.

She watched him grow lush, blossoming late in the fall when the leaves turned suntanned faces from the sky. In her dim memory she thought of others that had once existed, like him, yet different. They had been the mates to her and her sisters, helping the great orb become green. She had not seen any in a great span of time.

The Brown Woman looked outward; that day the outer world called to her to come and spread more seedlings, to heal the woundings. The leaves browned, the cold time neared and soon she would retreat deeper into her realm where the sharp-leafed trees still offered cover. Behind her, the brown limbs of trees waved their last leaves in sad remembrance of summer. The Green Man came up behind her and touched her softly.

He felt the outer world, too; it flowed through him. The pain of the great orb formed a tangible vibration. They felt the time to watch passing.

The Brown Woman felt something new fill the hole within her. The Green Man healed her as she had healed him. It was as if a small hot orb blossomed within her. They strengthened each other into something newer, larger – a new growth for the Green. But all the healing, the filling of the hollow could not be done from her small island. She again felt the pull of the larger Green as it beckoned, vibrating in sickness.

With spring, there would come the time to seed and to blossom. For now they would rest through the snowy wet days and form a bond to gather energy for the work of rooting deeper than they had ever gone before.

Symbiosis

Survival at any cost. This could be a tale of any place on earth, but here, surviving the hunter moves in a new direction on an alien, hostile planet.

The acrid cloying blood, the wet pulling apart of skin and muscle sluicing about her feet made her gorge rise. Keela swallowed reflexively, trying to rid herself of bitter saliva as blood blackly clotted the sand beneath her in the still night air.

She threw the pelt onto the sand, wiping sweat from her eyes, not to mention the tears forming hotter trails over her cheeks. Hateful work. Why couldn't the gods have sent something deserving of being killed? Why something as beautiful and terrifyingly efficient in its lethal way? They all had to survive, though, even the great cats, but Keela did not know if she could continue much more fighting, fearing, being a monster. Yet, weren't they all? Leaden exhaustion weighted her limbs and mind.

Keela tucked the serrated knife in its sheath and folded the skin into the pack, then strapped it to her back. It would serve as a sunbreak for Yasmeen as she healed… if she healed. Then Keela looked up at the boat of the gibbous moon, wishing it would carry her back to those first months when this had seemed just a small pastoral planet, teeming with nothing larger than the beaver-sized herbivores. Now, there were only twenty researchers left and three years to wait until the next supply ship. Their equipment had died first, prey to the vagaries of electromagnetic fluctuations and heavy metals. This howling wasteland of a parched planet was slowly eating them. The heat, the lack of water, the giant black and white spotted cats, canines curving down like a sabertooth's, all of it tried to expel the people for the invading bodies they were.

When Yasmeen had been attacked by this cat, Keela had shot an arrow that wounded it, then tracked it to a deadly winner-takes-all fight. She checked the suture patch over her arm, making sure blood was not leaking through. The night painted the blood a sinister substance and it spotted her skin as if she were a great cat too. Loading meat into the second pack, Keela then took bearings, hoping they could come back for more, should it prove edible.

She began trudging back to the base camp, searching for the one remaining white dome. It was clear how much they stood apart from this apparently simple planet. Everything flowed, sinuous, moving from one state or space with apparent ease. Wind undulated the sand into rippling dunes. Short grasses moved in waves. What sparse trees there were curved branches back toward the earth, as if afraid to bear the full brunt of the harsh white sun. The cats and the herbivores all seemed to flow, as if embodying the properties of the rare sightings of water.

Keela listened to the odd pops and snaps that filled the night air. She turned slowly as she walked, trying to gauge the landscape for movement, her eyes straining against the pale light. Cocking her head, she sniffed, feeling the taint of heat. Morning would soon be ripping away the evening. Muttering, "I want to live, I want to live," Keela tramped determinedly until the low rumble of the cats permeated her chant.

Another slow pirouette revealed three slinking shapes. That was it then; she would become part of the ecosystem by joining the food chain. She would fight. No… no use. There was no hope with three. A frozen silhouette, against the night's backdrop, she thought quickly, madly, not wanting to die.

Maybe, maybe there was one way to survive.

The gruesome clamminess was still preferable to feeling fangs sink into her flesh. Tears leaked from her eyes as the throaty huffs sounded closer. Gagging beneath the pelt, she felt her suture patch give way and the weight of the skin settle firmer against her. Something stepped on her – the great head-sized pad of the cat – and crushed her into sand and darkness.

Weight pushed onto her, squeezed the air out, and all she could smell was cat and dirt and blood. She stifled her nausea. Not moving, breathing slowly, shallowly, she let the spotted coat blanket her, completely conceal her in its gummy funeral gloom. She waited as one with it, believing she was nothing more, for so must the great cats believe that it was one of their own that had died.

Pain knifed through her, rippling in a spasm. They weren't attacking but one of her cuts might be infected. Still, she remained stationary as the cats moved off and the pain took her breath away, sealing blackness beneath her eyelids. Her breath was but a whisper.

———

Heat filled her. A hot breath. She rose, sloughing off the beast and stared at the other three. Her whiskers twitched as she swung her great head about. This was how she survived, flowing with the planet's ways. A metamorphosis of sorts. A growl escaped her throat as she cursed the heavens and loped off to the caves.

Exegesis of the Insecta Apocrypha

Would we recognize an insect in a human body and would it act any differently than a sociopath? I took a novel writing workshop in Kansas at the Center for the Study of Speculative Fiction (CSSF) where the term exegesis was used often. The word stuck, and I had an image of a woman covered in insects. This was one of the most difficult stories I've ever written. To research the stages of decomposition and which insects are involved was hard, but worse was writing the stages in which a sociopath grows into their disorder. I'm thankful though that I was disturbed because otherwise perhaps I would be a sociopath.

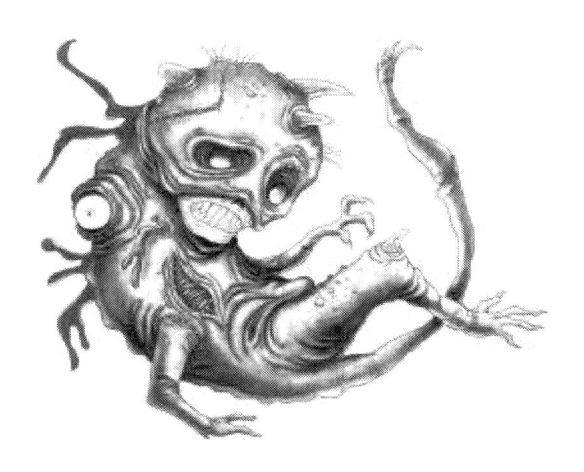

"In the beginning, it was a shift, a flutter of orange and black that caught her eye and held it, pulling her in to a new paradigm before she knew there ever was one. The opening of the butterfly's wings fastened her two-year old gaze forever." *Apocryphon I*[1]

The Apocrypha *first appeared on the worldwide web in the early twenty-first century. Their legitimacy as sacred writing was not considered for two decades, with arguments reiterating that class Insecta could never evolve to the state of written language, let alone into a mindset able to formulate histories and concepts of time. In light of the documented case of the child with compound eyes being born last year, as well as several climatic shifts that have increased insect populations, the* Insecta Apocrypha *are being analyzed for new interpretations. Whether they are indicators of a convergence of evolution and intelligence to a new level is not in the purview of this paper. What draws the eye immediately is the symbolism. Butterflies and birds have long been seen as forms of the human soul. Just as the Bible opens with Genesis, so does the Apocrypha begin with a genesis of sorts, and at the awakening of a child's conscious begins the search for the meaning of soul.*[2]

---

[1] Alice Rothwell, ed. Sacred Writings of the Modern Cult Movements in North America (New York: Random, 2014) *All subsequent Apocrypha quotes are from the same publication.*

[2] Rachel Urquhart and Roy Hammerschmidt, eds. Exegesis of the Insecta Apocrypha, Rabbi Joel Shapiro, Chapt. 1 "Interpretations of the Soul" (Numinous Press, Toronto, 2032) 14

APOCRYPHON I – DISCOVERY

Ever since that first erratic flight, Libby's gaze followed minute forms of locomotion. Whether a larva wriggling, a beetle scuttling, a dragonfly flitting and hovering, or the leap of a grasshopper, she watched intently, tracing its path as long as possible. At the age of four, she squatted in the garden, staring intently at something that shivered the long grass. Inhaling noisily, she wrinkled her nose at the cloying smell but stayed put.

Her father's words were less than a fly's buzz and her chubby little fingers itched to pick up one of the writhing white maggots that worked its way in and out of what was once a mouse. The grey brown fur was nearly indistinguishable under the moving carpet that gently trembled.

In that instant Libby understood that life was cannibalistic, feeding on itself, but taking different forms. Life fed on death, death generated life – an intrinsic cycle.

Early on, she noticed that people shied from answering her questions about death and decay. It disturbed them, especially when insects were involved in the decomposition. There was something about the mindless infestation of life feeding voraciously on the dead. A need was deposited in her, a small egg incubating, maturing the more attention she gave it until it could eat its way out of her. The larval thought was curiosity, but it was inherently tied to watching life and death.

Her father buried the mouse and its white pulsing attendants, digging a hole so deep that Libby never found the spot again.

One humid morning brought mosquitoes swarming from the creek in the back field. Libby had been walking with her mother, who had stopped to take a few pictures of plants. She listened to the whine of mosquitoes and held out her arm. They alighted, a half dozen or so, their needle thin proboscises piercing her flesh. They sucked and fattened on her blood. Although it itched slightly, Libby didn't interfere with their feeding until her mother turned and said, "Libby, what are you doing!"

Her mother frantically brushed the mosquitoes from her arm and dragged Libby out of the woods, swatting the whole time. At home Libby found her arm swathed in calamine. She watched it throughout the next day, fascinated by the reddish bumps that arose. If she scratched them long enough they enlarged and seeped a clear liquid before oozing blood, like small volcanoes erupting. She licked her wounds, feeling the heat of her skin and the slight sourness of the scabs.

She never shied from any insect, letting red-backed ladybirds and butterflies alight on her, moving her feet into the path of shiny, black carapaced June bugs, or walking into a spider's web so to induce the arachnid to crawl across her. Holding her mouth open, she would stick out her tongue, letting a few brave insects land so that she could feel the soft dance of their feet. Bites and stings often laced her skin and left her parents bewildered.

Children have a natural curiosity and, like cats, they will watch anything that moves. They are sometimes considered cruel when, in their discoveries, they tear apart insects or hit another child with a stick. Libby's early experiences, when read without the fictional embellishments, are within the normal range of a child's development and expanding consciousness.

It is possible that this early infusion of insect venoms laid the tracery for Libby's later metamorphosis. Her next stage, in Apocryphon II, *began at the age of six. Libby actively investigated the insect world and was ready to learn the depth of what they could do.*[3]

---

[3] <u>Exegesis</u> Shandra Radakrishnan, Chapter 3 "Psychoanalysis of the Messiah and Anti-Messiah in Relation to Major Religions" 39-46

APOCRYPHON II – EXPERIMENTATION

She found an orange striped kitten in the field behind her house. There was a small stand of alders near the creek and she stood under the fluttering leaves, holding the mewing kitten. Taking a string from her pocket, she tied one end around the cat's neck and the other end around a slender tree. Libby patted the kitten once, then walked away.

It took three days for the insect world and the mammalian one to intersect. Each day she strode quickly to the grove of trees and checked the kitten. The first day it struggled and mewed loudly when it saw her. She turned and left it. The second day, it lay on its side, panting, croaking out a feeble meow. Libby searched for insect activity and on seeing none, left. The third day, she bent over, peering at the prone kitten. Its eyes were open and glassy. The slightly matted fur did not move.

Libby settled herself in the grass, cross-legged, her elbows on her knees, chin in hand. Eventually, she noticed a miniscule flicker. She bent closer and watched fleas, which fed on the living, abandoning the carcass, some leaping off, some disappearing underneath, and even a couple of them crossing the surface of the corpse's blind eyes.

Next, the flies descended, buzzing and settling upon the creature, especially around its eyes, ears and nose. It had died with its mouth slightly open, the pink tongue showing swollen and dark. In crept a fly, glistening blue-black, and another, moving about, probing with insectile feet and mouth. The kitten's body crawled with insects, alighting and flying ellipsoid orbits. Libby removed the string from the cat's neck and returned home by dinnertime so as not to jeopardize her experiment.

Each day, she returned to sit and watch the insect activity. In just a few days, the orange and white fur began to move and ripple, like wind over grass. Glistening maggots tumbled from the mouth and eyes, feeding on necrotic tissue.

Eventually, ants and gnats and beetles crawled over the putrefying mass as the fur sloughed off, displaying the animal's liquefying organs. Libby held vigil through all of it, noting when flies grew bored with the carcass and when ants and spiders moved in to remove morsels. The kitten's body was a motel of activity. Only when the feeding slowed, with mostly bones and fur left, did Libby bury the corpse.

It was a couple of years later that she took a puppy into the same woods. This time she did not wait for death's slow claim but strangled the pup immediately, her hands choking off its whimpers as its black paws scrabbled in the air. When it stopped moving, she laid it on the ground, spreading out its silky ears.

Then she pulled a sharp kitchen knife from her pack. It glinted in the afternoon sun as she studied the black body of the pup. She placed the point against the soft, nearly furless area by the genitals and pushed in, sawing up through the skin to the ribcage. Only a small amount of blackish blood pooled out. Then she cut under the ribs in smaller strokes and across, forming a T. Pulling back the skin and opening the organs to the elements had already brought the flies. Her knife pricked the pink intestines that seeped a fetid black fluid.

Libby sat back as the flies settled upon her offering, humming their contentment. She twirled her wheaten hair, forgetting her hunger and almost missing the distant call of her mother. Scrambling up, Libby tucked away the knife and ran off.

Her diligence brought her each day to note earwigs and the black bowl of hister beetle backs moving in and out of the architecture of decomposing organs while maggots were born and grew fat on the meat. Within a few days the dog's black skin sloughed off the bloated body. Pupae from the flies eventually cracked their husks, emerging as a new generation.

Libby's interest only grew. Not far from her home was a two-story apartment building slated for demolition. The vacant shadows of the windows held only shards of glass. Plywood had been nailed up, but vagrants and teenagers had pried them away. Libby had already explored the place, seeing what insects lived in dark and dank rooms.

When she was twelve she found a little boy of about five wandering down the street. He seemed to not realize he'd strayed far from the familiar. Libby gave him a cellophane-wrapped candy, and as he popped it in his already sticky mouth, she said, "I've lost my puppy. Would you like to help me find him?" The boy nodded, pushing his stringy brown hair out of his eyes, but not saying anything around the candy in his mouth. Gummy sweetness streaked his chin with brown and pink.

She took his hand and he followed complacently. It was easy enough to get him into the building and have him sit while she grabbed an old rag and some rope. She deftly tied him and before he could whimper, stuffed the gag in his mouth. He began to cry, soaking the rag with saliva and snot. Libby ignored him while she readied her tools; tweezers and scalpel. A few alert flies already circled the boy's face. From her pack, she withdrew several small jars, each holding a flickering, insectoid mass. In one she had scooped up beetles and earwigs and other ground insects. Another held the agitated buzzing of wasps, while a third showed the constant flutter of color from butterflies and moths. Two more jars contained flies and caterpillars respectively.

She ignored the boy's muffled shrieks, refusing to hurry.

After her experiments, Libby retied the gag on the unconscious boy, most of the insects having abandoned him, and threw a blanket over his body. He would be a better stew in the morning. She left and came back a day later, looking at his welted belly and peering at his crusting arms. Flies buzzed about the trickling snot on his face, landing and walking over his sweat-matted hair.

Libby continued for a couple of days, watching how the fly larva grew on living tissue. The boy stared vacantly, drooling, barely making a sound. When nothing more could be gained from her observations, she untied him and watched. He didn't move, just lay on his side. Maggots dropped off his arms. There was no need to kill him. She packed up everything she had brought, removing jars, tweezers, scalpel and rope, leaving nothing behind. Libby walked away from the building, never to return.

Between the first Apocryphon *and the second, there is a shift of personality. What could be considered normal behavior for a child diverges wildly by the second writing, indicating sociopathic tendencies. Although Libby exhibits the escalation of brutality from animal to human subjects, she doesn't seem to repeat these offenses, which is atypical for sociopaths. However, her behavior in detachment and lack of empathy is typical.*[4]

Debate remains as to whether the Apocrypha only mark the first of each phase of Libby's experiments, or if indeed she only conducted one event at each stage. The first two Apocrypha remain nearly emotionless, whereas the third takes on a slightly different tone and it is believed that Apocrypha III and IV may have been written by Libby. Contention exists as to whether she wrote the first two, or if an unknown source fictionalized all of it.[5]

APOCRYPHON III – RESEARCH

She graduated from high school at sixteen and gained her doctorate in entomology by twenty-two. She became a forensic expert in decomposition and the insects that populated the fleshy worlds of the dead. The microscopic realm of insect biology was as interesting as discovering that first maggot-ridden body.

Libby laid her groundwork well, knowing cell structures, the chemical interactions that drove ants, dragonflies, leafhoppers, moths, and the basis of different groups of social insects. Colonies and hives were fascinating in the caste structure of workers and drones. Not all ant colonies had only one queen, and most workers were females, sometimes able to breed when necessary. Often drones lived only long enough to fertilize the queen before dying. In some species of wasps and bees the queens mated with multiple drones and stored the sperm, releasing it over time to fertilize the continuous cycle of egg laying at their discretion.

---

[4] <u>Exegesis</u> Radakrishnan, 53-56
[5] <u>Exegesis</u> Carl Purdy, Chapter 5 "Interpretations of Voice" 76-78

Libby stored the information, then began to study communication of hymenoptera; the bees, wasps, ants and their hives, colonies and social structure. She ordered yellow crazy ants from the Christmas Islands, Western honey bees and Buff-Tailed bumble bees, Asian giant hornets and German wasps. Besides hymenoptera, she brought in Kirby's Dropwing dragonflies from Namibia, Meadow Argus butterflies from Australia, lady bugs from Canada and a host of other species. She concentrated on the pheromone trails of ants and tried to see if she could colonize species that were not hymenoptera. She tried to form messages from light, from chemicals, from Braille-like forms. For five years Libby diligently tested many types of command and communication and searched for any effect on hive activity, caste structures or mating.

Her tests did not lead to any discernible change. Her research could have gone on forever. There were always many new paths to take in studying class Insecta. An estimated thirty million species were still unclassified, but Libby grew unsatisfied, feeling that she was not attaining her goal fast enough.

It dawned on her that, though she had concentrated on hymenoptera for their social behavior, she herself was not social. How could she possibly understand such behavior unless she undertook the final phase?

First tidying her lab, Libby took two weeks off, leaving as many insects with the department as she took. After all, she worked alone and was known to keep to herself.

She went downtown and entered a department store. For the first time ever, Libby felt a bit displaced, as if she were an ant that had lost all pheromone signals to the colony. Bewildered, she stared at the array of cosmetics, jars and pomades, lotions, scents, eye and lip colors that surrounded her. Turning a slow circle, she could not pinpoint a place to begin until a clerk approached her.

"I want…" She made a motion around her face, struggling for what to say.

The clerk smiled and beckoned her to follow. "I know. You've not worn makeup before. Don't worry, I'll show you what you need. With your features, you don't need much but we can enhance and highlight what you have."

Libby sat through the experience, finding it alien, then proceeded to buy clothes that were more than utilitarian.

Always a good study, she had no problem in applying the makeup. She slipped on a slinky red spaghetti-strap dress that showed her long legs. Red stilettos added to her color, and she made her way to where males swarmed. The lights and music throbbed around her, pulsating off her skin. She danced awkwardly but it seemed to matter little to the men that grabbed her about the waist and pulled her close.

The first man offered to take her somewhere else. Libby freely gave up her virginity in a car. But she did not stay, exiting for the next nightclub. The second man took her in the restroom, and a third in the back alley where they went to "share a joint". At the end of the night, Libby went with five men, finally finding herself in a threadbare hotel room with a naked flickering bulb. She pulled the closest one to her and kissed him, undoing his pants. When he tried to push her head down, she pulled back and sat on the table, pulling up her dress to take him in. It wasn't long before the others followed.

Libby repeated the swarming for a week, collecting as many men's semen as she could. When she felt she had accomplished that task, now holding enough sperm to release thousands of eggs, she shucked off the mating colors and set to work in her home, which bordered a large, state-protected park.

She brought out the terrariums with the various insects and arrayed them about her. From bees, flies, dragonflies, beetles, grasshoppers, moths, weevils, wasps and ants, Libby extracted eggs. She required special tools, often a microscope and careful incubation so that the eggs would not wither. Some she took from the hives about her place and others from the insects directly. When she had a good yield, Libby stripped off her clothing. Under a bright light, she made small incisions on her thighs, arms and abdomen, and inserted a different species' eggs into each opening. Although she felt the pain, it was an abstraction from the task at hand and it only aided her concentration. Overshadowing the pain was a flush of excitement, warmth that spread through her in ways sex hadn't.

As she laid each egg beneath her epidermis, she took out a glass case crawling with army ants. Pressing each bleeding wound shut, she applied the ants along the fleshy rim. The ants in turn seized the edges of the cut in their lightning fast jaws and locked on. Libby felt sharp pricks and then cut off the glossy black bodies, leaving the head and mandibles as sutures. She stood with her stitching of ant heads, and opened all containers holding insects.

A few variants of Apocryphon III *indicate that Libby prayed or cried at this point. These have largely been dismissed as additions by unknown sources that wished to humanize her actions. There is no indication in any Apocrypha that she ever showed intense emotion.*

It is argued that Libby was trying to become an insect and found the only way to communicate was to pass on her knowledge through her cells. Others believe that she had in fact been imbued with the essence of Insecta from birth.[6]

APOCRYPHON IV-A – METAMORPHOSIS

Naked, Libby walked out of her door and into the park. In the white heat of the day she stood beneath the trees, her bare feet burrowing into leaf mold. Feeling the slight ripples in the air about her, she spread her arms. It may be that she knew the secret language of insects and called her disciples unto her with the release of a pheromone borne on her words. In a high voice, she trilled.

They came, great black clouds of pixilating Insecta. The air rippled and thrummed with movement. The green bottle flies with their metallic sheen, the beetles with their chitinous clatter, the buzzing drone of bees, wasps and hornets, the flutter of moths and butterflies, the gnats, mosquitoes, the walking sticks and praying mantises. They came from miles around. Still they were only

---

[6] <u>Exegesis</u> Purdy, 112-115

representatives of the greater horde, but one came of every type, thirty million strong.

Onto each pore and hair the smallest insects landed, followed by others coating her arms, her legs, her naked torso, her face and eyes and ears. When nothing could be seen but the pulsating cluster, it rose into the air, higher and higher, like an enormous runaway swarm. Lifting to the heavens like a gyrating, buzzing black host, it grew smaller and then… dispersed, scattering insects like seed pods.

APOCRYPHON IV-B – METAMORPHOSIS

Libby walked naked amongst the trees under the moon's silvering light. Like Lilith in the Garden of Eden, she moved with confidence. The air seemed to blanket her as she raised her slim, bare arms to the heavens and she cried out in a voice like the chirrup of locusts. Into the skies, boiling from the ground, the myriad host arrived on the pheromone trail, the Insecta in their glory of gold and red, gunmetal black and blue, jarring green and earthy brown, a scintillating mass of color, of forms soft and furred, hard and chitinous. Sound rose like a roar, a thunder, an unearthly humming.

Those who heard the cacophony of wings and legs, the clatter of millions of mandibles, thought the end was near. The insects came from all around, swarming up her legs, onto her head. Then they burrowed, chewed and crawled within her. Some crept in her nostrils, others into her eyes, while flies and gnats filled her ears. Other vermin and plump larvae wriggled up her legs. All made their own way and she said, "I am of the hive. Eat of me and understand."

She did not scream, nor run but stood, her form limned in an odd moving pointillism. When an hour had come and gone, the insects pulled back as if one and departed. Where they had been, nothing remained; not bone, nor hair, nor flesh, nor sinew. It was as if she had never been.

Her name could have easily been Deborah or Melissa or Mariposa, as would befit a benefactor of insects. Swarmings happen from time to time near urban centers yet no specific incident can be pinpointed in North America where a woman was consumed by insects. There is no extent evidence that she existed under any of these names; that she wasn't a myth generated for a troubled world of the new millennium.

Is this a metaphor in which Libby imparts her knowledge to the insect race, raising them up to the next level of evolution? Indeed, praying mantises have been known to lose wings and then regain them in a single generation – a startling discovery even before the Apocrypha *were created.*

There are only four Apocrypha (Discovery, Experimentation, Research, *and* Metamorphosis), *which coincidentally compare to the four stages of insect growth: egg, larva, pupa and imago.* Since the appearance of the first Apocrypha, global warming and pollution have seen the extinction of many amphibious species that kept insect populations in check, and entomologists have recorded a change in hymenoptera hive and colony organizations and structure, as well as the evolution of some other orders into new, highly organized social structures.

The question most debated about the Insecta Apocrypha *is who wrote them? If Libby did exist and if she did not write them, then the only living beings that saw her deeds were the insects.*[7]

---

[7] <u>Exegesis</u> Shapiro, "Conclusion" 198-220

Sins of the Father

When we read of murderers and rapists and that often they have families, we may think briefly of their despair of learning a monster was part of their happy nest. I wondered: what must it be like for those victims as well? That knowledge can be a catalyst for many things, including change and purpose. This is probably my only story that I have actually placed in my city, Vancouver, pulling in aspects of the Downtown Eastside, the drug addictions and the homeless situation. It is about identity and moving beyond a family's past. And then of course, there is that fear that sometimes we may turn out exactly like our parents.

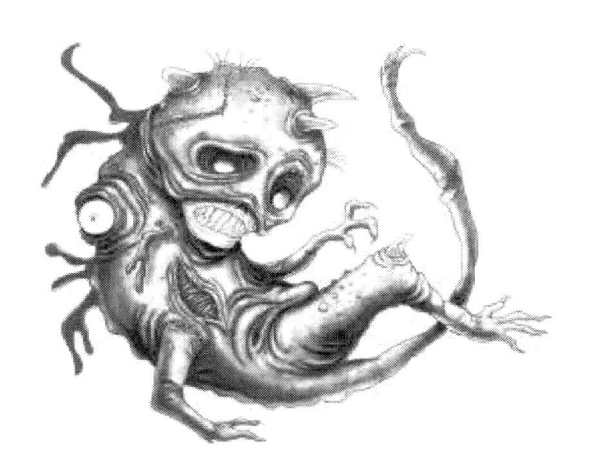

He was like Rasputin when they took him down. Sixteen bullets rammed into him while he peeled the flesh back from his last victim, loyal to his art until the end. Nine women in all he murdered. That last, too, did not survive. How could I correlate this reality with the loving father I had known?

He was more than just loving. He paid attention, read me stories, played chess and Frisbee toss with me. We went for walks, discovering flowers, trees, the unique patterns of clouds. Little did I know that he was using those outings to search out more intriguing specimens. He was quiet, attentive and a good listener. That too, I learned later, was how he teased out the pattern of his victims, like a detective dusting for fingerprints.

My mother was no harpy who drove him to seek revenge on women. They displayed a tenderness for each other that was as delicate as a butterfly's dance through blossoms. They went on weekly dinner dates to moderately tasteful restaurants, leaving me in the care of a babysitter. To many people, including my mother and me, our life was perfect.

Father victimized far more than nine women, of course. Those nine were the ones he tortured, and who did not have to live with the knowledge of what had been done to them. But he also seared the memories of those hapless women's families and friends. The horror was like the gap where a rotting tooth once sat, always being probed. No one ever thinks of the murderer's family, the unnoticed victims. My mother and I bore our scars and wounds, and our shame. The awareness of what he had been resided within us, germinating, giving us nightmares as we eternally replayed the possible reasons, what he had really felt for us. It was another way for him to inflict his dark desires, a legacy we could not purge. My mother withered away, her world chopped down like a forest's last tree by a heartless logger.

I grew up and changed my name. At St. Paul's Hospital, at the West End's edge, I cared for the ill. I changed bedpans, administered medicine and held the hands of the dying. Through the glossy linoleum corridors, the hushed hum of the rooms, I tried to gain strength and resilience in my psyche, understand the aches of the world, and lessen the painful throb that accompanied my heart every day.

St. Paul's borders the areas of disease and destitution. Those who prowl the streets or have found a home amongst refuse because their minds aren't fit for our institutions; those who swim in the fluids of their downfall; they are always around us, coming into the ER, courting death. Meanness and pettiness, greed and fear walked and limped through those doors. But sometimes they had a worse disease, just as my father did. Evil grows.

It was one of those dreary days when Vancouver weeps at the degradation of those in the Downtown Eastside, whose livers are eaten by the worm alcohol, or their minds by the needle-borne demon. I made my usual rounds to each patient's room, doling out their medications. I saw a hunched figure, definitely not her daughter, enter Mrs. Wylie's room. I went to check, and a man, grizzled and rank as the alleys, was pulling a ring off her finger. She flailed weakly, her withered hand grasping at him. He smacked her and pushed her hand away.

As she cried out, I yelled, "Hey! What do you think you're doing?"

The man turned, his hair like greasy snakes, and smiled. Then he thrust me aside and ran into the hall.

For a moment, I forgot about my duty to the patient. I did not burn with anger, but with something more fearsome – hate. A numbing cold raced through me. Like the dark fungus that reaches out in dank and moldering apartments, it took hold and blackness haloed my vision. I smashed the door open into the stairwell. Leaping down two steps at a time, I gained on him.

Shadows curled as I grabbed his collar. It barely registered that my fingers were charcoal-tinged. Twisting my hand into the fabric, I slammed the scumbag into the wall. The tamped-down hate and fear rushed through me and out my fingertips as they brushed his neck.

For a moment, all went black as a heavy blankness and confusion filled me. Then with absolute clarity, I saw every crime and dirty thought this creature had ever committed. Kaleidoscopic images flashed – taunts, beating dogs, sexual abuse, injecting viscous fluids, punching out a store clerk, losing jobs, more fights, jail, alcohol, fiery drugs. A panoply of pain and fear flooded me, and my distilled fears flowed back to him. Locked together, we were a conduit neither could break. We danced and jittered in the flickering neon stairwell, a pair of tangled marionettes. After a minute, an eternity, it ended. The destructive mold that had surfaced in me had now transferred to him. He crumpled to the floor, tears searing runnels through his dirt-smeared face, snot a slug's trail over his chin. He cringed and cowered, still shaking.

Rooted, I stared at a black fungus that had dried and powdered from my fingertips. I wasn't marked, but he was. Spots tinged his neck and hands and he whimpered as he scrubbed at them. Moments passed before I could snatch the ring and retreat upstairs, leaving him to an unknown fate.

I fled the hospital, complaining of a sudden illness, and locked myself in my apartment. I looked out my window onto English Bay, staring at the innocent white sails of boats, the joggers running along the waterfront. While I looked on the placid beauty I tried to tease out the tangled web of my thoughts.

I'm not a religious person. What has god to do with any of it? Why pray to a deity that gave his creatures free will and vowed to not intervene? And if he could intervene, then he was a sick bastard who let monsters like my father etch nightmares into people. It was what my father had called himself, when they found his meticulously written diaries. The Etcher, for he wanted to carve each canvas of human skin with his words, his teachings. But he never did explain why he did it, what drove him. It was all about technique and recording lessons. Is madness the same as evil? He was both, but what sort of monster was I becoming?

My father's blight had long since infected my soul, and it had welled up at last, leaving me neither mighty nor euphoric. I had been choked with nausea, but had been relieved when the hate had erupted from me, transforming into a wicked fungus like that which poisons dwellings in the soggy environs of the coastal rainforest.

In nature, mold is green, filled with chlorophyll, or brown and part of the rotting and renewal of vegetation. A natural cycle devoid of desire and deviation. But black mold feeds on the urban falsity of lies and plaster, the sins of betrayal and duplicity. It grows in the moist corners of gyprock, unseen behind couches and TVs. It permeates lungs and airways too, slowly eating at the dwellers until their mysterious illness is identified.

I was a product of my heritage and the land. Vancouver had claimed me, and somehow I had been chosen to exact revenge for the deeds of my father, and perhaps others. I wondered if my father was responsible for more victims who had gone missing and were never found. There were so many more than nine dead souls claimed by the man I knew.

I am my father's child. What happens to us in childhood shapes us for the future; the genetics, the environment, the love or abuses that touch us. I was made of love and horror. My father had betrayed us, a monster, a wolf in sheep's clothing, and I would never be able reconcile the split that had made up his whole. It's why, once I uncovered my power, I did what I did.

I took to prowling Vancouver's destitute areas, on side streets where prostitutes decorate the sidewalks like forlorn flowers, around Main and Hastings where decay and wasted lives spill out like industrial sewage, in alleys moist with human refuse where the crystal meth addicts try to consume others before they themselves are consumed. I took shifts as one of the street nurses who aid those in the Downtown Eastside. An itch grew in me, a feeling beneath my skin that I could alleviate only through movement. I did not consciously seek out evil, but it is always there in such places. Perhaps we are drawn to it unconsciously, as a plant seeks the sun.

Something drew me. As the weeks passed, it became more persistent. I had to peer behind that dumpster, look in that stairwell. Sometimes I found a person in need. Sometimes I found more.

One night, while my co-worker tended to a passed-out man in Chinatown, I felt compelled to explore the alley behind the red- and gold-lettered shops. I almost stumbled over the man raping a scrawny, unconscious woman, his hand clamped over her mouth. He didn't even stop when he saw me.

The cold swept down on me black and frigid; it singed my veins and cleared my sight. Without thinking I hauled him off the woman, throwing him into the brick wall across the lane. He slid down as I stood over him. I wanted to squeeze the horror from him but stopped with my hand on his throat. I would not be my father.

Instead, I pressed my fingers into his cheeks, increasing the pressure as his eyes came into focus. He scowled and reached up to my hands, but by then the black lanugo was creeping up his face. Time slowed and I watched the progression. He clawed at my hands but I held on; we locked together as the change took place. His face furred like some wolfman's, and his sins played out their reel to me, each bloody interaction; preying on drug addicts, weakened people. A parade of raped women. He had not cared if they had lived or died. I felt the same way about him.

He went slack, his hands falling, drool slipping down his chin, eyes wide, staring. I screamed at the barrage of images, oblivious of the presence of any observers.

This time, only he danced as I exerted more pressure, the black fungus crawling down his neck, under his shirt. But a call from my co-worker halted me. Breathing deeply, trying to bring light into my mind, I released my grip and turned away. The victim hadn't moved. I knelt, feeling for her pulse, pulling back her eyelids. Dead.

After the police dealt with the situation, I returned home. Sitting on my bed, fingers wrapped over my eyes and anchored in my hair, I rocked back and forth. What was I? What was I doing?

It felt as if someone had threaded sutures under my epidermis and gently tugged on them. While not painful, the need to move constantly crept through me. I could not sit still. The blackness in my fingertips faded away unless I hated. So I used it, filtered it, and turned my hate into a lesson for others.

I became a reluctant vault for all the terrible deeds of those I touched. No longer just my father's exploits – now I festered with a cinema of misdeeds. Night sweats soaked me, my stomach roiled. The more I tracked down the aberrant and infected them with the mold, the more I had to do it, to unleash the images that infested me.

I began to patrol the tracks by the sugar refinery, away from downtown. The large grey concrete cylinders look more like Cold War silos than a place to harness sweetness. Metal walkways, high fences, hidden cameras and the hulking shapes of railway cars added a disturbing, destitute mood. On the other side, away from the walkways, the inlet's oily waves lapped parasitically at the concrete as if it were a salt lick. The water sloshed and made throaty sounds.

I could not say why I was drawn to such an area, forlorn at the best of times, except for that strange intuition now hauling me here and there. The area whispered of neglect and sinister secrets. Mesh fences, razor wire, barred doors, and the sharp thorns of blackberry tried to hedge out the graffiti, the burned-out tins and piles of refuse that indicated a garden for the abandoned. Shadows were thick here, even in the day. At night, they were impenetrable. I carried a flashlight but left it off, walking softly, listening, feeling.

A train tunnel led from the south, to the bridge over the water. As I drew near, noting a security camera's shiny black eye, I smelled the salty fecundity of the ocean. The throaty sound now seemed more like a slurping, and my footsteps slowed. Dread quivered my belly, for the water was hundreds of yards away, and the sound was in front of me, echoing against the night-painted sides of the train tunnel. Shadows bulged, bloating and rippling. I wanted badly to shine my light, and just as much not to know what was there.

No longer able to wait and listen to the sad whimper of infinite pain, I flicked on the flashlight, its white beam wavering. Legs, a shadow, warty lumps, a green sliminess, black – no, red – puddles; a slideshow of images revealed in the unsteady light.

Was it Newton who said that for every action there is an equal and opposite reaction? My father's heinous actions led to my reaction, the ability to inflict the memory of one's deeds back upon them. But just as I had this power, could my deeds too create an equal and opposite force? Somehow, I felt certain that this reaction hunched in front of me, salty seaweed wafting from it, making me swallow and breathe through my nose.

The thing hissed and gurgled, turning. It was half woman, naked, beautiful, terrifying, dripping dank water from silvery hair. But the light highlighted a face that shifted, eyes that shone like a maddened horse's, a nostrils flaring, nightmarish teeth and a thick tongue lolling and dripping bloody gore.

What lay beneath the creature twitched, his face half-eaten away, an eye lying bare like an oyster in the shell of bone. I retched, bile hanging stringy from my lips. Half crouching, I advanced on the monster, forcing the black mold to my fingertips, but I hesitated. Did I really want to see the horrors in this thing's mind?

I had a mission; my father had branded me with a mark of shame and I could not shy away because of squeamishness. The thing trudged toward me, its victim dragged behind like a broken pull-toy. The man wasn't conscious but his hand adhered fast to its scaly greenish leg. I grabbed for the creature's throat and a jarring cold jolted my veins. Its scaly skin was moist and tacky, but the fungus tried to turn away, back up my hands. It was hard to see. My fingers slid off the slime.

The rotting seaweed stench permeated me as I tried to grip the monstrosity's neck again, and before I knew it I was heaving up everything in my stomach, over and over. The creature ignored me, flowing over the ground, toward the water under the bridge, its meal in tow.

It took me hours to return home, stopping to gag up a bitter residue. Shakily, I turned the key and staggered inside, sliding down the door. I managed to get to bed after rinsing my mouth.

The next two days I was pale as a water-bloated corpse and couldn't keep anything down. I had met my nemesis, a monster so terrible that it turned me to quivering jelly. I had not helped that poor wretch, and considering his state, it had probably been better that he died. I shuddered and slipped into uneasy sleep. Eventually the shakes and queasiness subsided and my thoughts bobbed to the surface.

Was I really responsible for bringing another monster into the world? I would have stopped then and there but the irresistible prickle within tugged me to restlessness. The fresh air, the rain made me feel better and I took to walking often under the perpetually leaking sky that can hit Vancouver for weeks. I identified with my city in a way I hadn't before, learning the layout of the streets, fascinated by the architecture and age of neighborhoods. Shaughnessy's rich and sometimes empty old dames, Chinatown's quaint yet slightly dilapidated buildings mixed with the new, East Vancouver's bohemian chic, the nondescript blandness of Champlain Heights.

I learned crimes happen anywhere. Not every alley or derelict building holds wickedness. The city, like any forest, houses those that prey and are preyed upon. There were always lawbreakers, but a jaywalker or a speeder did not deserve my fungal touch. In fact, there had to be a true touch of evil for the mold to take hold and dance the greater sins through their minds and mine. Fungus needs darkness in which to take root, so then why had that creature by the tracks managed to resist my touch?

I came across those whose vices were made evil by the drugs that took them over. Crystal meth morphed people into savages, and the drug nicknamed "bath salts," though as of yet infrequent, was worse. I hoped that the parade of past exploitations would move them away from a destructive road. Addicts were rarely evil, just desperate, but when I came across true malevolence it felt like rusty spikes being driven through my viscera.

Months passed and many monsters were jailed with my help, usually scratching and gibbering as the black fungus took root. The lesser evils, I left where I found them. I did not really judge them. The mold did that. And I was not free of the acts perpetuated. I knew exactly what they had done and that nest of vipers weighed me. My mistake was never wondering what happened to that lanugo that spotted their flesh.

One afternoon, as the rain fell steadily and cold, I walked the seawall around Stanley Park, the pewter plate of the ocean flat, obscuring its denizens. The sky melted into it, the drizzle creating a marriage of greys. October was fully entrenched and the season had descended like the apocalypse. Leaves moldered to treacherous sludge on the roads and walks. Worms writhed, drowning in their besoddened homes; mildews acted like it was a night at the ball. Only the hardy, like the jogger who passed me, braved the dreary climate. He nodded to me from beneath his jacket's hood, and ran on, a companion against the weather.

It was the fact that it was still day, though dreary, that lulled me. Deep in thought, I nearly stumbled over the creature pulling itself over the railing by the lighthouse, its grey and green scaly hide sluicing water. I backed away, watching it. Silver strands of hair hung like rivulets of cascading water. It turned flat brown fish eyes upon me, the horselike countenance baring massive, sharp teeth, large nostrils flaring. Then it shifted, like wind skimming the surface of the ocean, so subtly that I almost doubted my eyes. The snout flattened, the eyes grew bright, the figure straightened. A lithe woman, with skin the color of chrysoprase, hair silvery and tangled, ambled toward me.

No matter what the illusion, the fetid miasma of seaweed, rotting fish and dank cellars hit me with the truth. My mouth watered, bile surging and I swallowed, breathing through my mouth. I'd seen this same creature that night by the tracks. Had it been coming up to snare an unwary jogger or was it hunting me?

I backed up farther. The crawling surge of mold moved through me, tingling my fingertips. I wasn't sure I'd have any affect. I was about to turn and run when another jogger came up behind me and passed with head bent down. I yelled, but she didn't see the monster.

Lightning-fast, it snapped out an arm and the jogger went down. She lay stunned upon the path, rain pelting her face. The creature bent toward her. My stomach pitched, but I had no choice. I clasped its shoulders, forcing the mold upon its body. Again, the fungus wouldn't stick and my hands slipped off, but it hissed and turned toward me, swatting out at the annoyance disturbing its meal. I ducked and came around from the other side, panting as I tried to keep from vomiting.

It knelt by the woman and her eyes finally focused, going wide. She pushed at its chest and her hands adhered where mine had slid off. Its wicked teeth approached her face and she screamed.

I kicked its head, and tried to choke it from behind. It elbowed me and I fell, vomiting, onto the concrete. I crawled back, and laid my hand on its back, hating, loathing, calling up all the anger within, the horrendous deeds of past fiends, and channeled all the blackness through my fingers. They grew warm as I pressed my palm on its back. No images came to me.

Something sizzled and the thing screeched, arching back. It whipped around and a large webbed hand pushed me. I flew back, my head smacking soundly into the railing. Struggling, I could not swim through the darkness that pulled me down as the jogger shrieked.

When I came to, pain and horror surged out of me. I rolled to my knees and dry-heaved into the pouring rain. I looked around but only a thin scarlet streak trailed over the walkway, past the railing and to the rocks below. The rain was washing all evidence away and the sea thing had returned to its lair. There was no point calling 911, when I had neither victim nor perpetrator.

Sick and shivering I made it home, and suffered the same symptoms as before.

My father had a good life – his naive, loving family and freedom to pursue his morbid delights. I tried to lead a good life, do what was right, atone for his sins, but I'd lost all my friends, and I'd isolated myself with my feverish searches. *Feverish* was what I felt, for I itched and sweated, always trying to dig up the wickedness that skims just beneath the city's veneer. Is a person who generates mold slowly consumed unless the fungus can be spread? And I had done precious little to stop that thing from the water.

As inevitable as the sun setting, we would meet again – and we did. This time it came hunting me, not some hapless pedestrian. I walked home along Burrard Street and under the bridge along the waterfront, past the aquatic center and the high-rises. Vistas of the ocean and the breezes seemed to cleanse me, clear my sinuses that clogged now if I stayed indoors too long. The green grass cushioned me as I strolled, and for a while I could forget the ebb and flow of sinister influences. I just was, a part of the natural world, an organism moving through.

Early morning and the sun dried the tears of dew upon the grass, a rare nice day for the time of year. A chill added clarity to the air, and a few hardy sailboats and the freighters farther out waited to move on their journeys.

I felt the monster before it touched me, for my stomach twisted and tossed as if the calm seas had sent their storms internally. I whipped around, striking with an outstretched arm and a closed fist. The beast lost its balance as my fist struck its head. I wasn't foolish enough to think I had bested it. It tumbled to the ground, catching itself on a long clawed hand, and kicked out. I jumped back, and spit out some bile that surged up my throat. Breathing through my nose, I called on my ability to manifest hate into the fungal pitch that bloomed at my fingertips. It wasn't enough.

I poured revulsion and fear and anger into my hands, tugging on that invisible thread that wound through me. It was like having stitches removed, an unpleasant beneath-the-surface movement of alien material. Gritting my teeth, I concentrated as the fish thing advanced on me. Its dead milky eyes stared straight ahead and a long eel-like tongue moved over fleshy horse lips and sharp-edged teeth.

My fingers darkened and the lanugo moved up past my wrists. I had hurt it once before. I ran at it, pushing my hands into its chest, knocking it down as I straddled its rotting hide. Screaming, I poured my horror into it. It shrieked like a thousand bats being torn apart and black wisps wafted from its chest. The odor of kelp and seaweed and dead shellfish filled me and as my gorge rose, it batted me off. I fell and twisted to my side to vomit. Then the monster latched its teeth through my coat and into my arm.

I howled as scarlet oozed out onto the blue fabric. Using my boots to try and kick it loose, I clawed at the beast. Wounded, its strength was lessened and I managed to back away, crawling across the ground.

Something slammed through my brain and laced my nerves with acid. I couldn't even scream as I convulsed. I wouldn't have known if I had been devoured at that moment.

The fish-horse thing was shaking its head, stringy hair spraying water everywhere. I tried to focus, gasping for breath. Something had happened. Gathering my wits, I staggered to my feet, wondering where all the early morning joggers were. Alone with this watery demon, I tried to summon the mold into my hands but nothing happened. My arm dripped thick blood and the monster righted itself, growling now in pain or anger. It didn't matter; its goal had not changed.

Backing away, disgust and fear filled me, but the summoning would not come. Something bumped into me and I cringed. I sidestepped so that I didn't put my back to the greater threat, and a shape – possibly a man – stumbled forward. Sprouting from his head was a two-foot long stem, brown and black, wrinkled, fuzzy. Gluey fluids leaked down his head, seeping into his grimy collar. Flaps of his scalp hung down, where the growth had sprouted through.

He moved between me and the monster, and reached for it, his hands adhering. The creature snarled and slashed at him, and then there was another shambling man. I recognized this one, also with a protruding stem from his head. He was the first one, who had tried to steal the woman's ring. Lanky, taller than the first, he too shuffled forward.

Gaping, I saw the stems were mushrooms, fungal growths. They were my fruiting bodies.

The second man grabbed the fish thing and adhered to it as well. It bit his arm and fluids, yellowish and clear, oozed out. A third juddered in. Not one looked at me or each other. Mindlessly, they grabbed the monster, their eyes dull. It could not remove them. They pulled it down on the grass, all rolling around. A fourth joined them and I realized they had all been criminals I'd stopped, the ones who had not been taken by the police. I could only wonder if the ones sitting in cells now banged into bars, blindly seeking escape guided by the growth sprouting from their brains.

Numbed, I watched as the thing hissed and snapped. Skin tore loose, greyish and pink, but they didn't stop. They managed to pin its limbs and while three held it, the fourth opened his mouth and stuck his tongue between the pried-open horse jaws. He coughed into the fish-thing's mouth and it squealed.

The revolting menagerie dragged the convulsing monster over the grass and onto the sand. They didn't stop but moved into the silvery water's mire until nothing remained.

Shuddering, I went home and did not leave my apartment for four days.

The tugging left me, as did the power to bring on mold. Spring came and flowers bloomed. Was my ability seasonal and would it return with the fall rains? Was I no better than my father? I thought I would stop those criminals, and I had, but turning them into zombies had not been my intention. I do not know if I'll be able to use the mould again, but I'm afraid to. My father decided he could take lives. I did the same. I fear to use this power, if it returns. Perhaps then I will be the sacrifice to assuage the sins of my father, and the black mold will consume me from within.

The Healer's Touch

An invitation went out to several authors for this one and I thought I would try to write something that involved technology and healing, and the very real aspect of humanity that is required. "Physician, heal thyself" is a phrase that applies. This story looks at the degree of trauma that sometimes healing can cause to others but that to be effective in many areas of our lives, we must be healthy ourselves. I pulled on the very real and current issues of the war in Syria and the many refugees that have moved throughout Europe in a quest for a more peaceful life.

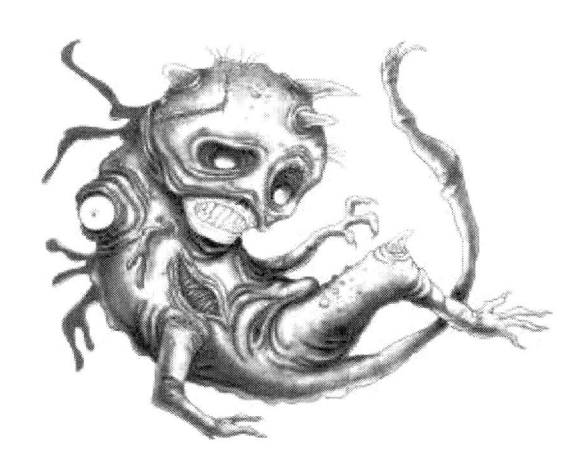

"Dr. Petrovna, we need you now! In the ER."

Hela's concentration broke, her visualization of muscle and bone disappearing as she looked up toward the door. The man's face flashed away from the opening. He left the door open, urgent voices drifting in from down the hall. The mending slowed on the child's leg, fractured in three places. The girl whimpered.

"Damn it," she whispered, not wanting to wake the child from the light sedation.

Bending over the bruised leg, she laid her tattooed hand over the bruised flesh and fracture again. The nanotechnology embedded along her inked design glowed a soft silvery light and her fingertips left pools of brightness on the girl's flesh.

"Dr. Petrovna, we need you!"

Keeping her eyes closed, she commented, "I'm not an ER doctor and I'm in the middle of healing."

The man moved closer, his voice gaining in volume. "Our ER nano docs are away; we're short staffed. There are at least a dozen people with third degree burns."

She gritted her teeth. "Give me one minute and I'll come."

Tuning out the sound of rushing steps, voices growing louder, crying filtering from the ER, she envisioned the femur, the tendons and muscles, and directed the nanotechnology injected into the girl's leg to speed the repair. The leg grew warm as nanobots moved quickly to knit bone, pulling the leg into a straighter line.

Hela sensed the nurse still hovering. When she knew the mending was well under way, she opened her eyes and stood. The man clenched and unclenched his fists, biting his lip. She moved toward him and grabbed him by the throat, pressing him to the door.

In a hard-edged whisper, she said, "Don't ever do that again!" Her face was right up to his, his breath warm on her cheeks.

His eyes widened. "I—I w-was told to get you immediately. S—sorry."

Get control, Hela! The cloying fear. She released the nurse quickly. "I could have done severe damage. Never interrupt a healing."

He cleared his throat, a hand rubbing where hers had just been. "Can you come now?"

Reluctantly, she nodded. She hated doing ER, with the crowded rooms and distressed people, the urgency. As they walked down the hall the envelope of antiseptic was pierced and shredded by the acrid taint of coppery blood, burned hair and flesh. Hela closed her eyes for one moment and tried to shore up her strength.

Then she was in it, stretchers everywhere, curtains half askew, people moaning, weeping, whimpering. Sweat beaded her brow and her breath grew shallow. Red, raw, lacerated and burned bodies. It was nothing new for a doctor but the onslaught nearly froze her. She was tugged in a direction, and narrowed her focus to the person in front of her, face like melted plastic.

People rushed to and fro, voices surrounding her with hushed urgency, carts wheeled back and forth, and metal instruments clanged as they were dropped into trays. Someone said, "Just stabilize them. We don't have time for full rebuilds." A nurse injected bots into the burn victim.

Hela breathed shallowly and began, gathering her strength, trying not to let the crush of people thrust her into the past. She touched the person's face, unsure whether man or woman, closed her eyes and envisioned the intricate structure of muscles, fascia, veins. She directed the nanobots to mending the subcutaneous tissues, where the third-degree burns had pressed deep. The dermis and epidermis would have to wait for later, when there was time. Heat generated from the accelerated healing mechanism would matter little to such badly burned people. She murmured once to another doctor, "The tissue is healing but they'll still need to be treated for trauma and shock."

She stayed focused and the pressure of the ER faded into the background, blending with the demon voices of her past. Hours later, she had no idea how many, she found a cot and slept.

Hela floated in a white fog, voices calling for help, pleading, growing silent. They were all dead. Then an accusing hand grabbed her, pulled her, shook her.

Gasping, as if she were drowning, Hela bolted awake.

"Dr. Petrovna! You were dreaming. You're at the hospital." The woman looked at her with concern. Her hair was pulled into a pony tail, clean and shiny, her nurse's scrubs fresh and without stains. New shift.

Hela swallowed. "What time is it?"

"Three p.m.," The nurse said. "They told me to wake you. You've only had about four hours sleep but Dr. Saeedi would like you to come to her office."

"Dr. Saeedi? The chair of surgery?" Hela rubbed her face as the woman nodded. "Okay, give me fifteen minutes to clean up and I'll be there."

She slid off the cot and went to the doctor's lounge to change and freshen up. Technically, she fell under the chair of nano-medicine, but Dr. Cohen was at a conference abroad. Dr. Saeedi barely knew her and she wasn't a surgeon in the typical sense.

She knocked on Dr. Saeedi's door and entered. A slouchy man turned toward her as she warily came forward, his hangdog eyes examining her.

Dr. Saeedi, a slim woman with warm brown eyes, stood and shook her hand. "Thank you for coming on such short notice, Dr. Petrovna. I'm sorry to drag you in, I know it was a long night."

She introduced Director Boscoe, from Public Health and Safety, then motioned to a chair and sat.

"Have I done something wrong?" Hela looked from one to the other, wondering if the nurse had complained.

"No," replied the director. "On the contrary, Dr. Saeedi has sung your praises. We have need of a nano-medicine doctor in one of our refugee centers."

Confused, Hela replied, "But surely you have doctors there already."

"Not enough. There has been an influx of refugees, from various countries that you've heard about. Some are in grave health and we need an expert. You came recommended as one of the best, and there are some cases proving difficult to heal to lesser experienced doctors."

She understood the unspoken part. The government wanted to look good to the media.

"I-I can't. I have too much to do here, many patients. The need is great everywhere. And I work best in less hectic environments."

As Boscoe dangled great remuneration, paid expenses, possible recognition from the Prime Minister, etc. Hela noticed Dr. Saeedi tapping her elbow, a hard look in her eyes.

But Hela saw crowds, a crushing mass of people holding their hands out to her, demanding she save them. She wanted to heal but on her own terms. It was the best she could do, instead of the masses accusing her when something went wrong.

"I'm sorry, none of that matters to me. I can't do it." Moving into all the unknown traumas was more than she could bear; her skills would suffer.

Dr. Saeedi spoke to break the stalemate. "Dr. Petrovna, your record is exemplary. More of your patients heal without complications than any other nano-med work. It takes a fine mind and great recall to map the body thoroughly. Dr. Cohen recommended you, and the hospital would like to be able to contribute to such humanitarian needs."

Dr. Saeedi smiled but Hela felt only the cool calculation of what prestige it would bring the hospital. The walls were pressing in, Saeedi's and Boscoe's eyes on her. "You're giving me no choice."

Boscoe said, "You'll be doing a great service for your government and saving many lives." He pulled a packet from his pocket. "You'll be flying in two days at six pm, to the center in Manchester."

"England? Wait, I don't fly. I can't."

Dr. Saeedi replied. "You must. Considering your outburst with a nurse last night, a change might be good for you."

"You don't understand." Hela tried to keep the panic from choking her voice. "I—I don't like flying."

Director Boscoe patted her back, making her jump. "Just think of what you'll be doing for your country and all those poor souls."

☙

Hela had not flown, *ever*, after that one time. Her hands shook so badly at the thought that she self-medicated with Ativan and several shots of vodka even before entering the flying tin can. The mix dulled her anxiety, but even with the quietude of business class she stood and walked around, trying to pretend she was not in the air. She wore long sleeves to hide the distinctive nano tattoo that laced her hand and arm, mixed with a design of her own choosing, a bird in flight.

Eventually even that was too much and she returned to her seat, ordering vodka, hoping to get some rest. A few hours' sleep finally smothered the cries and moaning from her past. All too soon the pillow jostled from under her head as they landed.

She stumbled off the plane, still fuzzy, trying not to gag on the thick oniony smell of ripe bodies and sour breath. Once Hela grabbed her one bag and was through customs, she saw her name on a card being held by a short woman with curly gray hair.

The chattering woman guided her to a taxi and to her hotel with a mention of meeting with the Director at four.

After locking the door to her modern design hotel room, she flopped onto the bed and closed her eyes, relieved to be on the ground and alone. Sleep overtook her and she missed her appointment. Hela ordered a vegetarian meal, happy to hide in her room. She stared out the window at the light rain, in between eating and reading about what awaited her: thirty-eight hundred refugees, three-quarters with health needs, a third of those were serious, etc. etc. The thought of so many desperate souls sapped her, so she opened the bar fridge and helped herself to the supplies there.

Regaining her equilibrium was important. She had been like a spinning top for the past few days. It felt like losing control, and Hela had worked years to put her past in a box and seal it tight. Being a healer was what mattered, what she had always wanted, and her purpose was to lessen people's suffering and give them a better quality of life. The nightmare of the flight was behind her. *Just pretend that you're back home, working as usual,* she reminded herself.

If she could do that, she could maintain control. But she'd insist they give her a room to bring each patient into, one by one.

Hela prepared in the small white room. There was an examining table and a tray holding twenty syringes with the healing nanobots. White labels for bone, red for tissue repairs, and yellow for cancers and tumors. There were only two with the green label for genetic fixes – disease and syndromes – the special category of inherited conditions. They were the most difficult. She lowered the cloth over the tray.

Checking her watch, Hela noted she had five more minutes before the first patient. Her list was long, and she doubted she'd get through all, but each patient had been prescreened: multiple broken bones, head traumas, lacerations and deep cuts, burns, crushed limbs – which were very hard to return to their original state – leukemia, heart attacks, severe anemia, malnutrition, etc.

Some would be able to walk out of the room, nearly whole, and others would take longer, even with accelerated healing.

Hela knelt in front of her first patient, a scrawny girl of about five. "Hi, Tasneem. I hear you're not feeling well and your legs hurt?"

The girl nodded, her braids momentarily giving the stuffed bunny in her hands a mustache.

"Let's take a look, shall we?" Hela lifted her onto the table. "This won't hurt; will you lay down for me?"

Tasneem looked over at her mother, waiting in the doorway. Hela beckoned her in to sit. She read the chart, noting the malformed legs, the toes curling under, bruised and scraped raw from a long journey to escape their country's border. They'd been traveling for months, on one ship or another, illegal passage, poor sanitation, not enough food. Rickets and malnutrition.

Hela swabbed the girl's leg and pulled out a syringe, keeping it below the eyeline. "Hold your bunny tight and take a deep breath. There will be a little pinch. Now breathe out." She injected the nanobots and put the discarded needle in the bio-hazard container. Washing her hands thoroughly, Hela dried them, then sat beside the girl, placing her tattooed hand on the leg.

Closing her eyes, she envisioned the physiology of the body, the bones of a healthy skeleton; femur, fibula and tibia. She sent the bots to mend and straighten the bones. Then she sent an auxiliary back-up of blood cells to heal and reknit the bones. Her hand, still glowing, stayed on the leg for another minute, monitoring the invisible helpers setting out to repair.

Opening her eyes, she looked at the girl, who watched her intently. "There, that wasn't so bad, was it?" The girl shook her head.

Hela wrote out a prescription for high dose vitamin D and a diet rich in bone broth and proteins. As long as the girl could eat properly, she'd recover completely. "Keep her off her feet for a week, and then ease back into normal activity."

Tasneem's mother cried as she carried her daughter out the door. Hela breathed a sigh, washed her hands and thought she could do this. Just like home.

The next few people had second degree burns or broken limbs that had started healing badly. There was no help but to sedate them, re-break the bones, align them and set the nanobots to mending them correctly.

The orderlies then carried in a man, delirious, with third degree burns to his face, which had happened in the overcrowded refugee camp when a kerosene lamp was kicked over. There was some infection, causing the angry wound to weep fluids. He would need antibiotics as well, but Hela injected him and laid her hand near his raw red cheek.

As she retraced the facial structure and the muscles she was jarred, as if she'd been pushing against a membrane that suddenly turned to mud. Her musculo-skeletal memory was impeccable but now it was as if someone had partitioned off the facial muscles. Hela couldn't reach them. Concentrating harder, her brow furrowing, she retraced every muscle, thrust the nanobots into the damaged tissue and directed the beginning of the mending process. Her fingers tingled, like getting frostbite, but she didn't remove them. Heat flared back into her hand but she held steady.

When it seemed the nanobots were finally working, Hela withdrew and opened her eyes. The man looked dazed, his beard half burned away, his eyes glassy and unfocused, but his wounds were still fresh. What was going on? She'd never run into this resistance before. Making a note on his chart, she told the nurse who guided him out, "Let me know how he's doing. There's something else going on here."

Several more times she encountered the same pushback phenomenon, something that she'd never seen before. One teenage boy had multiple contusions and lacerations patterning his back. He must have been whipped.

Another young woman, who was slightly malnourished, looked fine with no evident trauma but a question on a diagnosis of head injury. And a third, a man is his thirties, seemed to suffer a neurosis; paranoia perhaps, though he also seemed catatonic at times. Hela wasn't sure there was anything she could do for the latter but she used the green syringe, looking for underlying genetic markers. This form of genetic reconstruction was still new and no nano-medicine professional could map everything. All they could do was set the nanobots to searching out anomalies and hope repair would make someone better. It was risky but when nothing else was working, it was a chance at least.

When Hela looked at the clock, it was already 7p.m. She reviewed the list of people where she had pushed the nanobots harder, asking to be kept up to date. In forty-eight hours, she would know if the mending was working.

Exhausted, she returned to her hotel and ordered fries, or chips, as the English called them, unable to eat more. She had one shot of vodka, to help turn off her mind, and crawled into bed.

The next day blurred like the last. Refugees with various injuries, some requiring interpreters, came and went. Including another half-dozen patients where Hela met resistance. Her list was growing longer.

Two days later, Hela saw the patients on her list again. Outwardly, none of them showed much improvement. It was as if they'd had no intervention at all. Hela swallowed, feeling the dread build. There was no need to inject more nanos, so she placed her healing hand near the burned man's face, on his neck. There was that resistance again, as if his physiology was wrapped behind heavy plastic. Hela pushed, trying to clarify the image. She'd never had trouble envisioning physiology and anatomy before. Why these people and why now? Sweat dampened her upper lip but she kept her hand on the man. Then it was as if she were falling, vertigo sweeping up to swirl her around. If she hadn't been sitting, she would have fallen.

She dropped and dropped and fell onto a table. Something hit the soles of her feet, over and over, the soft bruising an incessant, unrelenting ache that grew intolerable. Then a cloth smothered her, blocked her breathing, causing her breath to choke back into her. Water rushed over her face, up her nose, in her mouth, in her eyes, choking her. Her body heaved. It wouldn't stop, it was killing her. Then, finally, a moment's respite.

She tried to pull a breath, gagging, spewing water and then it began again before she could breathe properly. Blackness closed around her, her light dwindling, her body spasming as life's nourishing air was denied her.

Hela came to, twitching, convulsing on the floor, the man on the examining table moaning and weeping. A nurse bent beside her. "Dr. Petrovna, are you okay? Dr. Petrovna!"

Scrabbling until her back was against the wall, Hela pulled in deep breaths, crying, thankful for the precious air. She rubbed her face trying to scrub the images from her mind. It had felt so real, as if she were there. "I—I need a few minutes. Please take him out."

She ran from the room, grabbing her purse, not caring that she was in scrubs. Hela walked mindlessly for an hour, not noticing trees or cars or buildings. She parked herself in a pub and ordered several shots of vodka. Her hands eventually stopped shaking. Staring at them, she admonished herself. *You can't run away. You have to help people. Face it.*

The dread settled back on her, like a demon sitting on her shoulders, digging deep its claws. It was tearing her carefully constructed world apart. It had taken years to get it right, perfect the mold. Her past was buried deep and she had thrown herself into her work, becoming one of the top nano-med doctors. There was no time for a relationship, she'd told herself. Her career came first; there were so many that needed her. And now this dark memory lurked, pulling at her, digging up her emotions.

She signaled for a cab to take her back to the center. The nurses came to her. "Are you all right? Did he attack you? What happened?"

Hela brushed them all away and said, "Just bring me one of the other patients on my list."

They brought the young woman, still without physical marks, guided by a gentle hand but not seeing the room she was in, nor Hela. Looking the woman over, she noted the lack of response, the dark bruised look that marred her brown skin. She picked up the woman's hand and then let it go. It fell without resistance or volition. Nausea swirled in Hela's belly, but she had to know.

Her fingers touched the woman's arm, the nano tattoo turning bluish white. She pushed again, trying to sidle her imaging around the barrier, trying to mesh with it, in the end tearing through it to find she was being held down, her clothes torn off, a man pushing into her, and then another and another, her body sticky with their fluids, her face covered in tears and snot. The bruising, the burning, the violation. And it didn't end. They pushed her head into their crotches, made her gag on dirty cocks, had her take them over and over. It never ended. Each day they used her, kept her in a dark cell, barely fed her. The only light she saw was from a high window before another foul-smelling body fell on top of her and tore her open where her soul spilled out, soaking into the dirt floor. She was fourteen, fifteen, sixteen. Every day for seven years, they treated her as less than meat. When she became pregnant they punched her over and over again in her stomach till she vomited and bled out what life might have formed.

She came to, screaming, the woman on the table mingling her cries with Hela's. She vomited over and over, unable to wash her mind of the memories. In the end, they both had to be sedated.

The black soothed her, comforted her, kept the past from her, and Hela did not want to awake. She groaned and tried to roll over, slowly waking, feeling as if a weight held her down.

Director Boscoe sat beside her, reading on his tablet. He looked up as she focused her gaze. "Dr. Petrovna, you gave us quite a scare. Can you tell me what happened?"

She tried to sit up and realized she was restrained. Taking a deep breath, she said. "Can you remove these? I need to pee."

Boscoe colored slightly at her request, but undid the straps. She sat up, realizing she was in a clinic room, then went to the bathroom. In the mirror, a haunt stared back at her. She splashed water on her face and patted down her hair.

Returning, she sat in the other chair. "These people."

Boscoe waited patiently, his hands folded in his lap.

"They…I don't know how but the ones I can't heal… That's never happened before. Those that aren't healing…they were tortured. I'm- I'm reliving their experiences. Their illnesses are in their minds."

Director Boscoe sat straighter, leaning forward slightly, a hard light glinting off his hazel eyes. "You can see what happened to them? How?"

She shook her head. "I don't know. Mostly it's feeling but I do see some of it. Light, once in a while a face. The terror and fear, the pain. It's…it's terrible."

He sat back, his thoughts hidden from her. "All right, I think you better take it easy. We still need your services, obviously. Do what you can."

What she did was find a bar close to the hotel, order up a baked potato, no meat, which the waitress seemed puzzled about. "Vegetarian," Hela said. Then she ordered a string of vodkas to blot the memory. A couple of men tried to engage her in conversation, which she rebuffed quickly. It was two a.m. when she fell into bed. Consequently, she didn't get to the center until 10:30, after a liquid breakfast. She knew it was unwise but she couldn't bear to face those patients without the numbing effect.

She handled a number of cases through the day, but sent away anyone where she met the resistance, before a woman walked into the clinic room. "Hello, Hela."

Hela looked up from the chart, squinting. The woman was petite, with a slight accent, her hair braided up the temples and forming a foam of black curls cascading down her back, the ends tinted purple. Her eyes were the most amazing shape in a face of the loveliest shade of deep brown. "I…know you. Ibby. Ibby Okilo!"

Ibby grasped Hela's hand, smiling. Hela pulled back, feeling…something…interest, attraction, curiosity. She surreptitiously wiped her hand against her leg. "What are you doing here? I haven't seen you since med school."

Ibby sat. "Oh you know, doctorate in neuroanatomy, neuropsychology, all those things to do with the brain. And I'm here because of you."

Hela crossed her arms. "I'm okay."

"Really?" Ibby looked at her curiously, her head tilted. "From what I've been told you're experiencing others' memories when trying to heal some refugees. If you don't mind the effect it's having on you, then you don't need me. Otherwise, if you continue without some help, you're going to lose it."

"Then I'll just go home. I didn't want to be here anyway."

Ibby leaned forward, looking up at Hela, who stood with her back to the wall. "You're not the only one this has happened to, Hela, but there are few nano-medicine doctors who have the unique combination."

"What do you mean, unique combination?" She was afraid she knew the answer.

"You're an empath, and combined with the nano-medicine, you're crossing into a feedback loop. Once established, you'll start experiencing it more often, and not just when you're healing."

"That's bullshit!" Hela grabbed her bag and stormed out. "I don't need this. I'm going home."

But she didn't. She went to the hotel bar, and then onto a pub, drinking shot after shot, nibbling on crisps, tearing apart radishes and carrots. There was no such thing as empaths. It was some weird effect of being in England, of being out of her element.

She was staring blindly at the back wall when she felt someone sit next to her. A glance told her it was Ibby. They were both out of business wear, in casual tops and jeans. Ibby ordered a cider.

"Where'd you go after graduation?"

Ibby didn't look at her but stared at the television, sipping her cider. "I went back to Nigeria for a few years. My parents were ill so I took care of them and set up a practice there, but I finally moved away. I wanted to do more research. I'm living in France these days.

"Do you remember when we were nearly finished pre-med and we got drunk that night, too stressed, needing a break from studying and medical terminology?"

Hela smiled. "We got pretty silly, didn't we? Singing, dancing on tables at that Greek restaurant, tearing up buns and throwing them at customers."

Ibby laughed. "Yeah, we really let our hair down. Do you remember what you told me, about your past?"

Hela stopped laughing and downed her vodka. "I was bullshitting you. No one really believed that story. Look, Ibby, it's good to see you. You look awesome and I'm glad you're doing well, but…" She stood and tossed money onto the counter. "I've got to go. I'm tired now."

"Hela," Ibby called as she walked away. She didn't turn back. "It's going to get harder before it gets better."

✶

The morning assaulted her. Too bright, and the sounds of cars and lorries going by beat at the thin membrane of control. She went into the center, hoping the work would keep the memories buried, but afraid of what she would find in other people's minds.

The day was a disaster. There seemed to be more muddy senses when trying to heal people. The director wanted a list of names, but also showed up, asking her to detail the tortures against each person. "I can't do it," Hela said. "It's too real."

"But it's not actually happening to you, Hela," Boscoe replied. "You can distance yourself. Otherwise, you're not really helping them."

"I'm not a damn psychologist. And I'm witnessing these horrors. Get Dr. Okilo, if that's what you want."

Boscoe steepled his fingers in a way that felt demeaning. "What we want, Dr. Petrovna, is a professional demeanor and to help these people. And we want a list of the war crimes. If you can heal these people, they will be able to testify, along with your corroboration. Dr. Okilo will be working with you."

Unable to face more memories, Hela hid herself for several days, but soon the patrons, the bartender, every damn person on the street was invading her thoughts, bleeding their feelings all over her. The alcohol was not dulling it and she could no longer get her nanotech to work correctly.

She ignored the hotel phone and pulled a pillow over her head. Whimpering, Hela felt lost. There was no escape, but she was afraid, afraid that if she faced these people's memories, her own would bubble to the surface. And she didn't want to remember the past at all.

She heard the door click and Ibby walked into her hotel room. Hela burrowed under covers, crying softly.

Ibby sat down beside her, and stroked her head. "Look at you. Shhh, Hela. You poor thing."

Hela tried to wriggle away from the touch. "Leave me alone."

"So you can tailspin into alcoholism or death? No, I didn't think so. I missed you, Hela, even after all these years. Even though you always pushed everyone away."

"I don't deserve anyone!"

She heard *tsk*-ing. "Really, Hela? A pity party?" Ibby laughed. She'd always had a sunshiny belief in the good of everyone.

Hela pushed back the covers and sat up. "I can't do it. Their memories are too terrible."

"I can give you some self-hypnosis techniques to help handle it, to view it from a distance, without feeling everything. You're not the first empath who has felt people's emotions too strongly."

"I don't want to see them at all," she sniffed. "It's torture."

"Yes," Ibby smiled, but it was such a tender smile of understanding that Hela paid attention. "It is, but without lobotomizing yourself you have to learn techniques to control it. It will lessen in time if you do this."

Hela wiped at her eyes. "Okay, fine, I'll try it. I can't stand this anymore." She got up to pour a glass of vodka, but Ibby stood and pulled it gently from her hand.

"No. This isn't helping you. It's making it harder to maintain a barrier, even if it dulls your pain in the meantime. And do you really want to add alcoholism to what works against you?" She smiled gently and pushed Hela back to the bed. Hela sat crosslegged and Ibby knelt in front of her. "Close your eyes, and I'll guide you into a visualization that will help you stabilize your mental barriers."

They worked at it every day for a week. It took a few days for Ibby to convince Hela to lay off the vodka. Hela continued to see the refugees, just the easier ones at first, leaving the broken ones, the ones damaged by torture, till the last. But when she tried again to help them, she still could not get more than lukewarm results.

She met Ibby later in a quaint little bar, and ordered wine, choosing to stay away from the vodka. She had only one glass, and made sure to have a good meal, vegetarian shepherd's pie.

Ibby smiled at her and finished writing on her tablet. "How is it going? Are the barriers working?"

"They are…" Hela hesitated. "I'm not picking up residual feelings from anyone here or at the clinic. Even when I'm healing the refugees, I can keep their emotions compartmentalized. I can now record the torture I've seen but it's still terrible. Nightmare images. And…I can't heal them."

She stared at her Cabernet, thinking how like dried blood it was in color, then pushed the wine away. Maybe white wine would have been better.

Ibby leaned onto her hand, her elbow on the table as she searched Hela's face. "I'll ask again. Do you remember what you told me that night we got drunk?"

Hela pulled back as if Ibby had slapped her. She had regretted ever showing vulnerability, ever revealing her terrible dark secret.

Ibby reached forward and ran a finger along Hela's chin. "You were twelve, with your parents in a small plane flying over the Himalayas."

"Stop," Hela whispered.

"The plane crashed, a blizzard, and everyone but you injured or dead."

Hela's hands gripped the table. Ibby didn't remove her hand from Hela's face. "You saw your parents die. The other people, you watched each one expire and you could do nothing."

"Please, stop." Hela sobbed, so afraid to hear the terrible words of condemnation. "Please," she whispered.

But Ibby was relentless, her wide eyes warm. "You were left alive and you stripped the bodies of clothes to keep you warm. Their eyes were frozen open, watching you. When help didn't come, you did what you had to do to survive."

"No no no. No." Ibby grabbed her wrists to keep her from leaping away from the table.

"You ate their flesh, Hela. You ate to stay alive. You were a child and they could not feel anything."

Hela wrenched her hands free, ran to the bathroom and vomited. The horror all over again. The dead watching, accusing. The terrible terrible secret. Sobbing, she flushed, then washed her face, staring at the face of a monster in the mirror.

She hoped that Ibby had left, but when she emerged, Ibby sat there, looking down into her glass of wine.

Hela sat, her head down, and whispered. "I am a monster. I've tried every day to atone for what I did."

Ibby clasped her face with both hands, tilting Hela's chin up. "Yes you have, but you are not a monster, Hela. You did what you needed to. You hurt no one. Do you think that there is anyone anywhere who has not done something they regretted? We all have monster and hero inside us. How we choose to live our lives is what matters. And consider this; I've known your secret for years, and I never hated you."

Before Hela could move back, Ibby leaned forward and kissed her, lingering until Hela's cold lips thawed and she responded.

Ibby smiled at her. "Accept that your past is your past and move on."

⸙

Hela entered the refugee center and noticed that there were fewer people. Maybe they were getting nearer the end, of those needing to be processed and those who needed aid. In the care room, she paced. This would be the final test. It was at least her third try. Could she heal those traumatized by torture?

The woman was lead in, raped repeatedly for years. A zombie. Hela sat her down, activated the nanotech, the blue glow from her tattoo softly kissing the woman's flesh. Hela envisioned the musculature, the bones, the connective tendons and fascia, as she had always done. She imagined the brain, its intricate convolutions, the hidden and nearly mystical energy that formed experiences and memories. She pushed past the plasticky layer and felt the emotions rising. Cataloging the experiences, she extracted everything she could; the stale cigar smoke, body odor, urine in one corner, the hot desiccated smell of the open desert, the bleached light that paled the darkest skin, the leering men's faces, the feeling of being nothing but an afterthought, not even human. Every feeling the woman remembered and so did Hela, but when she set to repairing what was so ephemerally and fundamentally broken, she could do nothing.

Frustrated, she opened her eyes and touched the woman's face. "I'm sorry," she said. "It's not your fault. You've suffered horribly and I can do no more for you."

Next came the man with the deep lacerations across his back, the bruising and the skittish mind. She chewed at her lip. No one should be made to suffer as these people had, yet how could she help more than the shell of their bodies? Trying again, Hela eased in past the barrier, recorded the sensations, then observed. The images weren't physiology nor anatomy. They were feelings, thoughts, fears. How had she dealt with her own?

While still in the man's thoughts she realized that the healing could not be done from a distance. Growing the nanobots into hands, arms, a visage, a body, she approached the man's image.

He was more a broken wooden toy, a marionette with his strings snarled and being pulled, a whip coming down again and again and again, splintering away wood. A voice said, "*You were always so willful, stealing, breaking your mother's heart.*" She blocked his view of the whip and took his wooden hands. Staring into his painted eyes, she said, "You are real. You don't deserve this. None of this is your fault and you're safe now."

She kept repeating the words, using the nanobots to build a safe structure, people laughing, and smiling at the man. Slowly, she noticed the wooden grain softening, the eyes rounding, turning back into human eyes. She said, "You don't have to be punished for your past. We have all made mistakes, we all have regrets. You've paid the price." The man blinked and looked around, a tentative smile quirking his lips.

Hela withdrew her hand and opened her eyes. The man was staring at her. She examined his back; the nanobots were finally working, new pink flesh closing the lacerations. "You're going to be okay. Just make today count. Don't let the past control you."

As she worked with the victims, in almost all cases they believed they were punished for their own pasts, for their regrets, the mistakes they made, that they should have been better wives, husbands, sons, workers, sisters. The key to healing was to let go.

Hela trembled, rubbing her eyes. It was time to leave. Not everyone had been cured, not everyone could be helped but with more research they would make headway into healing psyches. She yawned, and left the center.

It felt good. She didn't feel the dread sitting upon her shoulders. When the call came, Hela wasn't that surprised.

"Dr. Petrovna," rumbled Director Boscoe. "As you've noticed, the center has processed most of the patients, but there will be more refugees. I'd like to offer you a permanent job."

She went to meet Ibby in a quiet cafe. Smiling, she sat down. Ibby, her hair full of snaky black extensions, looked up from her tablet. "You came."

"How could I not? You've helped me a lot."

Ibby shook her head. "Not really, you helped yourself. I guess you'll be going back to Canada now?"

Hela reached out and took Ibby's hands in both of hers. "No. I think I'll stay here. It's a much shorter flight to visit France."

The Book With No End

When I wrote this for the themed anthology, a book about books, I wanted to play off of those adventure movies I loved as a kid, the ones that were emulated in The Jewel of the Nile and the Indiana Jones movies. I wanted to explore, again, the sociopathic mentality—in this case turning into one. This is a tale about sacrifice to get what you most desire but then when you achieve that state, will it be what you thought?

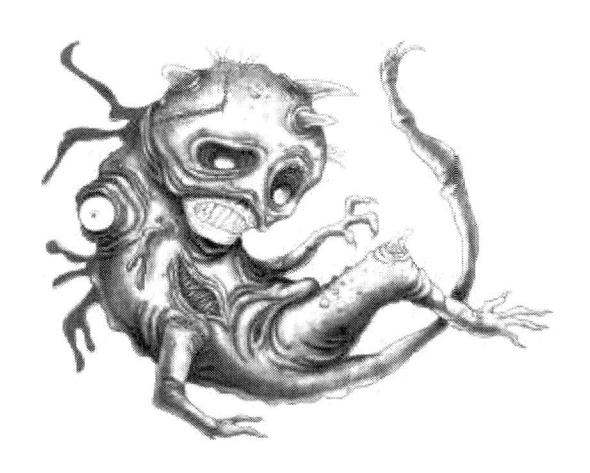

Lizbet feels much like an ant as she and the others slowly shovel and brush away the fine gritty dirt from the emerging walls. Her specialization in dead languages will give her an edge, but does not excuse her from being on hands and knees in the sand. She will decipher any cuneiform tablets uncovered, should they be lucky enough to find any. A month ago ground-penetrating radar indicated several buried chambers in the Sumerian city of Nippur, one of the seats of civilization and the home of the earliest form of writing.

The area has been picked over by hungry archaeologists for decades; it is the land where Gilgamesh and Enkidu went on adventures, where Inanna tromped the unknown caverns of her sister's realm to overcome death. If any truths are to be found, they will be in the oldest myths, when humans tried to crack open the world's mysteries. This is what Lizbet needs: to unearth the very genesis of when civilization awoke and grew in might.

What she wants is complete control. Being able to manipulate boys, men, and teachers has always given Lizbet a primordial thrill, as if she were the battery that ran the world.

Two grueling weeks under a sun that sucks the moisture from skin and withers everyone beneath its glare. Lizbet is ready to take a flight home at the end of the week. They haven't even found the foundations yet, just walls and more walls. Even an abandoned village would have a few artifacts. Maybe it is time to look at a more illustrious career, a faster road to what she wants.

Markus has just called a halt after twelve hours, a normal day when you're racing against the time a foreign government gives you. Back-breaking work; they may as well be ancient Sumerian peasants. Lizbet stands and stretches, running her tongue over dry lips. Sipping water from her Camelbak, she wipes from her eyes stray strands of hair now the color of dunes and peers at the sun lumbering toward its dusty bed. Another tedious day.

She turns toward the tent to find shade and takes a step when the ground capsizes beneath her. There isn't even time to yell as dirt and stone follow her into a hole.

Her plummet is buffered by sand and the old sandstone beneath her feet. She half-slides, half-falls in a cascade and lands on the hump of the water bag strapped to her back. Dirt and stones rain upon her. She opens her eyes to see a dark shape plunge toward her; she moves her head to the side barely in time to avoid the large piece of masonry. Blinking and scrubbing at the dirt in her mouth and eyes, she coughs and sits up. Her back is sore and her hip is already pulsing with pain. There will be a few bruises from the twenty-foot fall but no bones seem broken. As she stands, she moves each limb then, satisfied, slaps dirt from her clothes and hair. She sucks water from the tube, swishes, and spits out mud. As people's shouts filter from above Lizbet looks around, still rubbing dirt from her eyes. A treasure trove reveals itself: more artifacts than almost any Sumerian excavation to date.

Someone calls down.

"Yes, I'm all right. Just bruised."

"We'll find a rope and ladder and get you out."

Lizbet barely hears them as she walks around the rectangular chamber that is bathed in amber light and settling dust motes. She has discovered a mystery. The ancients built rituals around them: the Orphic rites, the Dionysian and Mithraic cults, the Eleusinian mysteries – all these had force and endurance. There is something here; she feels it at this ancient nexus of civilization where words were given power, and knowledge was stored for millennia. Lizbet's fingers tingle.

It is here again: that electric vibration, that thrumming resonance she senses when power is within her reach.

She runs her hands over the contours of three stone bulls and of petite, glazed clay bull dancers, looks at turned wooden bowls full of unsown seeds, and stops in front of a low pallet with the dusky bones of some past lord or lady. A wooden chest, several bronze blades, a folded pile of grayed fabric that would disintegrate on touch completes the riches of the funereal chamber. She circles the room again and is drawn to the skeleton, not laid out in any sarcophagus, bare of the shreds of any garment or of the telltale glint of ornaments. Stripped of everything but its bones. Devoid even of any desiccated remnants of hair or flesh.

What can one tell from the bones of the dead, those ivory sculptures no longer corrupted by the indulgences and errors of living? Only the greatest stories, the traumas that embed into a person's core, only those etch themselves on bones. And yet these are more pristine than baby's bones. No nicks, no mended breaks, teeth all present, perfectly straight and whole, no axe marks of any untimely death, no disease nor malformation have touched this body. Everything in the room is incredibly fragile and the air that now circulates could destroy some of the artifacts in days. She moves softly, almost reverently, and kneels beside the wooden bed on which the pristine skeleton rests. How could anyone in an age of primitive medicine remain unmarred?

The pallet is only about a foot off the ground; beneath it, Lizbet glimpses a shadow on the floor tiles that must have once been brightly painted. She reaches underneath and pulls out a stiff bundle tied with cord that crumbles in her hands. An animal skin, most likely cow, crackles and powders brown hair onto the floor. The bundle is as long as her forearm and twice as thick. Lizbet delicately folds back a tiny portion of the old hide and pokes her finger inside to feel a supple softness, slightly clammy and unpleasant. Tilting it to the light, she distinguishes some form of marking. A parchment or vellum with inked symbols upon it. Her heart thumps harder now than it did from her fall.

There is noise around the hole as people prepare to let the ladder down, and Lizbet knows she can't share this find. Quickly, she drains the water from her Camelbak and unzips it to wedge the package inside. She pulls off her shirt, leaving on the tank top, and puts the pack back on with the shirt tied to it so that the bulk is disguised.

"Okay, Lizbet."

She climbs the ladder and is bombarded with questions.

"What's down there? Some furniture?"

"That and more," she tells Markus, who keeps shifting from foot to foot. "Untouched artifacts, a skeleton; weeks of work." There is so much talk and chaos that no one even notices her overly full water pack; when she pleads bruises and needing to lay down, there are no questions.

Lizbet will return to the lab with the first shipment of artifacts: one tablet and a couple of pots with engraved cuneiform. Other quadrants have yet to be excavated. But she has enough, and wants to examine her find in private.

༄

The cracked animal pelt reveals three layers: papery gray leaves, several unknown powdery substances, and a sticky residue. Lizbet finds the inner layer is a skin or sheath still supple after millennia. She experiences such a rush that she has to sit down, as if she'd inhaled an opiate.

She works painstakingly for weeks to remove the integument from its chrysalis. With techniques perfected for burn victims, she immerses the skin in a stainless-steel water tank and doesn't unroll it until she's certain it maintains its integrity. Still, she peers at what she can with a magnifying glass, noticing the smooth, cinnamon brown color as well as the cuneiform symbols in red and black ink.

༄

After a second week of immersion, Lizbet carefully unrolls and cleans the skin. It is human.

This amaranthine skin is an entry to another world – like the Rosetta Stone. While it may be the key, it is not the full answer to her quest. The cuneiform script is not unusual, nor dissimilar from previously excavated tablets, but the arrangement of symbols can make a world of difference in meaning.

The earliest writings were tabulations of possessions. Soon after, people started to write about the mysteries, to create formulas and ways to cross into the underworld or the sphere of the gods. Gilgamesh, Odysseus, Herakles: the earliest adventurers walked in realms that held true control and the potential for fundamental metamorphosis. Lizbet feels that hunger and begins rereading all the epics, but only the most accurate translations. This skin is worth all the finds in the world.

The amaranth skin tests her knowledge and expands it as she unravels the tattooed script. It tells of a binding, readings, maps, immortality, and the greatest of powers: all will know the name of the wearer.

She knows it now; that is what she truly wants – immortality.

There are three different types of information in these inked markings: short phrases about the sheath's abilities when worn, riddles to solve, and instructions for attaining immortality. This is only the start of a long pursuit. The recipe is in every inch of skin covered in pictographs from the flap and eye holes that once covered the skull, down to the thin twists that were fingers and toes, but it does not list the ingredients except as clues, such as where to hunt. This could take years.

For the next ten years Lizbet travels the globe by plane, train, jeep, horse, mule, and camel. She ages. She reads numerous papyri, scrolls, tablets, stones, and texts, solving puzzles and riddles. Some lead to other artifacts or ingredients. The rarer spices, oils, and pastes, she ships to a post office box; the artifacts require a range of blackmail, auction purchases, and bribery. Her expertise in ancient languages allows access to most texts, whether painted on stone, engraved, woven, imprinted, written, or branded.

There are items that no longer exist, and those she must reconstruct. When unable to find the kudurru of Nebuchadnezzar's vision, she re-examines all such stones and checks the translations. The vision is engraved on the stone that held boundary allotments for King Marduk-nādin-ahhē. The museum won't release that kudurru, so she photographs it and has a jeweler meticulously carve a replica in black nephrite. Each reconstruction is worth the expense.

She dated the tattooed skin to be around eight thousand years old; it has not aged, is indeed, like amaranth, known for its long-lived quality. How is it that the sheath holds information about more recent civilizations and artifacts? That alone indicates some prognostication and hints that it might be a piece of the map to immortality. She discovers a clue on a worn clay tablet, tracing the lead through a partially burned manuscript back to an inscription on a weather-beaten wall. She must guess and think and try to parse these together into the precise instructions.

There are other tasks and tests set out in those books, yellowed scrolls, and slabs of marble and clay. Laced within the intricate symbols and tales are riddles to solve, revealing tasks to fulfill. Sometimes the message is repeated in different areas of the skin, in slightly different phrasings but always three times. Lizbet knows that early forms of chants and songs used repetition to memorize tales. She does not need to do this as she has the script on flesh plus all her notes.

Before she begins to undertake the list of tasks, she must verify that their order is correct.

The first requirement is relatively easy: *Segregate yourself*. For years her jealous obsession has made a recluse of her.

Next: *Examine the living*. She sits in libraries, funeral parlors, restaurants, and emergency rooms. She walks malls, parks, and campuses, studying people in all their states. Every test requires her to examine her own feelings and emotions, and then to list them. People are mere lab mice, and she finds them easy to understand. Her motivation is clear but not so her own emotions.

Examine the dead. She volunteers to do forensic archaeology on homicide victims. While the first few gory examinations revolt her, used as she is to the desiccated forms of the ancient world, she becomes curious; what murder method was used, did the victim experience pain, did she suffer long? Did the murderer feel anything – joy, anger, numbness?

Do not help those in need. She travels to Haiti, searching out the worst slums, the most destitute and ill. She strolls among them and, rather than compassion, feels revulsion at the scrawny limbs and the people with cholera. They are rotting and should be put down.

Be cruel. When Maggie complains of a sore tooth, Lizbet responds with "If you stopped eating candy, your teeth would be better off and you'd lose some of that weight you're gaining." When José shows up with his short hair gelled into spikes, she laughs: "That won't hide your bald spot, nor get you a date." No one willingly works with her anymore, but she doesn't need them. She continues this stage of the test: two women milling at the subway, she just pushes out of her way; she stares at an old woman bowed over by the weight of her wrinkles, and stays in her seat; she kicks away a street person's cup of coins. She feels no shame, only a small joy that she now possesses this power.

There are many tests; their goal is to eliminate her feelings and emotions. But when she has distilled them down to the last one, the exhilaration of control, she becomes stuck. She cannot get rid of pride, anger, exaltation, and the small thrills of command. She must hone herself into the perfect vessel or the process will not work. Once she attains immortality, then she can glory in it.

If she attains immortality.

The weeks stretch into months, and her frustration mounts as she feels the push of time. Emotion is her undoing. The more she tries to bury them, the stronger the emotions come, the stronger her attraction to drink becomes. To have wasted so many years, cut off from everything, all in the vain hope of gaining true power. All for nothing. She has failed.

She buys another five bottles of scotch. And then, another five.

Lizbet's binge rides her through several months, until she is numb, uncaring. One day, in a bleary stupor, she realizes that she cannot allow herself to care; it is the caring about the outcome of her quest, whether negative or positive, that brought her down. In the end the alcohol is her savior; she realizes she was a fool for almost letting that near-final step become insurmountable. She sobers up and repeats all the steps again.

This time around the tests are, paradoxically, both more demanding and easier. She watches and sometimes even participates in events, all without reaction; the more tests she undergoes, the less she feels.

On sabbatical, Lizbet spends more time alone, often in the dark, without food, to meditate on the cuneiform characters the sheath has shown. Loneliness doesn't matter. She is able to read the different messages; hidden messages become visible when viewed from dermis or epidermis side; head to toes; right arm to left leg; fingers then toes; areas where the flesh once covered organs, such as heart, kidneys, lungs, stomach; the eight chakras in a line from genitals to scalp. It is the ultimate topographic map; each layer of meaning is deeper, more profound.

Thus, she learns the rudimentary language of the elements. It would take decades of practice to fully master the skill, but she nevertheless stirs a leaf, ripples water, causes smoke to rise from a twig, and makes a bloom open, by simply pronouncing the right letters in the right order. She has no need to write down these arts; if her journal is ever discovered, any who read it will need to find their own steps.

There is one final preparation before she can undertake the ritual to bind the sheath to her. It will be the last time she can let herself feel emotion, and it must be convincing, most of all to herself. She goes to a club, drinks good scotch, and finds a man worth fucking. She forms no attachments but brings him to her place, then discards him once she's done. The act is repeated with a variety of men until she's sure the seed has taken. There must be no record, so she buys the pack of strips and waits for the color to confirm that she is pregnant. She waits long enough to make sure she doesn't lose the fetus; meanwhile she continues to study the skin, the Dead Sea Scrolls, hieroglyphs and pictographs, the Talmud, the Bible, the Quran – but only the earliest versions, the purest. She does not find any more clues or messages. The time has come.

※

Lizbet packs everything she needs: the artifacts, the skin, the unguents and herbs, water, food, and camping gear. She finds a cave that will not be visited until spring creeps out. Autumn has strangled the life from last leaves and they lie, discarded husks, upon the ground. The sky is clear and pallid as the weather cools, and she has enough wood.

In various nooks, fissures, and natural shelves of grey and black striated stone she places the scrolls, the stones, the vessels, and the statues that she procured from all over the world. They might not be necessary for the final ritual, but she leaves nothing to chance. Great sacrifices have been called for; she has met all but one last requirement.

※

The months have passed in contemplation and practice. Lizbet can now move water, wind, earth, and fire, though it is still a demanding feat. Winter has been cold and dry, and spring will heave itself from the earth soon. She does not mind the pain when the contractions begin. The circumstances of her labor do not matter; only that the fetus live.

The final preparation is the most explicit: suckle the baby for three days, then kill it while looking into its eyes. It cries as if it knows its fate. Its measly life will serve a greater goal.

Lizbet decides to strangle it; the neck is so small that she only needs one hand to encircle the soft pink flesh. Her fingers sink in as she squeezes. The baby flails and shrieks only momentarily before the blood supply is cut off. Fascinated, Lizbet watches the face blister red and the eyes bulge.

She brings the body near the fire and guts it with the curved gurkha blade she acquired in India. Blood pools like oil on the stone; she uses it to mark her skin with sigils. The entrails are set aside for later. She cuts through the skin and meat, and breaks the soft bones, puts all in an iron kettle to which she adds spices and water, and a few root vegetables. She eats the food thus prepared over the next three days.

Three is one of the great magic numbers. It stands for past, present, and future; beginning, middle, and end; life, death, and rebirth. Religious paintings were done as triptychs. There are many groups of three. Stories are often written in three parts. This is the final part of the trilogy.

It is the end of the third day as Lizbet checks for any residual emotions. She is full and ready. There is no elation. She will do as she set out to do those many years ago. It is time to begin the culminating ritual.

The intestines have dried into sinewy rawhide and lie upon the small wooden altar near the fire. The fire is built high for warmth and for the spirit to find her. Her clothes are piled within a niche in the cave wall. Her skin shines with the oils of datura, nightshade, and poppy. The obsidian blade used in Zapotec rituals to release istli through human sacrifice lies next to the amaranth sheath stretched out on the ground.

She has eaten nothing since she consumed her child three days before. Three days of feasting, three of fasting, a circle completed; what was taken in and transformed is consumed and excreted. The coils wind in and out.

She sits upon the tattooed skin and writes her final words in the journal. Lizbet closes the book, then picks up the blade and carves fine symbols into her flesh; she marks the chakras. Triangles, swirls, waves, circles – figures as old as time with the power of eternity behind them. Feet, ankles, knees, pubic bone, belly, chest, back, hands, wrists, elbows, neck, forehead – all have characters etched into them; blood oozes from her.

She binds the sheath to her ankles, then to her wrists, using her teeth to tie the knot. Next she fastens the amaranth sheath around her belly and neck with the sinew of her sacrifice. Lizbet lies down, the cuts stinging and throbbing in time with her pulse; on these next three nights of the equinox, she chants the words of power. As she is absorbed, she thinks: *I shall be reborn to live forever.*

Humanity is a book: their stories make up the world; their skins, like this skin, tell a tale. I am the reader who knows each book's ending. I have read the leaves left here by the binder. The stories often begin with a birth, but the tales differ, though they all end with my beginning.

I have two siblings. My first task is to kill the oldest, skin the body, and lay out the clues for the next binder. One is new, one is old, one is always in transition.

I look at the pattern of glowing symbols on my skin; they tell me the way. I call the wind and mist to veil me, to absorb me. Then I fade. I am everywhere.

We three are everywhere. Our quest was written at the beginning of time. Our touch reaches all and they will know our name. Some have called us Fate or Destiny but most people call us Death. Ours is the longest tale in the world. We are the book with no end.

Colleen Anderson is a lifelong learner and has been exploring the creative arts in one form or another since she was a child. She has a BFA in photography and design from ACAD and a BFA in Creative Writing from UBC. Colleen first explored writing for self-expression in her tumultuous youth. Coming from a family of voracious readers, the worlds expressed in SF and fantasy captured her imagination. She has attended workshops and retreats in Washington, Kansas, Vancouver and Ottawa. She has performed spoken word and read her fiction in Canada, the US and the UK.

Colleen has given critiques and blue pencil workshops, hosted a speculative reading series and served on Bram Stoker and British Fantasy award juries. She has been poetry editor for Chizine, fiction editor at Aberrant Dreams, and has co-edited two anthologies (*Tesseracts 17* with Steve Vernon, and *Playground of Lost Toys* [Aurora nominated] with Ursula Pflug) and edited *Alice Unbound: Beyond Wonderland* which came out in 2018. Next, she hopes to edit a dark fiction anthology.

In 2017-2018, Colleen received a Canada Council grant to work further on her writing. She has been twice nominated for the Canadian Aurora Award in poetry and longlisted for the Stoker Award in short fiction. Over 150 of her poems have seen print with some recent pieces in *Grievous Angel*, *Polu Texni*, *The Future Fire*, *Polar Borealis* and many others. Over fifty fiction pieces have been featured in numerous anthologies such as *The Sum of Us*, *Beauty of Death*, *By the Light of Camelot* and *nEvermore! Tales of Muraer, Mystery and the Macabre*. Colleen's next projects include putting together a book of poetry and a mosaic apocalyptic novel that captures stories from the same world and time. She also runs a blog where she does not devote enough time but sometimes discusses aspects of writing.

www.colleenanderson.wordpress.com

Vancouver artist Jenn Brisson, started her art career in Classical Animation and has since then become a prolific painter, illustrator, street artist and an international muralist, having painted murals for Vancouver, New York and Sicily, Italy. Her work is one part strange, one part saccharine and a touch of whimsy. Jenn loves taking viewers to other places, where odd quasi-human beings live against textural backgrounds. Jenn's art has been seen in galleries, comics, art books and young adult stories. Currently living and working in Mount Pleasant, Vancouver, Jenn continues to chase magic beings and is living life to the fullest.

www.jennbrisson.com

Printed in Poland
by Amazon Fulfillment
Poland Sp. z o.o., Wrocław